CAR

NOTHI.

CAROLA MARY ANIMA OMAN was born in 1897 in Oxford, the second of three children of Sir Charles and Mary Oman. In 1906 she was sent to Miss Batty's School in Park Crescent, Oxford, where she eventually became head girl.

In World War One Carola Oman was a probationary VAD nurse at the Radcliffe Infirmary in Oxford. After various nursing appointments during the war, she was discharged in 1919. Her first book, *The Menin Road and Other Poems*, was published later that year.

On 26 April 1922, Carola Oman married Gerald Lenanton, and subsequently devoted most of her writing in the 1920s and 1930s to a series of historical novels, influenced in part by her close friend Georgette Heyer.

In the course of a writing career of more than half a century Oman published over thirty books of fiction, history, and biography, among them several historical works for children, and *Ayot Rectory* (1965), set in the village where she and her husband had settled in a Jacobean manor, Bride Hall. In later years she specialized in historical biography. 1946 saw her prize-winning biography of Nelson, the book on which her reputation as a biographer rests. She was appointed CBE in 1957.

After two strokes, Carola Oman died at Bride Hall, Ayot St Laurence, on 11 June 1978.

FICTION BY CAROLA OMAN

For Adults

Princess Amelia (1924)

The Road Royal (1924)

King Heart (1926)

Mrs Newdigate's Window (1927)

The Holiday (1928)

Crouchback (1929)

Miss Barrett's Elopement (1929)

Fair Stood the Wind (1930)

Major Grant (1931)

The Empress (1932)

The Best of His Family (1933)

Over the Water (1935)

Nothing to Report (1940)

Somewhere in England (1943)

For Children

Ferry the Fearless (1936)

Johel (1937)

Robin Hood, the Prince of Outlaws (1937)

Alfred, King of the English (1939)

Baltic Spy (1940)

CAROLA OMAN

NOTHING TO REPORT

With an introduction by
Sir Roy Strong

DEAN STREET PRESS

A Furrowed Middlebrow Book
FM30

Published by Dean Street Press 2019

First published in 1940 by Hodder & Stoughton

Cover by DSP
Cover illustration shows detail from *Garden Flowers on a Cottage
Table* (c.1937-1938) by Eric Ravilious

ISBN 978 1 913054 17 5

www.deanstreetpress.co.uk

INTRODUCTION
By Sir Roy Strong

"LADY LENANTON, last Friday I eloped and married your niece." With that telephone conversation Carola Oman (1897-1978) entered my life more forcefully than before as the aunt of my wife, the designer Julia Trevelyan Oman. Carola was by then a formidable grande dame in her mid-seventies, whom I had first encountered as a Trustee of the National Portrait Gallery, of which I had become Director in 1967. What I only discovered years later was that she first woman trustee of any national collection, the other being the National Maritime Museum, the consequence of her acclaimed biography of Nelson (1946).

The Omans were a Scottish family from the Orkneys which had sought its fortunes in India in the late eighteenth century. Ann Chadwick (1832-1907), one of the heiress daughters of the builder of the Great Western Railway, had married one of the numerous Charles Omans, an indigo planter in Bengal who died early. She returned to England with her only son who became the great historian Sir Charles Oman (1860-1946), Fellow of All Souls and Chicheley Professor of Modern History. In 1892 he married Mary Maclagan (1866-1950) and Carola was their second child, the name a reflection of her father's frustration that their second child was yet another daughter.

Much of her childhood was spent in Frewin Hall, Oxford in a household which still had maids and morning family prayers down to the death of her father in 1946. She was educated at Miss Batty's and then Wychwood School, Oxford, although denied knowledge of Latin by her father. She grew up to be a striking young woman with an abundance of flaxen hair and blue eyes. Already by 1914 she had taken part in the long series of Oxford pageants which were such a feature of the Edwardian period. With the outbreak of the First World War that idyll came to an end and she became a VAD nurse serving in both this country and France. Her contribution to a book of verse, *The Menin Road* (1919) is increasingly recognised as significant as female writers of the twentieth century are reappraised.

In 1922 she married Gerald Lenanton (1896-1952), a timber agent who was knighted for his services in the Second World War. His wounds, sustained in the 1914-18 conflict, curtailed any possibility of children. Carola inherited a fortune from her Oman grandmother enabling them to settle at Ayot St Lawrence close to Bernard Shaw in an Elizabethan red brick house, Bride Hall. She lived there until her death, apart from the war period which was passed at Flax Bourton near Bristol.

Carola had close links with two other female writers. One was Joanna Cannan (1896-1961) whose father was Dean of Trinity College, Oxford and whose literary fame depended on a steady stream of books for children focusing on ponies as well as over thirty adult novels. The more significant friend was Georgette Heyer (1902-1974), the creator of the historically accurate dream world of the Regency romance novel as well as a steady stream of thrillers. Carola too was prolific, writing over thirty children's books, historical biographies and fiction. She was hugely patriotic responding fully to the challenge of the Second World War with novels, *Nothing to Report* (1942) and *Somewhere in England* (1943) among them, and more fully in historical works like *Britain against Napoleon* (1942) and culminating with her prize-winning biography of *Admiral, Lord Nelson* (1946).

Already in the 1930s she had begun to write historical biography working through a succession of Queens, Henrietta Maria, Elizabeth, Queen of Bohemia and Mary of Modena. After the war came larger, more ambitious biographical projects including Sir John Moore, David Garrick, Eugène de Beauharnais and Sir Walter Scott. Although well researched, most would strike the modern reader as ponderous and lacking a sharper critical insight and analysis. She was awarded a CBE in 1957.

The Omans had a strong sense of identity and belonged to that group we now designate as the intellectual aristocracy but whose life was not in her case passed in academe. Her brother Charles (1908-1982) became Keeper of Metalwork at the Victoria & Albert Museum and a distinguished antiquary. The furnishing of the mind with an abundance of historical fact and wide reading in terms of literature was taken for granted. She wrote during a period when, for women of that class, servants were a given and 'work' in the sense of what happened after 1945 was totally foreign to them. Right until the very end Bride Hall depended on a cook and a butler-chauffeur. The world of Bloomsbury would have been also totally alien to her as indeed what we now categorise as that of the 'bright young things' and the smart set of the twenties and thirties. Much of Carola's life can be explained as demonstrating to her father that she too was capable of writing history. She inherited from him too his deep Conservatism. In his case so extreme that as an MP for the University he was nicknamed 'Stone Age Man'.

What of her papers that survive I have given to the Bodleian Library, Oxford. Some of her travel diaries, I am told, are of interest. She left me half her library and in the dissolution of Bride Hall following her death I came eventually to inherit the desk at which she wrote. For over forty years I have written all my books at that unpretentious Victorian partner's desk which I remember so well in what was her writing room off to the right as one entered Bride Hall. Carola was also a formidable needlewoman and her memory remains encapsulated here in one of a series of tapestry chairs that she worked. On the back she has etched a view of Bride Hall against which, in the foreground, one of her beloved Dalmatians scampers after a bird. It is a tiny vignette recording a once secure world that has gone.

Roy Strong

PART ONE
1939

CHAPTER I
FEBRUARY 22ND

(i)

THE MOMENT that Miss Morrison woke up she felt that something pleasant was going to happen to-day. The hour was close on seven-thirty, she knew, for from the parlour below came the unmistakable sound of a fire being raked out to the accompaniment of heavy breathing. The day, said the calendar, showing the likeness of an Alpine meadow, secured to the wall by a drawing pin, was Wednesday, February 22nd, 1939.

Converted seventeenth century cottages, rich in oak beams and elm floors, have their disadvantages, reflected Miss Morrison drowsily. At Willows, Westbury-on-the-Green, for instance, it was absolutely impossible to say or do anything in the parlour that was not thrillingly audible in the bedroom exactly above. Nearly all the furniture, itself somewhat crooked with age, had to be pegged, because the walls and floors were uneven. Quite often, when she tugged out her glove drawer, the Jacobean tallboy gave an affronted grunt and moved off its pegs, to subside heavily into a threatening attitude. "I got that at that little shop in the Cotswolds, when I was motoring with Marcelle and Rosemary, that wet Easter," remembered Miss Morrison, staring at the piece of furniture facing her bedfoot. It certainly was a little big for the room, but she had never regretted it. The tallboy from the Cotswolds had six large and two small drawers. Its pretty acorn-shaped drop handles, and key-shields with a design of cherubs with blown-out cheeks, gleamed warmly, although the curtains were still drawn. Both brass and oak were well polished. Turning her head to look at her bedroom curtains, which were of a glazed apple-green chintz patterned with Victorian moss-rose buds surrounded by a plague of dots, Miss Morrison realized that at last the sun must be shining outside. A thrush was talking. There was a flood of rosy light around the short curtains, which were lined with shell-pink casement cloth. She remembered, in the same moment, with a rush—"It's the 22nd, and Catha's coming!"

The thought that to-day she was going to see again, for the first time in five years, one of her oldest friends, caused Miss Morrison to sing as she performed her toilet. Down in the small oak-panelled room where she took her meals, she could scarcely give her full attention to her boiled egg or her newspaper. The newspaper bore signs of having been pushed under a freshly-washed doorstep by a village urchin on his way to school. "I must speak to his mother, and to Doris," thought Miss Morrison, as she unfolded the damp sheet. "This is the second time this week that he's spoilt the Births column." Since Miss Morrison was, as everyone in Westbury knew, in her forty-third year, that column was not often of particular interest to her nowadays. Most of her contemporaries had already achieved their families, and few of their children were yet of an age to open nurseries on their own account.

"Marriages" was as a rule even less likely to contain news of interest. Miss Morrison scanned "Deaths" cautiously, opened to the centre page, and from what she read there was only reminded that her Anti-Gas lecture was at seven to-night. She gathered up her letters, satisfied herself that they would keep until after her friend had gone, and stowed them away in an already overfull pigeon-hole of the desk in her parlour.

Before she set out on her morning round, she rang the bell, and while she waited for it to be answered, picked up and read again a telegram in an envelope labelled "Confirmatory copy."

"Tuesday, please," it ran. "Arriving by car, one, leaving five-thirty, Catha."

When Miss Morrison looked up again, a solid form blocked the doorway. Doris always reminded her mistress of Shakespeare's Audrey, with a dash of an old Dutch Master thrown in.

"I am going out now, Doris," said Miss Morrison in clear tones. "I may not be in again until almost lunch-time, so I want you to be sure that there is a good fire burning in here by then. Light it at twelve, and keep on making it up. Don't just put a match to it, and go away hoping for the best. Lady Rollo has come straight from India, and will be feeling the cold.

"I have told Rose that there will be a chauffeur for dinner," she ended, frowning slightly at the cannibalistic sound of her sentence.

"Yes, miss," said Doris, who was fifteen and nine months, and whom Miss Morrison had first encountered lying in the scales at the local Infants' Welfare Centre. Less than her usual airy confidence seemed to mark Doris's extraordinary countenance, as she added in a gabble, "If you please, miss, on May 27th, might I have Saturday instead of Sunday?"

Miss Morrison picked up an engagement block entitled "Lest We Forget," and said, puckering her brow again, "That's Whitsun week-end. I am sure to have people staying. Do you want to do something special?"

Doris's orbs swelled. "I've been asked to be a bridesmaid, miss," she said.

(ii)

The hired car from London, bringing Lady Rollo to spend the day with her best friend, went through all the contortions usually performed by a large, strange vehicle arriving at Willows.

Miss Morrison had time, while the chauffeur reversed, baffled, into the lane, to run upstairs and fling off her outdoor clothes. She had a bird's-eye view, as she combed her springy fair hair, of a dark shining bonnet nosing its way cautiously through her scarred white gate. As she descended the stairs again, she perceived through its open door, that the windows of her dining-room were now totally obscured by the vehicle which had trembled to a standstill. She heard a familiar voice, which caused her heart to leap, and she caught a glimpse of a tall, unknown woman in a long brown coat, issuing some order about a bundle of papers.

The friends met in the narrow hall.

"Catha, darling!" cried the hostess, three minutes later, holding her guest at arm's length in front of the good parlour fire, "how impossibly London-ish you look! It's not to be believed that you landed from a storm-tossed vessel five days past."

"Don't remind me of it," begged Lady Rollo with a shudder. "I never knew an easy moment until I set foot on English soil, and then I was plunged in woe simultaneously by having to send my four trusting, beloved bull-terriers into six months' quarantine. However, here I am, and I put on my most becoming outfit partly for your sake, and partly in hopes of producing a good first impression on my future home. I could not tell you in my telegram, but all those papers which the man has dumped on your best *petit-point* chair are not my preparations for making the tail of a kite. Tim and I have definitely settled to be your neighbours. You and I are going to look at twenty-two houses this afternoon. By the way, Button, what has happened to hats at Home? Tim says that this one is a Fool's Hat. No thinking citizen could put such an object on her head. I've told him that it was much the most sensible of the lot I saw, and I went to five places in deepening incredulity. Elizabeth has brought back one from Paris consisting entirely of a bunch of flowers and a scrap of veil, lashed to her brow by a single strand of ribbon. But she's seventeen and a little monkey-face."

"I've got one upstairs, I'll show you later, which still gives me a shock when I see myself sideways in a mirror," Miss Morrison assured her friend. "They are like that, nowadays. Go on about the Orders to View."

But Lady Rollo could not desert her other subject immediately.

"This one is ghastly sideways too, now that I look at it in your glass," she murmured. "I should never be able to wear it down here, should I?"

"Well," said Miss Morrison with characteristic candour, "not this year, perhaps. But next year, for weddings and big sherry parties, certainly. And the year after that—no difficulty at all."

"I see," said Lady Rollo. "Still," with rising spirits, "after all, we're not decrepit yet, Button."

"We're not chickens," pronounced Miss Morrison in her clearest voice, at the same moment that Doris opened the door to announce that luncheon was served.

Miss Morrison's dining-room, which seated eight at a pinch, looked its best this sunshiny day. Before she had departed to the village, she had found time to arrange a bowl of aconites for the centre of her circular walnut table. The room was filled with linen-fold panelling, painted pale sea-green. "I had the same colour throughout the two cottages," she explained, "for economic reasons. It was a complete success, except in the parlour, where I found it killed my flower arrangements. I set to work to scrape it back to the oak, with old kitchen knives, last Bank Holiday. Your Tony—my Tony—turned up suddenly from Oxford, bringing three friends. They all slept in the summer-house on mattresses, as there was a heat wave, and scraped all day. It was a riot."

A slight shadow appeared on the fine brow of Lady Rollo at the mention of her first-born. She said hesitantly, as Doris departed for an inner fastness, bearing a loaded tray, "Button, you've been such a saint, keeping in touch with Tony. Do tell me honestly what you think about him. Tim, of course, feels strongly, so strongly that at times I scarcely dare mention the poor lamb's name."

"Oh well," began Miss Morrison, sounding large-minded. Doris had reappeared, and was semaphoring from the sideboard.

"I don't think that there's much harm in a young man being a bit 'Left' when he's still learning, so to speak," pronounced Miss Morrison, rising to dissect roast chicken.

"Sometimes," said Lady Rollo, regarding the portion set before her with unseeing blue eyes, "I simply can't believe that I have a son taking finals at Oxford, and a son, six feet high, at sea, and a daughter ready to come out."

"I know," agreed Miss Morrison, hitching her chair sympathetically. "And it does seem a joke when one looks at you, for you're a sylph. We red-heads certainly score when it comes to tresses too."

"Button!" exclaimed Lady Rollo urgently, "have you seen poor Violet lately?"

"No," said Miss Morrison.

"She came to meet the Boat Train," said Lady Rollo. "I must admit, I was touched. She brought a large gilt basket of orchids tied up with shaded ribbon, and her hair is tomato-colour now, much, much brighter than ours was even when we were in our teens. She didn't bring the new husband. Have you set eyes on him?"

"Indeed, yes, I'm the baby's godmother," replied Miss Morrison firmly. "They've been here several times. He's a frightfully affable little bloke—Rinaldo, I mean. His looks are against him. But I believe—I trust—that he has a heart of gold. I really hope that poor Violet is going to be happy this time."

"What's the infant like, a boy or a girl?" enquired Lady Rollo.

"A boy; rather a pity, I feel. I haven't actually seen it yet, as I was in Madeira for the christening," said Miss Morrison. "I saw poor Violet just before it arrived, however. She came over here to ask me to be godmother. She was rather typical, and explained that she had thought the matter out and decided on me, because, as I had no husband or children of my own, and lived in two converted cottages, I would be able to give my full attention to the job."

"What did you say?" asked Lady Rollo, looking as indignant as it was possible for so gentle a character.

"I said, 'Violet, it may surprise you to know that I have already nine godchildren, in whom I take deep interest, and my various ploys in this village worry me quite as much as any husband could do. In fact, like Queen Elizabeth, I can truly say "To this realm I am wed." (Westbury-on-the-Green, not Great Britain, being my realm.) However, as I have known you since we learnt the polka and many useless things together, and I should anyway be interested in your child, I will do as you ask. I warn you, that if I find you upsetting the child's education by dragging it to the Bahamas in term-time, and starving it on roots and orange-juice, as you do yourself, I shall feel it my duty to interpose.'"

"Poor Violet," said her tender-hearted old acquaintance. "Perhaps she was feeling rather low and apprehensive. I think it was, in a way, a promising sign that she came to you."

"She told me, twice, that the obstetrician she had engaged to come down to the country to her was accustomed to Crowned Heads," said Miss Morrison. "I have always been sorry for Violet. I consider that her mother was responsible for her hopeless first marriage, and the second was an almost inevitable reaction. But in my heart I know that the poor creature has no sense. I sometimes attribute it to her having not a drop of Scottish blood."

"'From the giddy and godless South,'" quoted Lady Rollo, "'Good Lord deliver us.' But, if it comes to that, Tim is almost entirely Welsh, and you couldn't call him frivolous. The fact remains that we are both very fond of Violet, and I honestly believe that she is fond of us."

"We are probably," suggested Miss Morrison unbendingly, "about the only normal people left in her acquaintance."

Doris had set before each lady a green Wedgwood dessert plate in the shape of a vine-leaf, provided with an embroidered green muslin mat of the same design.

"How charming! Did you make them yourself?" asked the appreciative guest.

"Portuguese peasants made them," replied Miss Morrison, shaking her head. "Once I had six. Now the set numbers five. A Pioneer of Female Education, who came to lecture to the Institute, ate one. She was very old and noble-looking and, I suppose, shortsighted. I was just thinking how well the green plums matched the rest of the effect, when to my horror I perceived her cutting up plum and mat together with a good sharp fruit-knife. Her niece noticed presently, and said, 'Aunt Harriott, you cannot eat Miss Morrison's mat!' The dear old thing was frightfully distressed, and started tearing shreds from her jaws in grovelling apology. But it was too late."

"I once saw my father-in-law eat a whole paper ramekin full of cheese soufflé," recollected Lady Rollo. "But he was in a rage at the moment. I can't tell you, Button, what a relief it was to me when Tim announced that we need not live in the north now that the old gentleman is gone. I was terrified, since it all happened so shortly before we were due to come home, that Tim might feel drawn towards settling in his birthplace. People do, and it was a horrible house. Although it was quite old, it never really looked so, because it was built in that dark red sandstone that only blackens with age. The very thought of it used to damp my pleasure in the prospect of coming home. Every time I saw the photograph of it on Tim's study table it gave me the grues."

"I've seen that photograph," nodded Miss Morrison, "taken on a shiny wet day, when there was not a single leaf on a tree. It always made me think of 'And no bird sings.' Let's go next door now, and have coffee over the fire, and look at your house-agent's suggestions."

(iii)

The hired car stole out of the gates of The Grange and took the road to Crossgrove.

"Anyone in the East, feeling homesick," said Lady Rollo with feeling, "ought to be transported on a magic carpet to undergo our experiences of this afternoon. Never in my life have I seen five houses so perfectly unattractive in entirely different ways."

"Six," corrected Miss Morrison. "If you count the one where we drove away from the gates because you couldn't fancy an avenue of monkey-puzzlers."

"There was the one with lots of white-painted woodwork buttonholing round the gables," began Lady Rollo, ticking off her failures on her elegant fingers.

"It had a squash-court, and fitted basins and parquet flooring, and absolutely up-to-date central-heating throughout," her companion reminded her.

"I don't care. It made me feel as if Tim and I and Elizabeth and the boys would have to sit out under pergolas in tennis things, sucking drinks through straws and looking like an advertisement. Then there was the one we've just left, which the owner now finds he doesn't want to sell."

"I'm glad," explained Miss Morrison. "Because I couldn't have let you take a house built in 1860 and calling itself The Grange, which has no farm buildings attached, and no history whatsoever of connection with a monastery or feudal lord."

"Well," said Lady Rollo, "next we come to the quite new house with the back door round in front, and two dustbins with their hats on crooked, waiting to be collected. The hatefullest, I think, was the Old Rectory, with mossy tombstones lolling against the garden wall, and the church bell scaring one to fits in black stone passages. I've forgotten our sixth disappointment."

"It was the one with the Saxon moat, which you had liked the sound of so much," said Miss Morrison. "It had the young couple breeding Airedales in every room, who said that we would find we could get Bridge in the neighbourhood any afternoon."

"Oh, yes. Well, I hated it for their sakes, even if it had possessed water and light," said Lady Rollo ruthlessly.

"You must remember, dear," said Miss Morrison, smoothing the fluttering papers on her knee, "that the present owners of these houses are the one thing that you won't be buying."

"Let's cut out Crossways, it's sure to be abominable, and drive straight home to Willows and wish we could blow it up to four times its size and all live there in bliss," suggested Lady Rollo. "I haven't yet seen the tail-feather of anything that I like a thousandth part as much as Willows."

"It's not Crossways, it's Crossgrove, and it's what the agent calls 'a period house,'" said Miss Morrison, proof to flattery. "I know you will like it, because I have once been there to a Village Fête. I've been keeping it to the last, because I knew it was much the best of the lot they've sent you here."

"But it has carp-ponds, and a deer-park and about three hundred and sixty-five bedrooms," said Lady Rollo dismally. Her voice underwent a sudden change. "Oh! Button, is that the Cathedral spire poking out of the trees on the river bank down there? Do let's go home now, through the town, and get out, and sit for five minutes looking at that."

The weather, in spite of the sunshine, was too cold, in Miss Morrison's opinion, for a newly-returned exile to sit *al fresco* with safety. The friends dismissed their car at a venerable gate which led to the North Walk of the precincts. Half-past four sounded harmoniously from high above their heads, as they paced slowly towards a vista of spacious greensward and majestic trees. Willows were dipping pale yellow pointed leaves into glassy ice-cold waters. There were tufts of snowdrops on the river banks, and across the brilliantly green shorn turf, the cathedral spire was laying a long-fingered shadow. Overhead the sky was a youthful light azure. An old lady leading a fox-terrier, and two boys scrambling on a scarred cannon, were the only human creatures in sight.

"Listen to the rooks," said Lady Rollo. "Oh! isn't it English, and peaceful, and lovely?"

"Rooks always seem to me to be crying 'Far! Far!'" said Miss Morrison, watching them. "Do you remember when we wore pigtails, and read the *Oxford Book of Ballads* together, and went out into the garden and pretended to be Proud Maisie, and make out what the birds were saying?"

"I must find a house close enough to this town for me to be able to come in here whenever I want," said Lady Rollo. "And I must find it soon. Tim told me not to wear myself out, and said that we'd got the rest of our lives to search for the perfect home. But I know he loathes hotel life and service flats, and even staying with people he really likes."

"I want you to come inside, to look at just one thing, that always seems to me to epitomize the pleasures of the country life," said Miss Morrison, bending her steps towards a cloister door shadowed by a spreading yew.

"It's what they call a 'watching chamber,'" she explained in a whisper, three minutes later. "It used to have a monk inside, up at one of those windows, day and night, watching to see that nobody stole anything from the Saint's shrine. The carvings on the cornice dividing the two storeys are what I always come to see. Look at the little shepherd in a felt dunce's cap and jerkin, piping to his lambs, and the milkmaid on her stool, in a horned head-dress, with dozens of buttons down her jacket, and the two gaffers in top-boots, gathering apples, and the dog after a hare, and the hooded men stooking corn. They're supposed to show the things country people do during the Twelve Months. Aren't they neat and waggish, and isn't the oak a lovely silvery colour?"

"Quite perfect," agreed Lady Rollo. "How long should you think they've been up there?"

"I know," said Miss Morrison mildly, "because they've got the Hart, the badge of the unfortunate Richard of Bordeaux, on the south side."

"I am longing to see some really good plays," said Lady Rollo with gusto, as they attained the outer air. "We're going to the play *en famille* this evening, and on to supper at the Savoy.

Crispin is coming up from Devonport, so we shall be a four. Oh! it is lovely to be back in England, and to be tottering with one's oldest friend, round a cathedral close, and to know that one's going to sup in the bosom of one's handsome family on the banks of the Thames. It's too lovely," decided the returned exile, searching for her handkerchief. "It makes me feel almost creepy to say this, Button, but I solemnly declare that I should like things to stay, transfixed, just as they are at this moment, for evermore. I can't help seeing that I shall probably never be so happy again in my life. After all, I've now got what I've never had since I married—my husband and my three children all well and happy around me. Everything has turned out so propitiously for us lately—even Tim getting this good job, which means that we must live within reach of London. I used to dread his being unemployed when we came home, for he thrives on hard work, and when he's bored he gets ill. I know he dreaded it too, for when he handed me the letter from the War Office, he said, 'This will keep me from becoming an old man.'"

As their car climbed the steep hill up from the cathedral, Lady Rollo said, turning to lay a hand on her companion's arm, "You don't think there's going to be a war, do you, Button? What do people like you, at home, think? I felt almost crazy last September, when things looked so bad, and I had the sea between me and my three."

"I'm hoping for the best," said Miss Morrison. "But personally I'm being prepared. That's to say that I've taken my First Aid and Home Nursing again. By an odd chance, on the day that I was going in for the First Aid, I dug out the paper of questions put to us last time. I thought it might give me some sort of an idea as to what they asked one. I found that I was sitting for that examination on the exact anniversary of my last shot at it—quarter of a century ago—January 16th, 1914. And what's more, under the questions, I had scribbled, in the high spirits natural to sweet seventeen, 'Never again! not if I know it!' Before I returned that paper to its file," said Miss Morrison, "I added the words, 'First Aid taken again January 16th, 1939. *I did not know.*'"

"No, we do not know," agreed her friend. "But when I look at things like that cathedral spire, I feel it is impossible that we may be plunged in chaos again, at any moment."

"That spire," said Miss Morrison, "has seen the Normans come, and the Peasants' Revolt, and Marian martyrs being burnt in the plat below, and King Charles I on a tired horse, riding north to give himself up to the Scots, and moustachioed officers of Bonaparte's army arriving to be prisoners of war in the Gate House. I can well remember myself having a furious quarrel, under its shadow, with a quartermaster who accused me of having abstracted a pair of royal blue patient's trousers from her store, without permission."

"Had you?" asked Lady Rollo.

"That I can't remember. It was all silliness anyway, as I felt when I glanced up and saw that spire looking down on the animated pigmies in uniform."

"I don't feel I could bear it all over again," murmured Lady Rollo. "The other day I opened a copy of the *Illustrated London News* or something, in my dentist's waiting-room, and it had a picture of Hitler reviewing troops right across both middle pages. Being so large seemed to make it more real, and the letterpress said that it had taken the troops four hours to march past, and he'd kept his arm out at the Nazi salute nearly all the time. I had to shut it up quick. It made me feel quite sick."

"Looking over houses is notoriously one of the most exhausting things in the world," Miss Morrison reminded her companion. "Here we are home again, and I've ordered you a crumpet to your tea. So don't dare to tell me, as Violet did, that crumpets are death to female charm."

CHAPTER II
FEBRUARY 22ND

(i)

THE GUEST SAT at the kidney-shaped, chintz-skirted dressing-table, pulling her bizarre hat on to her wavy red-gold hair. Catha Rollo, whose features were short, would always have something of the child in her face, as well as in her heart, reflected her friend. On the gravel beneath purred the yellow-eyed monster which was to bear her back to London. She said, waving a hand at the view framed by the small window beside her, "Just look at that picture!"

Mary Morrison, standing silent behind her, looked. The picture was tiny, but perfect, resembling somewhat, in its sentiment and colour, the country scenes enclosed by a capital letter in a missal. Royal blue dusk was fast enveloping Westbury-on-the-Green. In the foreground, a Siamese cat with turquoise eyes was climbing delicately over a thatched shed roof. A gaggle of geese, whose shapes shone in the fading light, were moving purposefully towards the pond which reflected all that was left of a romantic pink sunset. Across one of the many narrow roads which meandered around and through the Green, a man was driving a herd of mired cows. He was a little, bandy-legged fellow, dressed in earth-hued garments, and helping himself along with a gnarled stick. He shook his stick and shouted, "G'yon thurr, G'yon will yer. . . ." A collie, barking on a high note, endorsed his order. The cows, shoving one another with their throats, staring wildly, staggered and slipped towards a gate tugged open by a gesticulating boy. The noise passed. In the distance a cock crowed. In a cottage on the further side of the Green, four squares of lemon yellow light sprang into life, making the dusk appear much bluer. Close by, under the garden wall of Willows, the legend on a signpost with a single arm was just visible. "Footpath to the Church," it said. The air was cold, but remarkably pure, faintly scented by wood-smoke and haystacks. In the darkling sky a single star flickered.

Catha Rollo gave vent to a sigh which contained no sadness. "Thank you for a lovely day," she said. "It's been like a dream come true, to see Willows for myself at last. I've talked about myself and my own affairs all the time, though. . . ."

"On the contrary," interrupted her hostess. "You've scarcely mentioned India, about which I intend yet to hear a great deal."

"I only want to know that you really are happy and content here, Button," said the guest, turning on her stool. "Of course you're so clever, you've made this dear little house quite a home. I was only afraid that sometimes you might miss Woodside."

"Everyone's sorry for me, living in a hovel almost in the shadow of my ancestral hall," said Mary Morrison. "They can't think how I can bear to do it. Actually I chose it, but I wallow in their sympathy. Even if I could keep five gardeners nowadays, I shouldn't want to go on living at home, like the last sardine in the tin. It was awful there during those last few months with Mother, when I knew it would kill her to leave and my sole reading was accounts rendered. Never again, thank you. And I'm delighted that the place is a school. I don't think I should have liked people who filled it with silk cushions and pottery dwarfs."

"And you don't find the long country evenings, all alone, very boring?"

"They aren't, you see. Nearly every night something takes me out. Besides, if I ever feel dull there's nothing to prevent me going up to London where I belong to an excellent club."

"I can't bear to think of you staying at a women's club, Button. Even the best of them always seem to me to be filled with females glaring in corners, and all on wires, as if they were waiting to be dragged to the tumbrils. Now, thank goodness, you can always come to us. We must, before I go, settle a day for you to lunch and meet the children. Your engagement block is downstairs, you said, and Tuesdays and Thursdays are always hopeless for you." Lady Rollo gathered her handbag and gloves, as if preparing to rise, but sat on staring out into the night. "I must thank you again," she said, after a slight effort, "for being so angelic to my Tony. You don't know what a comfort it was to get your letters, and know that someone understanding was keeping an eye on the poor boy. Tim has got an idea now that second sons are the thing. Crispin and Tony have been so different from the moment they were born. I sometimes feel that the first-born is always an amateurish effort. I was as bold as a lion before Tony arrived. The streets were full of bouncing babies; everyone seemed to have them. But when I'd got him I fussed over him like an old hen. It must have been bad for him. I remember I used to hop out of bed several times a night because I couldn't hear him breathing and thought he might have died. He was a completely healthy baby until he got that awful asthma. . . ."

"He's completely healthy again now," his godmother assured his mother. "Only suffering from acute retarded growing pains."

"I can't help seeing Tim's point of view," continued the mourning parent. "I never shall forget a ghastly night, just before we left. I was dressing for a big dinner, just putting on my stars, when Tim clanked in and pushed something under my nose. He said, 'You've been complaining we get no news of your eldest son,' and clanked out. It was a newspaper cutting about some idiotic speech on Misrule in India that the poor boy had made at the Union. I suppose you saw it. I could see it was rotten luck on Tim. But I always point out that Tony hasn't had the same chances as Crispin."

"He very nearly has," said his frank godmother.

"Oh no, dear! because when we sent Crispin home we sent Elizabeth too. Neither of the younger ones has ever been the sole child left by us at school in England. One time, when you were in Spain, and none of my relations seemed available, we had to get my old Chesterfield Street aunt's butler to bring Tony down to Southampton to see us off. They looked like something out of Dickens as they stood side by side on the quay, and the boat moved out in that heart-rending way. Tony was in his first prep. school clothes, which I'd ordered to allow for growth—vain optimism. However," said Lady Rollo, rising at last, "I must confess that he wrote afterwards to say that he and the butler had much enjoyed their return journey to London in the restaurant car of the special train, and had gone afterwards to a new cinema, where they had occupied *fauteuils* upholstered in imitation leopard-skin."

(ii)

Mary Morrison took out the clutch, and let her ten horse-power saloon car run gently through the gate of Willows and into the thatched shed which was large enough to house two such vehicles if parked by experts.

A sound as of metal subjected to sudden and violent pressure rent the night air. She dismounted calmly, and detached from her running-board the flattened form of a tin bucket. "One of these days," she said to the garage walls, "I shall murder that boy." She collected a pile of paper-covered literature from the back seat of the car, switched off its headlights, and stumped rather stiffly towards her dwelling.

The girls had all been disappointed that the grant for their uniforms had not arrived; the lecturer had been suffering from an undisguised cold in the head, and the hut had been over-heated. She was feeling tired and hungry. Exasperation swelled in her breast when she perceived that the windows of the parlour were still wide open, as she had left them after casting on the fire the contents of two ash-trays filled during the afternoon by herself and Catha Rollo. Doris, however, had not let the fire out, which was always something.

Miss Morrison cast down her armful of papers, and flicked on the light in the parlour. A loose-limbed form, which had been crouching in front of the large open brick fireplace, arose and shambled towards her, blinking at the sudden brilliance.

"Hullo, Tony!" said Miss Morrison, who made a point of never being surprised by this guest. "Have you been sitting all alone in the dark here? I'm sorry I was out."

Tony Rollo, still blinking behind remarkably thick horn-rimmed glasses, gave his sponsor an ice-cold hand, and muttered, "It was all right. They told me you were coming in for supper about ten, so I just waited."

"If by 'they' you mean Doris, you might have seen that she shut the windows," said Miss Morrison, snibbing her casements fiercely.

"I never noticed that they were open," said Tony in the accents of one who is above the cares of the body. "I kept up a good fire though. Whatever-her-name-is asked me not to let it go out."

"Considering that you are so keen on the down-trodden classes," said Miss Morrison, with regrettable acidity, "you might remember Doris's name. I've had her for nearly two years now."

"Do you tread Doris down much?" asked Mr. Rollo, interested.

Miss Morrison did not deign to answer. She had removed her overcoat, unassisted, and stood disclosed in a startling costume of scarlet cotton, with a pocket for a fountain pen attached to the bosom.

"Hullo! Been out on Blood-Sports again?" asked Mr. Rollo, upon whom the flaming colour seemed to have produced the result guaranteed in young bulls.

"Anti-Gas Lecture and Practice. Seven to nine," said Miss Morrison wearily.

"Don't attempt to deny that you revel in it," said her godson.

"We arranged to-night to jump through a gas-filled waggon next Wednesday afternoon, which is the afternoon I'd just fixed to lunch with your mother in London," said Miss Morrison. "And if you imagine that I revel in that sort of game at my age, you're wrong. Still, it had to be, for Wednesday's early closing down here, and half the girls get no other afternoon off."

"I'm sorry," said Tony. "But if they are such lunatics as to let you bully them into leaping about in gas-filled waggons, I'm afraid I can't take much interest in them."

Miss Morrison remembered that her godson was probably, like herself, cold, tired and hungry.

She said, "Come on in next door. I told Doris and Rose they could go to bed. There's soup in a thermos, but I think we might cook some sausages and mash, since we've got the excuse of one another."

"My lady mother visited here this afternoon, I gather," said Tony, staring into the fire again.

"She did, and she was looking lovely, and we had a heavenly day," said Miss Morrison.

"I suppose," suggested Lady Rollo's first-born, "that you had all the usual propaganda. My younger brother, who is good at games and work, never causes anyone a moment's anxiety, whereas all I can do is to write for the gutter press."

"No, Tony! have you really had something accepted?" asked his audience with unaffected pleasure.

"Humph! One thing last week. It wasn't much good, and they cut it down. To tell you the truth, I don't think they would have accepted it but for my name," said the author gloomily. "My father's name, I should say."

"Actually Catha merely said that Crispin and you had been different from birth," reported Miss Morrison. After a pause for consideration, she added the anecdote of Lady Rollo rising from bed several times a night to ascertain that her first-born was still breathing.

Tony Rollo cast an unnecessary log on the fire and kicked it to a blaze before saying in controlled tones, "Mother-love, unfortunately, seems to be almost as fatal to its victims as infantile paralysis. There ought to be a cemetery full of tombstones labelled, 'Here, but for the dissuasions of his female parent, lies a Prime Minister of Great Britain.'"

"Your mother would be charmed if you ever did anything on this earth, as you well know," said Miss Morrison, leading the way through her dining-room to her kitchen. "Here are the sausages, and that's the saucepan hanging up in that corner. You'll find matches to light the gas in the drawer of this table."

"I've got matches in my own pocket, thank you," mumbled Tony. "Would you mind if I produced my pipe too, while we cook?"

"No," said Miss Morrison nobly, for she was well able to imagine the resultant odours.

As she prodded the leaping potatoes five minutes later, she asked, "How is work going, Tony? Any hope of a First?"

"As far as I can see, if I swot till my eyes fall out, I shall get a Second. And if I don't do another stroke of work, I shall still get a Second," said the future Prime Minister.

"Is that what your tutor says?" asked Miss Morrison quickly.

"It's what he probably thinks."

"I should advise swotting," decided Miss Morrison. "You may be a border-line case. If you got a First, it would give you a pull for life. You might go on and get a fellowship somewhere. Then you could become a Young Red Don and make yourself no end of a nuisance, and be enormously popular."

At the thought of becoming a Young Red Don, Mr. Rollo appeared to his observer to flush darkly. But the result might have been due to the effort of frying sausages while smoking a very new pipe.

"If you don't get a First, what are you going to do?" asked Miss Morrison presently.

"Don't ask me," said her godson.

"But I do ask you," explained Miss Morrison. "What use would it be for me to ask anyone else?"

"It doesn't matter much to anyone else, anyway," said Tony, voicing a lonely soul.

"I fancy it will matter to your father," suggested Miss Morrison.

Tony approached the real object of his unheralded call.

"As a matter of fact," he said, "I've definitely decided to explain the situation to my father. You may have heard that I haven't been to see any of the family yet. I thought I should like to get things clear before we met. I've written my father rather a good letter. I've got it here. Would you like to see it?"

Miss Morrison's heart sank. "After supper," she said.

"You see," continued Tony, "I realize that while I'm entirely dependent on my father, he may think he has the right to object to my publishing my views. There has been an ominous silence since my last speech on the mess they are making in India, and I know that was fairly widely reported. So I've simply told him that if he feels like that, I am willing to go down from Oxford at once, without taking a degree."

"And what do you imagine his answer will be?" asked Miss Morrison.

"He ought to cut off my allowance," said Tony gloatingly. "But I doubt if he has the courage."

Miss Morrison, too, doubted this. She remarked, "It wouldn't be an economic step on his part, after all he's expended on your education. In his place I should insist on your taking Schools, and see what you got. However, I suppose you've formed some plan for supporting yourself if he agrees to your leaving Oxford now."

Tony hunched his shoulders, and looked not more than sixteen, and a very ugly hobbledehoy at that. He muttered, "It's so beastly difficult to get things published."

Elegant Catha Rollo's first-born was low of stature and heavily made. He would, his hostess thought, as she surveyed him, have been much the better of a little of his brother Crispin's reputedly imbecile affection for ball games. Tony had inherited the rough dark hair, lowering brow and dusky complexion of his Welsh ancestors. "Goodness," thought his godmother, looking at him as she prodded her potatoes, "he has a hard row to hoe, with that temperament." She remembered sitting out on the stairs at Christmas parties, keeping a firm grip on Tony, while crackers were pulled in the dining-room by children who enjoyed loud, sudden noises. "Of course," she thought, "though I can't say this to his father or Catha, it's as plain as a pike-staff. Tony's got plenty of the old gentleman in him. So had Tim himself, if it comes to that, and I know for a fact that he and the old gentleman used to tear one another in pieces. I wonder, though, if Tony has got any of their drive and ability."

The potatoes were ready to be mashed.

"You might get me the colander from the scullery," said Miss Morrison, over her shoulder.

"The what?" asked Tony with a dropped jaw.

"It's a round, white enamelled basin, with a hollow handle, and it's full of holes, so that you can drain boiling water off things," explained Miss Morrison. "You'll find one invaluable if you're ever driven, by force of circumstances, to be your own *chef.*"

But since she was fond of her godson, Miss Morrison belaboured the potatoes together with a liberal allowance of butter and milk, and added careful sprinklings of sugar, salt and pepper, before arranging the result artistically around the sausages with a couple of forks.

The odd companions proceeded to the dining-room, and began their feast.

"If you feel rotten about taking an allowance from your father while you stab him in the back, so to speak," said Miss Morrison between mouthfuls of pea-soup, "why don't you get a tutoring job to tide you over the vacation?"

"Putting a backward and delicate through Caesar and Elementary Maths—no thanks!" said Mr. Rollo scornfully. "Besides, if I am still taking Schools in June, I shall have to work during the vac."

"You could well do both. You would almost certainly get your evenings free, although you might be expected to dine with the family," surmised Miss Morrison, not very kindly.

Mr. Rollo swallowed something more than sausage.

"Lots of decent young men with no means do it," said Miss Morrison. "We had processions of them through the house while my brother was failing for the Army. One of them married one of my aunts."

"How lovely for him," said Tony. "Or wasn't it?"

"It depends upon your views. Last time I saw him, he was addressing a packed political meeting. He's been Member for a mining constituency in his wife's part of the country for seventeen years, and is much liked by all parties, I believe. He's Labour," added Miss Morrison.

Tony Rollo fell to the bait, and half an hour later was still explaining to his godmother the necessity for the nationalization of credit. They had an uncontroversial and almost genial chat over the good fire in the parlour, before Miss Morrison departed to her airing cupboard to hunt out linen for the unexpected guest. As they bade one another good night, Tony said, "By the way, I suppose you didn't hear anything special about my fashionable débutante sister?"

"I heard that she's brought an impossible hat back from Paris, which sounds correct for her age," said Miss Morrison. "But I doubt if, at seventeen, she can be seriously considered as a leader of fashion."

But nobody except himself was to be allowed to cast a stone at Tony's only sister.

"Elizabeth's a very bright child," he said, nodding his shockhead portentously, "and well up to standard in looks, I should say. You'll get a surprise when you see her."

It was only as she watched his battered two-seater disappear through her gate the next morning, that Mary Morrison realized, with a start of relief, that Tony had gone off without showing her his rather good letter to his father.

CHAPTER III

MARCH 16TH—MARCH 17TH

A HAILSTORM was sweeping Westbury-on-the-Green. It caught Mary Morrison, without raincoat or umbrella, two hundred yards from her house. Three weeks had passed since Catha Rollo's visit. In the green fields around Westbury there were wild daffodils, and in the gardens crocuses and scillas. At Went Park, where Mary had gone yesterday for a meeting of the Nursing Association, her ladyship's Adams hall had been garnished with several hundred pot hyacinths pink, white, blue and purple.

Mary Morrison lifted the latch of Westbury Post Office and darted into shelter. Before her eyes became accustomed to the warm gloom inside, she recognized the voice of Aileen Hill. The three Hills, Norah, Sheilah and Aileen, lived in Bury Cottage on the Went road, just off the Green. Norah kept house, Sheilah bred bloodhounds, and Aileen grew flowers and sold them to the owners of London houses. Their father, the late Canon, had been a rosarian, and their mother an Irish lady of considerable attractions, but far from regular habits.

"Hullo, Miss Morrison," said Aileen in her cheerful and rather loud young voice. "Are you in a hurry, because I'm afraid I've set Mrs. Crippen rather a job? I want to send a letter to Canada, Air Mail, and she's lost the sheet of instructions, telling one how much it is."

"That I 'ave not, Miss Aileen, so don't you go saying so," remarked a muffled and preoccupied voice from behind the counter. "I 'ave the sheet 'id up safe somewhere, that I know, for I mended it only last week, after 'er ladyship's plum-pudding dog laid 'is pawer on it when 'er ladyship brought in the letter for India, Air Mail, to 'er sister."

Mrs. Crippen retired into an inner fastness, her down-at-the-heel slippers clapping fiercely, and Mary Morrison assured her companion, "It's all right. I don't need anything except a book of stamps. I came in principally to keep dry."

Aileen Hill bent to peer out of the bottle-end windows of the Post Office, which were much obscured by jars of boiled sweets and festoons of bootlaces. "Golly! it's coming down," she exclaimed. "How's your garden, Miss Morrison?"

"Pretty good, thanks," replied Mary, "though I've been too busy lately to do much about it. How is the flower trade doing? I was sorry to hear from Norah that your car broke down on the arterial road after one of your London trips, the other night."

"It wasn't much fun," agreed Aileen, "because, of course, there was a fog. However, I only gave twenty pounds for that car, so I can't complain. Sheilah nicknamed it 'The Wreck' the day I brought it home. I'm doing quite well, thanks. I've found two perfectly useless women who want me to come up twice a week throughout the season, whatever that means, to do their houses for them. I did a dinner table for twenty-eight before a dance yesterday—Fantasy tulips and chionodoxa. Sloppy, but showy."

"Any hopes of a wedding?" asked Miss Morrison.

"What?" gaped Aileen.

Miss Morrison told herself that she had not realized before how good-looking Aileen was. The youngest Hill was tall and slight; her brown hair had golden lights in it, her features were neat and her complexion was glowing. This morning she had adorned her large, well-shaped mouth with lip-stick of a ruby hue. She was attired in a well-worn leather jacket, a crocus-coloured head-handkerchief tied under the chin, a brief tweed skirt of startling green and yellow checks, silk stockings, woollen socks, and brogues.

"Norah told me the other day," explained Miss Morrison, "that you were hoping to get orders to decorate churches for weddings."

But Mrs. Crippen had returned, triumphantly waving a sheet of printed matter. "I'd put it in me Bible to press after I'd mended it," she announced.

While Aileen counted out coppers, and Mrs. Crippen affixed with a bang an oblong blue label which she procured from a lofty drawer labelled "Air Mail," Mary Morrison flicked over the selection of post cards exposed for sale on the counter. They were all glossy sepia photographs, and cost, she knew, twopence each, or a shilling the packet. The set included St. Nicholas Church, Westbury-on-the-Hill; The War Memorial; Went Park; Greetings from Westbury-on-the-Green (six views); Went Junction and Woodside from the West.

Mary Morrison picked up the portrait of her old home and said, "I thought you told me, Mrs. Crippen, that the headmistress at Woodside had said you might send up your nephew to take some new photographs."

"That she did, miss, last August," admitted Mrs. Crippen, "but the young fellow, being in camp then with 'is Territorials, wasn't able to get over. I've told 'im 'e needn't trouble till May now, when the long avenue will be at its best. But I'll let you know without fail when the new stock comes in. I'm expecting a good sale to the visiting parents of the young ladies. Tut! tut! it's the weather makes these sheets stick. I'll give Miss Morrison her five-shilling book first, if you don't mind, Miss Aileen."

Mrs. Crippen, in trouble with her sheet of fivepennies, vanished again.

Mary Morrison prepared to take her leave.

"It's over, I see," she said, bending to study the landscape. "I'm too late now to do much before lunch. I think I'll take the chance of looking up poor old Sally Bates."

"Mrs. Bates, in my opinion," said Aileen Hill in resonant tones, "is Public Wet-Blanket Number One. If she walked a bit more and talked a bit less. . . ."

"But she really has been having rheumatism all the winter," objected Mary Morrison. "And I don't think she means to depress one. She's wonderfully cheerful herself always."

"Jolly good of you," said Aileen. "I shall stay here and put my letter in the box outside with my own hands." She added awkwardly, "It's rather a special letter, you see."

"Oh!" said Mary Morrison, with only the hint of a question mark after her interjection.

"You see," said Aileen Hill, staring down at her listener with lustrous brown eyes, "you gave me rather a start when you said that about a wedding, because I've just settled to have one myself."

"Oh!" repeated Mary Morrison. "Well, this is good news. I'm delighted to hear it, my dear."

The neighbours shook hands warmly, but with some embarrassment.

"It's not news yet," said Aileen warningly. "I'll let you know when it is. You see, until I hear from him again I feel rather like Mahomet's coffin. I can't go yelling round the Green that I'm engaged, until he knows too."

"Naturally," agreed Miss Morrison. "And he is in Canada?"

"Vancouver Island," nodded Aileen. "I believe it's lovely. He says that he thinks he could get home early in September, if that's all right for me. I must say I'm thankful, for the journey out, even if I go Tourist, is almost exactly what I made on the flowers last quarter. He's Scotch, and six months younger than I—twenty-three. I haven't told anyone yet, not even Norah and Sheilah. Well—so long."

"*Au revoir*, and the best of good wishes," said Mary. "I think he's very lucky. Please tell him so next time you write."

Miss Morrison proceeded towards the house of the lady stigmatized by the bride-to-be as Public Wet-Blanket Number One. "However," she reflected, "after hearing a good piece of news like that, I defy even old Sally to get me down."

Mrs. Bates, who was the widow of a medical man, lived in the most attractive house on Westbury Green. It was a Queen Anne doll's house, small, but perfect of its type. Every time Mary Morrison entered it, she was obliged to stifle a regret that Dr.

Bates could not have passed away insolvent. This morning a flowering peach and two yellow forsythias were spreading brilliant branches in front of the red-brick façade, and on the small lawn separated from the road by white painted posts and chains, a number of birds with shining backs were excavating diligently.

Mrs. Bates was at home, seated in front of an electric fire in full blast, although she was wearing a full-length outdoor coat over a woollen costume. She was a tall, large woman with a complexion of extraordinary pallor, which contrasted strangely with her vigorous address.

"Come in, come in," she cried. "I was hoping that I should see you this morning when I noticed you caught by that storm. You're not wet, I hope."

"Not at all, thank you," said Mary. "I sheltered in the Post Office. Most unexpected, wasn't it? I hope you were not out."

"I was not," chuckled Mrs. Bates. "I said to myself when I woke this morning, 'Bright, but treacherous!' I very nearly stayed in bed for lunch. I'm glad I didn't, as you've dropped in. It's a long time since you've been to see me. But I hear you're very busy with your nursing, these days. Is it true that you've volunteered, if there's a war, to go off into the blue and nurse total strangers? I had quite expected that you would be having your poor sister-in-law from London to live with you."

"Heaven forbid!" thought Mary Morrison. Aloud she said, rather weakly, "I wanted to volunteer, but they are not very keen on officers leaving. Marcelle hasn't said anything about moving from her London flat, and she loathes the country, I know."

"Help yourself to a cigarette," commanded Mrs. Bates. "I'm sorry I can't get up this morning. They're in that box with the Barbola flowers on the lid. You might give me one too. Thanks. Well, I'm surprised your sister-in-law isn't going to leave London, when places like Woodside are preparing to pack up in the event of war."

Mary Morrison echoed the name of her old home in a decidedly agitated voice.

"The Mental Hospital outside Went is going to become a Military Hospital, as of course you know," affirmed Mrs. Bates, with relish, "and the lunatics are going to be put into Woodside."

"Are you positive?" asked Mary Morrison. But in her heart she knew that Mrs. Bates was always right. Her spirits sank to zero. She scarcely heard Mrs. Bates detailing the drawbacks of the West Country residence into which the girls' school was going to move.

"And now," said Mrs. Bates, drawing a long breath, "tell me all about Crossgrove."

"Crossgrove!" exclaimed Mary.

"You don't mean to say," said Mrs. Bates in obviously rising spirits, "that you haven't heard about Lady Rollo's coming down and taking it."

After a short silence, Mary rallied sufficiently to say carefully, "Catha Rollo was down here house-hunting, three weeks ago, and we fixed a meeting in London, but I had to fail her. Then she went north, and the last I heard was that they were house-hunting in quite another direction—Berkshire, I think she said. But I am spending the day with them all in London to-morrow, so no doubt then I shall hear everything."

"I certainly hope you will," said Mrs. Bates sympathetically. "I said to myself when I heard that Lady Rollo had taken Crossgrove, 'Ah! that'll be because of Mary Morrison.' But she's left you quite in the dark!"

"Well, actually," said Mary valiantly, "I did recommend it to her, and we very nearly went to see it together. I expect in the end she came down in a hurry one morning, and hadn't time to telephone to me!"

"She's been down three times," mentioned Mrs. Bates, "but it was only settled last week. Well, that's very disappointing, that you can't tell me anything. They're putting in a swimming pool, I hear (though goodness knows why anyone should want to plunge themselves in cold water in this county), and for some reason they're tearing out all the lovely old panelling from the hall."

"Electric light and central heating, perhaps," suggested Mary, rising.

"How was Aileen Hill when you met her in the Post Office?" asked Mrs. Bates, retaining her guest's hand.

"Looking very pretty," said Mary. "She has the best large white tombstone front teeth I ever saw. Good-bye."

"I wonder how she'll like Canada," shouted Mrs. Bates.

But Mary Morrison was already out of hearing.

(ii)

On winter mornings, if Mary Morrison wished to catch the 8.50 express to London, she was obliged to rise and attire herself by artificial light. Her London clothes, viewed in the mirror of a country cottage bedroom at 7.30 a.m. always appeared to her a vision of elegance, but she knew that by the time she reached the cloak-room of her club she would find herself saying gloomily to her reflection there, "A policewoman!" Still, if you wanted full value for your day-return ticket to London, the 8.50 was the only possible train. It halted at Went Junction in a condescending manner on its thunderous career down the valley, but not for long. If you met a flock of sheep, or even a large lorry between the Green and Went, you were likely to lose the 8.50.

This morning, since the day was March 17th, Mary was able to dress by full daylight, but although the skies outside were bright and the sun was shining, she shivered as she brushed her hair. The scene, viewed through the tiny window on the left-hand side of her dressing-table, was a Christmas card picture.

The legend on the signpost in the foreground was hidden; the Green was white, and beyond silver-roofed cottages wreaths of mist were rising from unseen fields. There had been a fervent frost overnight. She placed her second pair of gloves inside her handbag, and fetched from its cardboard home her new hat. A single glance at it decided her not to assume it until the last possible moment. Downstairs, she hurried through her breakfast, and stowed her letters, unread, beside her clean gloves.

Doris was not a blithe riser on cold mornings, and Miss Morrison's small car often shared her maid's distaste for beginning work on such occasions. By the time that she shot through the gate of Willows, Mary knew that if she was to catch the express, she must drive faster than she deemed wise. The square tower of Westbury church rose picturesquely against a dazzling background of limpid blue, but a draught sharp as a knife was stealing round the nape of her neck. The lane had glossy dark streaks on its surface, and in the hedgerows faded long grass and bowed foliage sparkled like crystallized fruits.

She heard the whistle of the train in the cutting, as she ran her car into the shed opposite the station-master's cottage, and as she snatched her ticket from the booking-clerk, she panted, "As soon as you can, Henry, nip down and make sure I've not left my engine running." The damp timber platforms were covered by a glistening powder, and she was wearing high heels. As she crossed the steep bridge to the London side, she saw the express drawing in beneath her. To ascend from the platform at Went into the 8.50 was a feat difficult to perform without assistance from above or below, if you were carrying a closed wicker basket, a handbag and an umbrella. Miss Morrison was conscious of a pumping heart and a heightened colour as she took her seat in a warm compartment already containing several occupants obscured by open newspapers.

One of the newspapers descended, and a courtly voice remarked, "I am glad to see that you are evidently in rude health, Mary."

"Good morning, Sir James," said Mary. "I know I'm lobster in the face. My car wouldn't start this morning."

"I was just reflecting," said Sir James, "that the windows of this compartment resemble those of an aquarium." He cleared the opaque cloud from a portion of the pane nearest to him, and commented, "Went Junction, yes, of course," and then proceeded, "I am afraid that you are unlucky in your choice of seat. We have all been avoiding that corner this morning, because, as you will soon discover, there is a volume of heated steam emerging from beneath the cushions. Let me introduce my young guest David Cox, who will, I am sure, be delighted to exchange places with you. Mr. Cox is on leave from the Frontier, and about to enjoy a day's racing at Sandown Park."

Some confused movement followed, during which the protesting Mary was ousted from her unenviable corner, and the middle sheets of two newspapers escaped from their owners. The surprising fact was disclosed that the stranger with the appearance of an elder of the kirk, who was seated next to Sir James's lady, had been poring over an article headed "Why I liked the Chink best of my five husbands."

"He got in at Titterington. None of us have any idea who he is," explained his neighbour to Mary, in the really efficient whisper cultivated by those accustomed to live with the slightly deaf.

The travellers settled down to the intermittent conversation usual amongst those aboard the 8.50. The future of Crossgrove was a topic which interested everyone, except Dr. Greatbatch, who only uttered twice, and on neither occasion to the point. He said, twiddling a battered silver pencil-case in his long fingers, "How are you getting on this morning, Sir James? You've got 'Oppidans,' naturally. 'Tempera' I considered clever, and the clue fair. But seventeen down beats me."

"How many letters, my dear Greatbatch?" asked Sir James in his most ambassadorial voice.

"Only six," mourned Dr. Greatbatch, "and if I've got nine across right, then the two middle letters must be l and z, which fills me with doubt."

"Try 'Balzac,' sir," said Mr. David Cox suddenly and loudly, blushing to the roots of the curly fair hair which gave him a deceptively infantile appearance.

Lady Wilson, after a piercing gaze at her late guest, as if viewing him in a new and unpleasing light, continued her conversation with Mary. "Well, my dear, if you tell me that they are nice people, and likely to be of some use to the community,

I shall make a point of calling as soon as possible." Raising her voice to the scream of a macaw, as the train fled into a tunnel, she enquired from her *vis-à-vis*, "Dorothy! did your husband ever meet anyone called Rollo when he was in India?"

"Tim Rollo" came the answer. "Rather. Peppery little chap. Good at his job, though. Rolfe got on with him all right, I believe. I know everyone liked Lady Rollo, although she was hopeless on committees."

"A good Conservative?" probed Lady Wilson. But Mary's assurances were drowned by a whistle from the engine as they emerged once more into the light of day.

"I wouldn't have believed it," announced Dr. Greatbatch, putting his pencil in his pocket in a final manner. "They've used 'Borzoi' twice in ten days. The real fellow must be on holiday—or perhaps down with 'flu."

Twenty minutes later, the express groaned to a temporary standstill, and, on a lower level, an electric train sped past, inclining perilously. As it neared London, the 8.50 always became noticeably tamer. Presently the backs of many pitifully blackened small houses, all exhibiting washing, began to draw slowly past the windows of the express. At last a grey and echoing dimness enveloped the travellers. The noise of newspapers being folded and umbrellas reclaimed alternated with the click of doors, opened prematurely.

Sir James's lady said, as she held up an imperious finger to attract a porter, "We shall be taking a taxicab to our hotel. Can we lift either of you—Dorothy? —Mary?"

But the young Member of Parliament's wife was being met by her mother, and Mary, who knew without needing to be told, where the hotel patronized by her friends was situated, explained that South Kensington was out of her way.

The country neighbours scattered and were swallowed up in a crowd of figures pacing towards the adventures of a London day.

(iii)

Mary Morrison went by Underground to her club, where she freshened her appearance, and was compelled by the head-porter to take a ticket in a sweepstake on the National. She then repaired by bus to Sloane Street, where she identified and bought a packet of needles of a type unobtainable in Went. She had been meaning to do this on her last five visits to London, so she felt a glow of triumph as she left the shop.

Catha's telegram had said "Shall expect you 11.30," and the hour was still only 10.50 when Mary emerged from Green Park Station. She strolled down St. James's Street, found the block in which the Rollos had taken a service flat, and handed in the covered basket. Although Willows was already fully furnished, she never could resist the chance of improving her collection at a reasonable cost. She knew that "The Property of a Gentleman, including Antique Furniture, Oil-Paintings and Tapestries" was on view in auction rooms not fifty yards distant. Big Ben was sounding eleven as she ascended the bare brown staircase towards one of her favourite London haunts.

Fortunately, this morning no great temptations awaited her. The tapestries were all of a size more suited to Westminster Hall than Willows. They represented the Three Kings, more than life size, and with enormous curls and eyes; the Massacre of the Innocents, taking place amongst many pillars, and a very stout Esther gesticulating before Ahasuerus. The best pieces of furniture were a refectory table, and fourteen mahogany dining-room chairs. She lingered affectionately for several minutes in front of a small walnut bureau, but as it was reputed to have belonged to a famous Georgian minister, she deemed it unprofitable to consider its purchase. The auction rooms were not crowded. Shafts of sunshine full of dust-motes lit the figures of several gentlemen with dark complexions, wearing tumbled overcoats, who shuffled about muttering in various tongues. The only people moving rapidly were bare-armed men in baize aprons. A young lady, with curls the colour of the yolk of an egg, was attached to a bearded cavalier in a sombrero, who was making her look up numbers in a catalogue. They paused below a not very conscientious copy of a portrait of Strafford, and the young lady, having failed to realize that some of the pictures exhibited today, belonged to another sale, read in the voice of one who reserved her judgment, "A view near Fountains Abbey, with cattle and a rainbow."

Mary reached the block of service flats exactly on time, and a young man in a dark blue suit stepped aside briskly to allow her to enter the lift first. As they were wafted aloft, she took a second look at him. He was holding a bowler hat in his hand and looking cheerful. "Good morning, Crispin," said Mary. "You won't remember me, but I'm Mary Morrison."

"We met last on a platform at Waterloo, where you delivered Elizabeth to me for a Christmas journey to Wales," said Crispin Rollo promptly. "We were both hoping so much that we should not miss seeing you to-day."

It was not possible, Mary Morrison decided, that either Elizabeth or her brother could really have hoped to meet a middle-aged crony of their mother, but Crispin Rollo managed to make his statement sound heartfelt. He wrung her hand warmly, and beamed upon her.

Crispin Rollo was one of the best-looking young men that Mary Morrison had ever seen. He was, as his mother had warned her, now six feet high. He had flat, yellow hair, a ruddy complexion, bright blue eyes and a prominent chin. Before they could speak again, the lift boy said glibly, "First door on the right, sir," and the gates of the lift opened upon an electric-lighted fourth-storey landing.

The entire Rollo family, with the exception of her godson, was enclosed in the suite of four rooms into which Mary was now ushered. She first met Sir Daubeny, who was seated in sunshine at a bow window, writing cheques. The frown cleared from his prominent brow as he recognized his visitors. He got up saying,

"My dear Button, this is delightful!" and then raising his voice, "Elizabeth! tell your mother Button is here, and Crispin!"

A bang sounded on an inner door which Crispin hastened to open, and through the entrance came slowly a large glass container filled with flowering boughs, carried at arm's length by an unsteady walker. Elizabeth Rollo's face, seen through interlaced branches, dotted with almond blossom, was a very pretty sight indeed. She landed her load on the top of her father's desk, rubbed her palms on a vivid chiffon handkerchief, and cried, "Aunt Button! how heavenly of you to leave us those gorgeous flowers."

"I can't have that forest of stuff on my desk," began her father with a light in his eye.

"But darling," explained the débutante, "you're being frightfully rude! They're Aunt Button's flowers, and I've spent twenty minutes doing them, and I had to get that vase thing up from the basement. The only one in this flat had silver kingfishers on it, and only held one drop of water."

The floral arrangement stayed where it was, to Mary's secret amusement, and Elizabeth continued, "How do you like our flat, Auntie Bee? Isn't it perfectly ghastly? It costs untold gold, and there's nowhere to put one's clothes, and on Monday the typed *Menu* for lunch stuck up in the lift, said 'Lion chops.'"

Mary suggested tactfully, "It's very central."

"It's not as central as Eros, and twice as noisy," complained Elizabeth.

"I agree," said her father violently. "For my part, I shall be thankful when we get down to Crossgrove."

"You're not to tell her about Crossgrove, Tim," came faintly from an inner chamber. "It's to be my Surprise."

"You're living in a Fool's Paradise, my dear," replied Mary in flutey accents. "I've known for twenty-four hours, and I've got a footman for you."

"How marvellous!" came from the wings. "We've got a butler who'll quarrel with everyone, I prophesy. He was in Tim's old regiment. Tell me about the footman. What's the matter with him?"

"He has spectacles," admitted Mary, "but he's matchless at separating fighting dogs. He was pantry boy at Woodside, and has never been happy since."

Catha Rollo entered, saluted her guest and her son, and said vaguely, "Oughtn't you to be starting, Tim?" She explained to Mary, "They are all going to Sandown, while you and I buy curtains and carpets together. But I told you to come now, so that you should see them."

"I like them very much," Mary assured the parents. "They do you both credit."

"Do you really think I'm all right, Auntie Bee?" asked Elizabeth anxiously. "I've only been to a Point-to-Point once before."

"This is the third time this morning," announced Sir Daubeny, "that I've told you the Grand Military Meeting is not a Point-to-Point."

"It's a coat and skirt and flat shoes, though, isn't it, Auntie Bee?" asked Miss Rollo. "Auntie Bee knows what I mean. Or do you think as it's so close to London, I ought to wear Mummy's lovely new fur coat?"

Sir Daubeny was of the opinion that his daughter ought not to wear his wife's lovely new fur coat.

"Besides," he informed her, "you're too small to wear one, ever. You would look like a dormouse."

"The other day, when Mummy lent me it because I had a cold, Tony's decorator friend said I looked all Hollywood and Heaven too," said Elizabeth reminiscently. "I had a husky voice, because of the cold. I wish I had one always."

"Oh! no, dear, it made your poor little nose as red as a cherry," said her distressed mother.

"You will never have anything but the form and voice of a Nippy, my dear Elizabeth," said her male parent, "so you had better resign yourself to your fate."

"Good gracious!" ejaculated Mary.

"What is it, dear? Have you forgotten something?" asked her hostess.

"Yes, I'm afraid I have. I've just realized I never told Doris to feed the bantams, and it's my garden boy's day off. They'll starve. I must send a telegram."

"I can do that," said Crispin, handing his sister a brand-new shooting stick as he left the room.

Elizabeth was enchanted to be the owner of a shooting stick the exact twin of the one she had coveted every day this week on her homeward route, but had been unable to buy, owing to her more pressing need for a *diamanté* evening bag. She hurried after her brother.

"Elizabeth, go and put on your hat," called her mother. "You can thank Crispin in the car. Now Button, do sit down. You must be exhausted by our family pandemonium."

"Elizabeth," called Mary, "Crispin doesn't know my telephone number."

"All right, Mummy," cried Elizabeth. "All right, Auntie Bee. He must have looked it up in Mummy's address book, for he's on to Doris already. I can hear him."

"And now, I suppose," said Sir Daubeny, seating himself posed with a hand on either knee, and with sparkling eyes, "we shall miss the first race."

"Oh! no, Tim, why should you? Crispin is getting the car, and he's always quick."

"But he doesn't know the garage."

"He'll find out from the porter or someone."

"I see I shall have to go myself," said Sir Daubeny, making his exit.

Disregarding the fact that she must be interrupted at any moment, Catha Rollo began to open her heart to her old friend.

"Button, I've two things I'm longing to tell you. Crossgrove you know about, but you don't know that Tim got a long letter from Tony this morning." Mary managed to say "Oh!"

"Such a good letter," said Tony's mother, with shining eyes. "I feel truly thankful, and as if a cloud had rolled away. Do you know that the dear boy—entirely his own idea—has gone off and got a post as a tutor for the vacation? He explained to Tim (a little pompously, of course, but that's just his age) that since he was afraid Tim could not approve of views which he could not refrain from publishing, he would prefer not to draw his allowance. That's all nonsense, of course, but he genuinely is going to coach somebody's son—rather a dreadful family, I'm afraid, and naturally I shall miss him terribly. . . . The great thing is that it was such a manly letter, and Tim's pleased. He said to me as he handed it to me, 'My father might have written this.'"

CHAPTER IV
APRIL 14TH—APRIL 18TH

(i)

THE ROLLOS moved into Crossgrove on Friday, the fourteenth of April. The house was not, of course, nearly ready for them, but they were more than ready for it. Mary entertained all of them during the preceding month. She had Catha to lunch and tea five times, and caught a roaring cold in the head spending a busy but chilly afternoon with her friend in the empty house. She had Elizabeth and Tony down for a week-end, Crispin for a single night, and Tim for three nights. She had considered asking Sir James and Lady Wilson to meet their future distinguished neighbour at dinner, but as Sir James did not play Bridge, she decided upon her Member of Parliament and his wife, and—since she was not herself a player—Dr. Greatbatch. This arrangement meant bringing down a bedroom chair, and as far as Bridge was concerned, was a flat failure. The three gentlemen gloried together in the dining-room until ten-thirty. When they reappeared in the parlour, they continued their discussion of the European situation throughout the only rubber achieved.

Mary had Mrs. Bates to tea to meet Catha, and Mrs. Bates discovered that Elizabeth was going into a nursing home to have an impacted wisdom-tooth removed, which reminded her of the case of another débutante, also an only daughter, who had perished under the anaesthetic. Catha, however, thought Mrs. Bates a nice cheerful woman, and did not seem at all moved by the information that no housemaids would stay at Crossgrove because of the bus service, and that the little room which she had chosen as her sitting-room was the one in which a previous owner had qualified for delirium tremens.

Friday, the fourteenth, was, to Mary's satisfaction, the most beautiful English spring day imaginable. After breakfast she wandered out into her orchard, and deliberately wasted twenty minutes, strolling beneath budding fruit-trees, and occasionally picking a particularly fine sweet-scented narcissus or trumpet daffodil. The morning was one which made one want to walk slowly and draw long breaths. She was anxious to see how the cowslips were coming on in the field beyond the orchard, so let herself out by the small wicket gate in the hedge which marked the end of her property and the beginning of that farmed by Mr. Giddy. Willows had no view, except of the village green, but from this noble fifteen-acre field there was a wide and peaceful prospect. The sun beat down on her hatless head as she made her way towards the ditch above which cowslips were generally to be found. The blackthorn was in full flower against azure skies. Beyond it stretched a patchwork pattern of almost level pastures, and on the skyline, shimmering so that they seemed to move, rose the angular shapes of several large sheds. These marked Went aerodrome. They appeared to be cut out of powder-blue cardboard, and above them several aeroplanes were circling in the lavender-tinted sky, looking like silver moths as the sun caught reflections from their wings. Before Mary had time to reach her goal she heard a swishing sound, and turning, saw an aproned figure with skirts held high, struggling through the wet grass' of the orchard. She muttered, "Oh! bother. Telephone," but when she came within earshot Doris uttered breathlessly, "It's Missisix miss."

"What?" asked Mary.

"If you please, miss," said Doris mincingly, "could you spare a moment to see Missisix?"

Albert Higgs was the late pantry boy from Woodside whom Mary had recommended to Catha Rollo. She had not seen Albert's mother for many years. Albert and his widowed parent were standing in the hall of Willows. Albert looked unfamiliar in a much pressed and brushed but far from new dark suit, a size too small for him. Mrs. Higgs, who was tiny, but whom Mary knew to be a woman of iron will, bore a striking resemblance to a mole. She had a waxen face, eyes the colour of skim milk, with very puffy lids which she blinked incessantly, no hair visible under a grey felt hat pulled well down, and jet earrings. Her figure to ankles and finger-tips was entirely eclipsed by a brown coat of teddy-bear cloth. She carried an umbrella, grey thread gloves and a basket decorated with orange wool fruits, and was wearing mustard stockings and grey kid strap shoes with pointed toes.

"Well, Mrs. Higgs," said Mary, "this is a pleasant surprise!"

"We took the liberty. Miss Mary," said Mrs. Higgs, speaking in curiously indistinct tones, "to call in to thank you on our way to Crossgrove."

"How very nice of you!" said Mary. "Do come into the parlour."

"Thank you, Miss Mary," replied Mrs. Higgs, preparing to do so. To her son she added in an aside that brooked no question, "You stay out in the hall, Albert." Albert, turning his hat in his hands, swallowed but obeyed.

"Do sit down, Mrs. Higgs," said Mary. To herself she said, "Now I wonder what's coming."

Five minutes later she was forced to the conclusion that Mrs. Higgs had no object in excluding Albert from the conference except to show her authority.

Mrs. Higgs was in good health, but glad the winter was over. Her sailor son was still in China, and her married daughter had the five under four now, but her husband still out of work. Mrs. Higgs herself was going to live in rooms in Merle End, rented to her by the baker, an acquaintance of her childhood. She would thus be nice and near to Albert at Crossgrove. She was extremely obliged to Mary for recommending her son to Lady Rollo. They had taken Willows on their road from Went Junction, where they had hired the taxi owned by another old friend, to transport them and their belongings to their new homes.

"Is that dog yours?" asked Mary, glancing out of the window as conversation languished.

The words were scarcely spoken when the door burst open and a large animal of indeterminate breed charged in to greet Mrs. Higgs as effusively as if she had just returned from Australia.

"Yes, Miss Mary," said Mrs. Higgs tonelessly. "Down, Tiny, will yer?"

"What's his name?" asked Mary, unable to believe her ears.

"The young fellow from w'om I got 'im was not quite frank," explained Mrs. Higgs bridling. "'E said 'e would never grow no larger than wot 'e then was w'ich was w'y Albert and me christened 'im Tiny." She added with reserve, "One of 'is parents was a very good fox-terrier, smooth 'air," as she rose to drive her pet forth, adjuring him in a ferocious undertone, "Keep off them clean steps."

Tiny, who evidently knew all about clean steps, retreated with his tail between his legs, to greet the driver of the taxi as a long-lost ally.

"You'd better go and ketch 'old of 'im, Mother, or 'e'll be in again," advised Albert with surprising spirit.

Mrs. Higgs made her farewells, and took her seat in the taxi while Albert obtained his interview. His conversation was much more colourful than that of his parent, and it was a curious fact that only when addressing his mother did his diction resemble hers.

"I'm glad to see your mother looking so well, Albert," said Mary.

"She is well, miss," said Albert heavily, "and she was to thank you for your kindness in helping her with her teeth. But I shouldn't be surprised if she never passed a remark on the subject. Such a tussle I had with her this morning to make her put them in."

"Oh!" said Mary. "Won't she wear them?"

"Sundays, and not always then," reported Albert tersely.

"I hope you'll be happy at Crossgrove," said Mary. "It's a nice house."

"I wish it could have been Woodside and yourself, miss," said Albert suddenly in a voice that sounded to Mary quite beautiful.

"So do I," she answered. "But after all, people have to leave houses. And it isn't as if Woodside had been ours for ever. We came from Scotland, you know, and only bought Woodside early in the eighteenth century. My family did not build the house." Changing the subject a little hastily, she went on, "I am sure you will find Lady Rollo a most kind mistress. I told her you were good with dogs."

Albert's eyes lit behind his goggles. "Four bull-terriers there's to be, coming out of quarantine in early September, her ladyship informs me," he said. "I understood also from the butler that there was a question of her ladyship getting a brace of Dalmatian pups from Lady Merle meanwhile. That breed don't fight," he ended with a note of regret in his voice.

Mary took her courage in both hands, and said, "Sir Daubeny has been many years in command in India. You will find that he is accustomed to a very high standard of punctuality and smartness, I expect. But . . ." her voice trailed away.

"I hope I shall be able to give every satisfaction, miss," said Albert, who was not stupid. Rolling his eyes to the ceiling, he mentioned, "In the first situation where I was in the North, my lady's first husband, who was a frequent guest, habitually threw his boots at me if they were not polished to his liking. The gentleman was a Russian nobleman."

Mary longed to say, "You have lived, Albert!" and, "Sir Daubeny won't do that," but contented herself with, "You'll find Crossgrove a nice change then."

"And after that," continued Albert, apparently revelling in the memory, "I went on to the gentleman from South Africa, what was killed motoring. Another very hot-tempered gentleman. My late master, who had the accident with the rook rifle, only had his moments of being put out, so to speak. More melancholy-like, one would say."

"I'm afraid you've had rather a rotten time since you left us," said Mary. "It's so difficult to keep in touch with everybody, and your mother didn't write until Christmas as usual."

"My appearance has been against me," explained Albert, stating a fact. "But her ladyship, when she saw me in London, asked nothing except had I ever been bitten in a dog-fight, to which I was able to reply, 'Time and again, m'lady. It was part of my duties, so to speak, when I was pantry-boy at Woodside.'"

As the taxi was coaxed into action three minutes later, Mary perceived that in addition to Tiny, Mrs. Higgs had brought a canary to keep her company at Merle End. The canary, in its cage, firmly wedged on the roof of the antique vehicle between a corded tin trunk and two strapped paper suit-cases, was singing its heart out, delighted with the sunny warmth of this beneficent morning.

Mary Morrison said to herself as she watched the taxi out of sight, "Well, I hope to goodness that's going to be a success."

(ii)

Mary Morrison, seated at her writing desk, lifted the receiver from her telephone, and the voice of Catha Rollo, sounding very close, exclaimed, "Button! when are you coming over to see us?"

"I've been delicately waiting to be asked," explained Mary. "I thought you might be in some confusion still, and not needing visitors."

"Could you come to lunch to-day?" asked Catha. "We should be alone. This is to say, every single room is full of men drinking tea out of tin mugs, and saying what they'd like to tell the Führer and his Nasties."

Mary thought rapidly, and replied, "I'd love to, if you don't mind my not arriving until about twenty to two, and leaving at three sharp."

Catha's voice said, "That'll be perfect, for Albert has just introduced a young man looking like the poet Keats, in a pullover, who says that he wants to do things to power plugs in my sitting-room all morning. One-forty, then."

Mary replaced the receiver, and applied her attention once more to her morning's post. All her letters this morning had been suitable for storage in the pigeonhole of her desk blandly labelled "Difficult." But the one over which she had been knitting her brows as the telephone bell rang was marked "Urgent" in block capitals. Her late brother's wife invariably wrote in haste, on royal blue notepaper, with weakish ink. She further obscured her meaning by eschewing all stops except exclamation marks, underlining conjunctions and leaving out essential letters and even words. By the time that she had puzzled out an epistle from her sister-in-law, Marcelle, Mary's strongest feeling was usually exasperation.

"Dear Mary," she read now,

"Thank you so much for your cheque *and* you cannot think how much ye appreciate all ye tongue in bang." "No," decided Mary, "that can't be right." Gripping her brow, she flicked over the page and found, "Flowers at my flat." "She's got the things I sent for her birthday. That's all right," said Mary aloud. But the next line brought disillusion, "should have told you I was going away few days."

"Oh dear!" exclaimed Mary regretfully, "and I'd put in two dozen of those new jonquils. I suppose they simply died in the unopened basket. And she said in her last letter that owing to hard times she was never able to go away, even for week-ends. . . . However, she seems grateful."

Mrs. Morrison was grateful. On the third page of her letter she came to her point. "Such difficult times," read Mary, "*and* poor Rosemary quite impossible . . . stay on in L. and be bombed . . . so feel that as *deceased wife of your only* brother. . . ." "She can't mean that," frowned Mary. "She must mean only wife of your deceased. . . . No, that wouldn't be right either. Oh! good heavens!"

"Accept your long-standing invitation to come down to Willows, *then* we could have a chat about my staying on *in Event of War*," read Mary. "You, I know, will be so busy with yr hospital work out all day v. likely but loneliness alas! no novelty to me and if I cld have a south room on ground floor no matter how cottagey! Expect you will keep on running yr car so would not feel utterly cut off from civilization. . . . See there is a train arriving Went 12.50 Saturdays."

"Marcelle wants to come to live here for the duration!" announced Mary to her elder Siamese cat who had just entered the room noiselessly, and stared back at her with cold aquamarine eyes before heartlessly resuming elaborate cleansing of his hind legs. In the same moment the telephone bell rang again.

"Westbury Green 250," replied Mary. "Oh! Mrs. Gibson. Yes, this is Mary Morrison speaking. Good morning. Yes, I got your letter. Only this moment, though, as it had been addressed 'Lower Merle' and we're 'Went' here. Yes, about your daughter. No, I'm terribly sorry, I can't take her as a Member yet. The rule is that all Members must be over seventeen. Next September. Well, that means that she's only just over sixteen-and-a-half, doesn't it? I'm sorry, I can only take her as a Probationer. She's taken her exams, at school. That's splendid! Yes, I'm sure she is. Will you explain to her, and tell her that I shall hope to enrol her as a Member in September? Yes, I know, but you see she can't be just yet, because of her age. I shall be delighted to enrol her as a Probationer and see her at our meetings, though. No, I'm afraid she must not, because you see the rule says that Members must be over seventeen years of age. She will have to get Probationer's uniform. Yes, I daresay she does, if she's as tall as that, but you see she has to enter her date of birth on a form. Well, I don't know much about the other voluntary women's services. Oh! Dorothy Yarrow looks after them, I believe. You could always ask her. But I should doubt if anything could take her until she's seventeen. Oh! yes, so do I with all my heart. I thought the news looked a trifle better this morning, didn't you? Oh! no, she couldn't be sent abroad till she's over twenty-one. Just one moment. I'm being interrupted. . . ."

The interruption was caused by Doris, as spokesman for the driver of the railway delivery van, which had halted outside the parlour windows, turning day into night.

"The man says, please, miss," said Doris in her customary gabble, "w'ere's 'e to put the grand piano?"

"The what?" asked Mary.

"'E's got a grand piano for Willows. It's addressed to you, miss," said Doris, enjoying the sensation her words were creating.

"This must be some mistake," breathed Mary. But the label produced by Doris was indeed inscribed in a familiar handwriting.

"I expect there's something about this in a letter I haven't opened yet," said Mary. "Tell Saunders to put it in the garage. No! there's Mr. Tony's two-seater in there till Sunday! I've got a committee in here at twelve. . . . Look here, you'll just have to tell them to put it in the passage temporarily. We shall just have to squeeze past it until I've found out why it's come and how long it's staying."

The letter from Mrs. Thomas Morrison's daughter, Rose-mary, explained the grand piano in its postscript. Rosemary's epistle, which was blessedly short and legible, although evidently composed under stress of strong emotion, stated in a large round hand that, as Mummy was now quite impossible to live with, could Auntie Bee "have" Rosemary until she had completed her training at the Dramatic Academy, and got a good engagement with a touring company? "I hope," said the postscript, "that you won't mind my sending down my fencing things and piano now, as Mummy said last night that she might be shutting up this flat at any moment and leaving London for an unknown destination."

(iii)

The drive over to Crossgrove through country scenery in the height of its spring beauty, soothed and heartened Mary. When she dismounted from her car to open the first gate leading to her old friend's new home, she felt a pang of unfamiliar, child-ish excitement. When she resumed her seat, she discovered that her heels were infested with small stones, partially coated with a glutinous black mixture. She looked at the surface of the drive and said to herself, "I suspect Tim." The old yellow gravel ribbon of road through these undulating fields, although full of pot-holes, had certainly been picturesque. The park itself was not particularly interesting. It was somewhat sparsely dotted with budding oaks, and a few chestnut and white cows glared at her resentfully as she sped past them. At the second gate she collected more small stones, and clambering back into her seat, kicked one of her ankles, leaving a long black smear on a silk stocking. But a minute later she came in sight of a line of giant sentinel yews stretching straight across the approach as if set to guard some treasure. She passed between them, and found herself under the very eyes of Crossgrove, in a small grey-flagged courtyard, entirely surrounded by yew hedges. Her spirits rose as she returned the friendly gaze of four and twenty large round-headed sash windows, lighting lofty rooms, panelled in wood.

There were signs of a struggle in the hall, where spring sunshine caught many reflections from polished black oak. Two saddles, a dog's lead, a gun-case, a glazed chintz sewing-bag and a bottle of embrocation were grouped around a circular pottery bowl filled with drooping cowslips. Catha Rollo's inordinate fondness for pets, whom she left to the care of others, was a leading feature of her character, and Mary was not surprised that the silhouette of the butler advancing towards her was followed by that of a liver-spotted Dalmatian wriggling her quarters ecstatically.

"Well," said Mary to her slightly harassed-looking hostess, as she unfolded her table-napkin, "how do you like it? Personally, I am more than satisfied."

"We like this room very much," said Catha, glancing around. "In fact, we think now it's really the best room in the house. It's got perfect proportions, so two people dining in it don't look silly, while you can seat two dozen. I'm not enamoured of the mantelpiece—bulbous Cupids morbidly conducting oxen to a funeral. The Fox and Grapes one in my room is much more amusing. Have you noticed that these are the chairs that we got together at that sale, and they are exactly right for date? The curtains, I need not point out, are Tim's study ones. That's why they're covered with British lions, and a foot too short. I wish his room was ready. It is wretched for him having to come back after a long day in London, to sit in an all-white saloon amongst alabaster vases of lilies. But we shall get into my little room to-night. It's a crashing disappointment, so far, but when a few dogs have sat on them, I daresay the covers and cushions won't look so smug."

Mary agreed that this seemed likely, and asked how Sir Daubeny liked his new home.

"We took it because of the shooting," explained Catha, "so I hope that may prove all right. I'm sorry to say we've had words already about the drive. I see you've collected some of it on your stockings. I shall tell him. Elizabeth had a roll in it, dressed in a woolly white coat and shorts, on her way to play squash, on a bicycle, on our first morning here."

"It'll settle, I expect," suggested Mary. "Please say nothing about my stockings. I hope to be invited here again."

"The kitchen is part of the original Elizabethan house," continued Catha. "Its walls and floors are all crooked, like yours at Willows. Unfortunately, the kitchen-maid set down thirty plates on one of the dressers, just as we drove up to the doors on Friday. It fell forward, and hit another dresser. She got out of the way in time, but by an extraordinary chance, a two-pound pot of jam on the top of the second dresser got loose and hit the under-housemaid on the side of the head. She's in the Cottage Hospital now with slight concussion. The Matron sounded such a nice woman on the telephone. I expect you know her."

"I do," nodded Mary. "She's got fuzzy toffee-coloured hair and gold-rimmed pince-nez, and conceals the iron hand under the velvet glove."

"She sounded rather like that," agreed Catha. "Well then, yesterday an errand boy, with a heavy basket of groceries on his handlebars, took the corner of the new bit of drive too fast, and whizzed into the lake instead of up to the backdoor. However, Albert fished him out, and nothing was lost except a hundred boxes of matches. I don't think anything else has happened as yet, except that a number of people with the most intimidating names and addresses have called already—mostly while I was out, I am thankful to say. Remind me, when we get into my little room, to show you their cards, and ask you all about them."

"I certainly will," said Mary severely, "and I am sorry to hear you say that you are glad that you were not here when they came. It will be your duty, for Elizabeth's sake if not for your own, to spend several long, fine afternoons paying these people back in their own coin. If you don't begin by doing this thoroughly, the rumour will spread that Lady Rollo is always in

London, or a little queer in the head, and people will ask Tim
and the boys to shoot and then wash their hands of Crossgrove.
How is Elizabeth?"

"You will see for yourself in a few minutes," said Catha.
"She is having an early lunch somewhere miles away with some
people who want to show her a mare which they think might
suit her."

"Tony told me I should be surprised when I saw her," said
Mary. "But even so, I was surprised."

"No, dear, she's not pretty," said Catha brightening, "but
even as a mother I can't help admitting that I think she's a
nice-looking little thing. It's wonderful how much difference
eighteen months in Paris has made to her. I don't altogether
like her eyebrows, do you? They've left her too little, I consider.
Though when I look at Tim's, I see her point. And then, when she
has just emerged from the hairdresser, her little head reminds
me of my old astrakhan coat. However, when I remember how
terrifyingly sallow and skinny my poor little black monkey was
at thirteen, I feel that I have nothing of which to complain. I
used to tremble for her. Of course I could not foresee that by the
time she was due to come out, it would be quite correct to be the
size of a pea. She's naturally sweet-tempered. I do hope she may
have a happy life. . . . As a matter of fact, I rather drove her out
to lunch to-day, because I thought that Violet might be coming
here. I shall have Violet here, of course, but if possible I do not
want Elizabeth to meet her as yet. I want Elizabeth just now to
meet people of quite a different type from those who, I feel in my
bones, surround poor Violet."

"It must be fun having a débutante daughter," said Mary
hearteningly.

After lunch the friends made a tour of the house, in so far as
it was possible, and Mary admired again the oaken central staircase, with balustrades of much elegance and variety, which had
been part of the original structure. In her secret soul she was
not favourably impressed by the long saloon, which Catha had

decorated entirely in chalk white, with a view to a dance for a débutante. Even on this day of spring sun the room looked cold and formal, and when Catha switched on the lights concealed within six cut-glass chandeliers hanging from the ceiling, Mary caught a glimpse of herself and her friend in a full-length mirror, and noticed that she looked eighty-five and Catha eighty.

"And now," said Catha, "since we can't get into Tim's study, I think we may consider that we've completed our tour, and have coffee in my little room before a stroll in the garden."

Mary, looking up at the ceiling of ornamental plaster above them, said, "I've seen the painting from which this was taken. It's Aurora strewing flowers before the chariot of Apollo, and it's by Guido Reni and it's in the Rospigliosi Palace in Rome."

Albert, who had been hovering around his mistress unhappily, withdrew, evidently appalled by so much erudition.

"There," said Catha, two minutes later, emptying into Mary's lap a shower of visiting cards. "Now please tell me who all these people are, and which of them I shall like. You're not in a draught, are you?"

"No," said Mary. "It's beautifully warm in here. But do shut that window if you've got a cough."

"I thought you had one," said Catha, sounding puzzled.

"You'll like this couple," began Mary, reading from the first cards found by her. "Sir James and Lady Wilson—locally known as our Ambassador and Ambassadress. That all happened so, long ago that scarcely anybody alive can attest to the fact. He's rather deaf and lame now, but a perfect lamb. Lady Wilson is one of those little shrivelled-up, well-born Scottish ladies, with enough spirit for ten. It always gives one a slight shock to discover that she's not a spinster or a widow, and does not live brewing tea in a *pension* in Florence, or controlling missionaries. They have no children, but are very good to young people, and often have clean-looking subalterns and young men from the Foreign Office to stay. It is my duty to warn you that although

Lady Wilson has a heart of pure gold, she is not at her best at the Bridge table."

"Thank you," said Catha. "'Miss Catha Taylor, The Rectory, Westbury,' is, I imagine, the Rector's sister. I must have put him in the basket. . . ."

"Rather a trial," sighed Mary, "and would not be so nice to you if you were Albert's mother—if you take me. You will be opening the Fête this summer, dear. New residents always have to. Poor Dorothy did, the year her husband got into Parliament. She's particularly young and attractive-looking, and it was pure good-nature on her part, as Westbury is not in Rolfe's constituency. The next year Mr. Taylor arose to introduce Norah Blent, who's quite our age, and said, 'This year we are fortunate in having our little gathering opened by one of the Younger Set."

"I remember now," sighed Catha. "I put him in the basket because I was in when they came. And I am opening the Fête. And we're having it here, because the Rectory garden is so dull and they have no maids at all. I felt truly sorry for them. Don't let us meet our troubles half-way. Tell me about Major and Mrs. Albany Mimms and Miss Rosanna Masquerier and Lady Norah Blent."

"Oh, dear," mourned Mary, "I suppose all the duds and oddities always do turn up first."

A sudden blast of music, which lasted for half a minute, startled both ladies into dumbness. They watched fascinated while a young man crawled out on all fours from behind the sofa on which they had been sitting. He said, after coughing apologetically,

"The Radio-Gram is now ready for use, madam," arose to his feet, and flitted from the room.

Catha broke the ensuing silence by saying triumphantly, "He is like Keats, isn't he? And now I know what it was that Albert was trying to say to me before we came in here. And neither of us has got a cough, thank goodness."

(iv)

"How did you enjoy the Grand Military, Elizabeth?" asked Mary.

Elizabeth Rollo screwed up her eyes in the effort to remember something which had happened five weeks ago.

Since she was seventeen and very slight, she looked a charming little figure of fun attired in jodhpurs, and a jersey with a polo collar.

"Oh! it was lovely, Auntie Bee," she said. "I think it was the loveliest thing I ever went to. I never enjoyed a day so much in my life. You see, the sun shone the whole time, and there was a band playing up in a kiosk on a hillock covered with spring flowers, and we had a stuffing lunch in Daddy's club tent, and Daddy gave me a ten bob note, so that I could have a bet on every race. . . ."

While Elizabeth burbled on about her perfect day, Mary, scarcely listening, echoed in her heart Catha's words of half an hour past. "Dear little monkey. I do hope that she may have a happy life!"

Presently her attention was arrested by a name.

"David Cox," she repeated. "I've met him. He's a young man with lamb's-wool yellow hair and a pink face, just back from India."

"Do you know David, Auntie?" asked Elizabeth, with dancing eyes. "Mummie, isn't it extraordinary, Auntie Bee knows David? Now it will be quite all right for me to go in his car to Mrs. Jackson's sherry party, won't it?"

"What is all this?" asked Catha, in a fair imitation of her husband's manner.

"His name's David Cox," explained Elizabeth, "and I met him at Sandown, and he had mud on his cheek because he'd just ridden a winner, which was frightfully exciting, because he had never expected to ride at all. Only that morning he'd got a wire from a friend who'd got jaundice, saying 'turn up at all costs.' The friend had tea with us too, and he was all yellow round the eyeballs, and couldn't touch plum cake. And then I met David again at lunch to-day, and Mrs. Jackson was there too, and she is giving a sherry party and asked us all, and it's only twenty-five miles and David's offered to take Anthony and me. Actually he offered to let me drive his new car, as he didn't know that I've not passed the test yet. When I said that you might be needing me, Mrs. Jackson was so sweet. She said, 'Just tell Catha you're going to Violet's party at Muriel's house, darling.'"

"Ah!" said Catha. "I begin to see light. Violet Jackson has invited us all to a sherry party which she is giving in the house of her long-suffering married daughter, twenty-five miles distant— probably thirty from here."

"Is Lady Muriel Gidding Mrs. Jackson's daughter?" asked Elizabeth, opening her eyes wide. "But Mummy, she was there to-day too, and she looks at least twenty-eight, and wears a frump's hat, and talks about sitting on Evacuation Committees."

"Violet Jackson is the daughter of a North-country factory hand, who made a fortune in linoleum. She married first at seventeen," mentioned Catha, sounding a trifle impatient. "Very well, dear. Go in and change now, and tell Symonds we shall be needing the big car at five-thirty. Who is Anthony?"

"He's Tony's friend from Oxford, who decorates people's houses for them," Elizabeth reminded her mother. "You must remember how fussing it was, both of them being 'Anthony' really. If we're going in the big car, I suppose we shall be taking both David and Anthony. Only that would mean that they would have to come back here rather late, to pick up David's car."

"The young men will be wanting to return to places like Oxford and Aldershot," said Catha. "I expect it will be best for them to make a separate expedition." "Oh! but Mummy," protested Elizabeth, "I don't believe David really likes Anthony much. They never met till to-day, and I am their only link, so to speak."

"Your father is extremely worried about the European situation. I cannot let him return to find his house full of strange undergraduates and subalterns," said Catha definitely.

Elizabeth, who evidently was sweet-tempered, retired looking only a little downcast.

"What fun it must be," quoted Catha to Mary, "to have a débutante daughter."

They were out on the terrace, where stone vases filled with spreading wallflowers and erect narcissi were exhaling a heady scent. Below a flight of steps overhung by lilacs in bud, lay a moist lawn, on which magnolias were shedding shell-like petals. Beyond the lawn stretched a dark wood edged by wild cherry-trees, where bluebells would soon be glowing dimly. The cry of lambs sounded from an unseen field.

"The next six weeks are my favourites in the whole year," sighed Mary. "They're what I call the real 'Shakespeare's England' weeks. Oh, Catha! I was so depressed when I set out to come here this morning."

"I was plunged in gloom until you arrived," exclaimed Catha. "Surely nothing awful ever happens at Willows?"

"I know one should never think of oneself," began Mary desperately, "but I cannot help seeing that if Marcelle and Rosemary come to live at Willows my whole manner of life will have to be altered."

"Marcelle!" said Catha. "That's your widowed sister-in-law. But I thought you said that she never turned up."

"She's written to say that if there is a war she might like to live at Willows," said Mary, "I can't refuse to have her, for she was George's wife, and he was killed in the last war. Oh, dear! I will not say 'the last war' as if we were bound to have another."

"But Rosemary is her child by her first marriage," pointed out Catha. "She has no earthly claim on you."

"That's the worst of it," said Mary. "Poor Rosemary seems to have no earthly claim on anyone. And she and Marcelle don't really get on. She's not at all a bad child. I can't refuse to have her, either."

"Button dear," said Catha, pausing in their walk, "we have eight spare bedrooms here, even when the children are all at home. I have never met poor Mrs. Morrison, but if she is really afraid of staying in London, could you not tell her to come to us? I am sure we should scarcely notice her. Oh! I don't mean that unkindly."

Mary gave a hollow laugh before replying. "You are an angel, Catha, but little you know what you are offering to undertake. No. My duty is clear. I shall have to have them. Oh, dear! all through lunch I was thinking of how to re-arrange the furniture."

"And I was wondering if we should ever get settled in here," said Catha. "Last night, lying awake, it seemed to me that we are raving to have bought this house just now. Poor Tim has been coming home so depressed, Button. He won't say how bad he thinks things are, and I don't ask, but I can see that he's worried to death."

Mary took her leave an hour later. She had left some traps in Catha's bedroom, and while she was collecting them a trunk call from London was put through to her hostess. She blew a decisive farewell kiss to Catha, who was dumbly signalling to her to stay, and tiptoed from the room. On the first floor landing, where there was a large window with a cushioned seat, she encountered Elizabeth.

"Sister Anne! Sister Anne!" quoted Mary lightly.

Elizabeth, who had been sitting with her nose glued to the pane, leapt to her feet, shaking out a skirt of many pleats.

"Look, Auntie Bee," she said, thrusting forwards a little bare arm bearing a frivolous-looking muff composed entirely of Parma violets. "I got this in Paris. It's a handbag too, really. Do you think it would look silly at a sherry party in the country? Mrs. Jackson wears lots of diamond clips, even at lunch."

"It matches your frock perfectly," said Mary.

"I thought that if I took it with my blue frock, Mummie would notice and say 'No,'" said Elizabeth. "It's rather frumpish really to have things matching nowadays, you know."

Mary, who was herself attired from head to foot in shades of beige, said kindly, "I think it would be a pity to leave it behind."

As she passed through the hall, she reflected that to a débutante she probably appeared so old that fashions were of no moment to her. "How one can tell age from a handshake," she thought. Elizabeth's moist and boneless paw conveyed a pathetic impression of childishness.

When she had started up her engine Mary did not immediately drive away. She could hear the sound of another vehicle approaching. A small sports model slipped quietly between the yew hedges. Cardboard placards bearing the letter L in block capitals, decorated its bumpers. It drew to a standstill at a respectful distance from the house, and Mr. David Cox alighted cautiously. Mary was just about to bow and smile in passing, when she perceived that this visitor had no eyes except for a first-floor window of Crossgrove. He stood slightly astraddle, raising an arm to return a greeting.

"It's absurd, of course," said Mary to herself, as she passed through the gap in the sentinel yews, "but something tells me that I have just seen Catha's future son-in-law—or at least a candidate for the post. This decides me that I may as well continue to wear an all beige outfit, and be rather frumpish."

(v)

Miss Morrison did not sleep well after her busy day. When she went to bed, at half-past ten, she noticed that a cow, somewhere nearby, was mooing repeatedly. But being tired, she fell asleep, almost at once. She woke, shortly before midnight, and after that heard the grandfather clock below tell every hour until six a.m. During that time the cow never ceased complaining. Its lament was not pathetic. Persistence was its outstanding characteristic. But Miss Morrison had lived too long in the country not to know what it meant. "They've taken away her calf, of course," she told herself, as she hit her pillow, and turned and turned again in the dimness of her old room. "I know that to-morrow, when she's had her feed, she'll cheer up. And by the day after to-morrow, she'll have forgotten about it, as far as one can tell.

I never can get accustomed to it, though." As she drowsed into sleep again at six-thirty, she thought, "I'm glad I wrote at once to say I'd have Rosemary Wright."

Three hours later, as she walked across the field-path to the church, on her way to interview Mrs. Potts, with special reference to Ted Squirl and the Territorials, Miss Morrison heard the cuckoo for the first time in 1939. She thought, as she waited for a moment hanging over the stile, "I don't know why people say the cuckoo's annoying. In April, when his note is still so high, it always gives me a thrill." She made a mental note to make a pencil note, "Heard the cuckoo," on her engagement block, and thought as she made her way slowly towards Dolphin Cottages through strong sunshine which made her feel sleepy, "I'm glad I live in the country."

CHAPTER V
WHIT-SATURDAY, MAY 27TH

(i)

"JOHANNA PRATT is a very remarkable character," said Tony Rollo, looking at his audience severely. "Upon mature reflection, the most remarkable character I have ever met."

His listeners were his godmother and her sister-in-law's offspring, Rosemary. The scene was the parlour at Willows, and the hour breathless noon on Whit-Saturday. Tony must, Mary feared, have heard from one of his parents that amongst the guests expected at Crossgrove this afternoon were the Lord-Lieutenant and the Bishop. Tony's attire consisted of an open-necked brown canvas shirt and a pair of much-stained leather shorts, such as are worn by Bavarian mountaineers. As he was a dark and hirsute youth, his costume did not become him, and made him appear less than his actual age. Rosemary

Wright, on his first appearance this morning, had asked, in all innocence, if he was interested in Scouts.

"I must," thought Mary, "make an effort to get him to change into something else before we set out."

"How is she remarkable?" asked Rosemary, turning round on the piano stool.

"It's an odd coincidence," thought Mary, looking at her connexion by marriage, "that I should have two such unwashed-looking guests this week-end."

Rosemary Wright was not bad-looking, in an untidy, gipsy-like fashion. She had wild black hair, large, sleepy black eyes, and a long countenance of somewhat melancholy features. Her movements were coltish, her skin was sallow, and she was wearing a white muslin blouse trimmed with peasant embroidery and a thick green tweed skirt. Her voice and her smile were her best points. Unfortunately she smiled seldom, and was rather silent for her age, which was twenty-three.

"Well, to begin with," said Tony, staring right through the attentive Rosemary, "she absolutely refused to let her mother give a dance for her, or anything like that. When she was eighteen, she simply stayed on in Munich, continuing to study the subjects in which she was interested. Her people had to go out and fetch her in the end, I believe. She had given up answering their letters when they became unreasonable."

"How did she get on for cash?" asked Rosemary in deep tragic tones, laying her arms across the top of the piano, and sinking her face upon them.

"She does not care for anything of that sort," said Tony, waving a hand. "Her tastes are utterly simple. Fellow artists befriended her, I expect. They would consider it a privilege. She is startlingly beautiful, you know."

"I daresay that if I were the daughter of a millionaire I should have simple tastes," reflected Rosemary. "I wonder if she knows any managers. Julia—-Julia Marvell, you know—has promised to give me an introduction to an elderly one who's taking a company to South Africa next month. Shakespeare and all that. She says he's notoriously addicted to fair débutantes who can't act, and she thinks there might be a hope, as he's just finished a shattering affair. Unfortunately I'm not exactly a débutante, nor startlingly beautiful. Wasn't Johanna Pratt's mother disappointed that she refused to come out?"

"The wife of my employer," said Tony, "I prefer not to discuss."

"What's the boy like?" wondered Mary.

"Impossible to believe that he is Johanna's brother!" said Tony with vigour. "As backward as she is brilliant. However, I hope to be able to shove him through his exam. The moment you see Johanna, you will realize. . . ."

"Oh! we're going to see her, are we?" asked Mary.

"She's coming here for lunch," said Tony, looking surprised. "Perhaps I ought to have told you before. And, by the way, she said on the telephone that she might be able to stay the night."

"Do you mean here—at Willows?" said Mary, rising, and falling over a treasured footstool in her dismay.

"I particularly do not wish to ask any favour from Crossgrove, since I am—so to speak independent now," said Tony, scowling.

"But look here," said Mary, "Rosemary's mother is arriving this evening. I am absolutely full up, with the three of you."

"Mummie may not come," said Rosemary, sounding more and more like Mrs. Siddons as Lady Macbeth.

"You know what she is. This is the third time she's been coming. She may rat again as soon as she discovers that I'm still here."

"But," said Mary, "I cannot run the chance of her arriving and finding that there is no room for her."

"I thought," said Tony, "that I could sleep on that camp-bed thing out in the summerhouse. It's pretty warm."

"So you could, if it wasn't for the wedding," explained Mary.

"What wedding?" asked Tony, rumpling his hair.

"Ted Squirl is marrying Florence Potts at Westbury Church at two this afternoon," announced Mary. "He's second gardener at Merle now, but we had him at Woodside for eight years, so I'm having to go. I've promised the camp-bed to Mrs. Crippen's nephew Syd, the photographer, who's coming from Croydon to be best man. My Doris is Ted's first cousin, and she's being a bridesmaid. That's why we're having cold lunch. Let me get to the telephone, Rosemary. Tony, do you really mean that this is definite about your employer's daughter wanting to stay here?"

"Absolutely," nodded Tony.

"Lady Wilson is always kind," considered Mary feverishly. "No! on second thoughts I think I'll try Sally Bates. She's nearer, too."

Mrs. Bates was at home, and sounded interested at the prospect of becoming hostess to the brilliant child of Tony Rollo's employer. "Is that your godson? The one I always say looks half-baked?" asked Sally's voice. "Are they engaged? She's the only daughter, isn't she? Didn't her father get a peerage in the New Year's Honours? Will she be needing dinner? Why aren't they both staying at Crossgrove? Will she be bringing a maid?"

"Yes," answered Mary. "No, no, they're not. Yes, she is, I believe. Yes, he did, I believe. No, she will be having all her meals with us. Just one moment." Turning round, she repeated, "Will she be bringing a maid?" Tony's gesture was enough. "No, she won't. Her tastes are utterly simple," quoted Mary.

As she passed towards her kitchen, Mary heard the trundling sound produced by a sewing-machine. That noise ceased and gave place to a burst of carolling. Up in her attic bedroom, where the mantelpiece was crowded with curling picture postcards of renowned film stars, Doris was blissfully engaged tacking to the front of her bridesmaid's gown a large bunch of crimson cotton roses. Mary could picture the scene, for she had been obliged to suggest to Doris yesterday that it was not seemly or practical to attempt to combine putting dog-tooth stitches into the hem of a buttercup artificial satin picture gown, with skinning tomatoes. She had given Doris the morning off, and lent her the sewing-machine.

In the kitchen, Rose was upset. She pointed out, with reason, that a couple of grape-fruit cannot be fairly divided amongst five persons, that the lobsters were unusually small, and that the strawberries, though large, were few in number. Since the day was Whit-Saturday, she could only suggest that Doris should be sent on the bike to ask the Duck Farm to oblige Miss Morrison. But last time that a duckling had been supplied at short notice, Mr. Tony himself had said at table that it seemed a shame to eat the winner of the National, which witticism Doris had repeated to the Duck Farm. Mary ordered her cook to open a cold tongue and add a Swiss roll to the supper menu.

"I can't send Doris anywhere this morning," she said. "She's still making her dress, I know."

"She was in the garden, laughing at Ted Squirl, five minutes ago, miss," said Rose.

"Ted Squirl!" exclaimed Mary. "Is he up here?"

"'E is, miss," said Rose. "'E's 'elping the boy stake your sweet peas. And if you asks me, 'e looks like spending the afternoon at the task."

"What do you mean?" asked Mary. "But he can't! The wedding's at two."

"Ted's saying that 'e don't know that 'e'll turn up at no wedding," replied Rose. "Ted's saying that 'e don't know that 'e wants to get married. I wouldn't put it past 'im to act silly at the last."

Mary walked into her kitchen-garden through a wicket gate overhung by brilliant laburnum tassels and heavy double lilacs. Just inside the gate an unmistakable scent invited her to linger. Hundreds of lilies of the valley were hiding between their pointed leaves, in the shade of the potting-shed wall.

Ted Squirl, when he heard his employer's step upon the gravel path of her kitchen-garden, made a vain effort to conceal himself in the cage.

"Good morning, Ted," cried Mary cheerfully. "I was glad when I woke this morning, to see what a fine day you've got."

Ted, who was a thick-set young man of five and twenty, with a slightly fishy pale eye and a remarkably thick neck, was breathing heavily. Strangers, at their first glance, always received the impression, which was entirely unsupported by fact, that Ted Squirl belonged to the criminal classes. This morning he made an elaborate business of cleaning his boots of soil before stepping onto the path, and replying that a nice bit of rain was what the strawberries were needing.

"I am coming to the church," continued Mary mercilessly, "though not to the Legion Hall afterwards, for your party, as I had promised to play tennis at Crossgrove this afternoon, already. Has Sydney Crippen arrived yet? He is sleeping here, you know."

Ted replied in a mutter, with his eyes cast on the ground, that he was sure he could not say whether or not his best man had arrived.

"How is Florence?" pursued Mary. "She showed me her dress when I went to see her mother last week."

Ted, looking up at last, repeated suddenly and ferociously the sentence reported by Rose in the kitchen.

"What do you mean, when you say that you don't know that you want to get married, after all?" asked Mary, looking far bolder than she felt. "You're twenty-five, aren't you, and sound in wind and limb, and you've got a good job, and you are very fond of Florence, aren't you?"

"I am very fond of Florence, miss," stated Ted, looking at Mary with the glazed orbs of the calf hurried to the shambles. "And I am glad to say I am in good 'ealth and with a nice job up at the Park. And I know I'm lucky. It's the fuss I can't face," he brought out, to Mary's unspeakable relief. "Bridesmaids and photographers, and standing up there waiting for 'er like a Stuckey, w'ile they all stares," he added. "The Reverend Taylor," he went on, drawing a long trembling breath, "'as told Florence not to be late. Very short with us, 'e was, w'en we went up to see 'im. 'Don't be late,' says 'e to 'er, 'for I'm expecting the Bishop at three.' I was for asking the Reverend Mallet, over at Merle, to marry us, quiet-like, in the morning early. The Reverend Mallet is a nice gentleman. But Florence was all for bridesmaids and two o'clock at Westbury."

"It's very natural that she should be," said Mary. "Stop thinking of your own feelings for a moment, Ted, and think of Florence's. This is the happiest day of her life, the day every girl looks forward to. Besides, you needn't think that anyone will be looking at you. Dear me, after a wedding I've often felt that half the guests are saying, 'Was there a bridegroom? I forget. Yes, of course there must have been. There always is.' But nobody takes the slightest notice of a bridegroom, even before the bride arrives, I can assure you. There are the flowers to look at, and people like myself, who are fond of you and Florence, will be kneeling down and saying a prayer that you may have a happy life together." Foreseeing the frightful possibility of reducing both her audience and herself to tears, Miss Morrison hurried on, in clarion tones. "There is no necessity for you to stand up at the altar rails like a stuckey. Sydney Crippen and you can very well wait, behind the pillar by Abbot Wayne's tomb, until the very last moment. Come, Ted, Florence is not asking you to do much for her. No doubt she is feeling very nervous herself just now."

"I give up the Territorials to please Florence's mother," was Ted's sullen answer to all this eloquence.

"I was sorry to hear that, and I think it was wrong of Mrs. Potts to ask you to do such a thing. I have been down to tell her so," said Mary.

"I've 'ad it 'anging over me for some time in a wye, miss," said Ted, delighted to expatiate on any subject other than his own nuptials. "W'en I gets the job at the Park, I sez to myself this may mean 'aving to give up the Territorials. But 'is lordship made no difficulty and I went into camp last August just as usual."

"Of course his lordship wouldn't want you to give up the Territorials," said Mary. "As a matter of fact, his lordship himself ran away from public school to go out to the South African War." Conscious that she was being lured from her point, she ended firmly, "Well, Ted, I must be going now, but don't forget what I told you about waiting behind that pillar, and remember that by three o'clock it'll be all over, and you'll be on the way to the sea. Florence told me on Tuesday that she had actually never seen the sea. Think what a treat it will be for her!"

(ii)

At ten minutes to two, Mary turned her car into the yard of the antique-dealer's shop, half-way up Westbury hill. Eight years before she had received permission from Mr. Wookey to use his premises as a parking place whenever she visited, and never before had she found the yard already full.

"This would happen to-day," she told herself, as she prepared to reverse, and try Dead Woman's Lane, a quarter of a mile further up the hill. "Now I shall arrive at the same moment as Florence—or after her."

But just as she began to move, a car from the furthest corner of the yard started into action, and Dr. Greatbatch, letting down a window as he drew alongside, said mildly, "I think that if I go forward and then in again, I can make room for you."

Mary thanked him, the manoeuvre was effected, and the two owner-drivers began to walk across the road towards the church-yard. A portion of the staring crowd prophesied and dreaded by the pusillanimous Ted, had already assembled on either side of the path leading from the lych-gate to the south porch of St. Nicholas' church. There were a number of old ladies with remarkably furrowed faces, clad in many black garments, who looked ready to mount broomsticks at any moment. The wail of infants whose mothers were determined not to miss a show, burdened the air. A mongrel dog, pursued by two small boys, ran with practised cunning between Mary and her cavalier.

"Oh dear!" sighed Mary. "Every time I come to a wedding here, the population seems to have increased."

"It probably has," said Dr. Greatbatch. "There are eighteen new cottages on the Went road. Still, this is nothing to what turns out for a funeral. My hat!" He stopped dead.

Mary knew Dr. Greatbatch well enough to realize that his exclamation meant that he had left his headgear in the car. "I'll come back with you," she volunteered. "I am out of temper and in need of exercise."

"Now what has been happening?" asked Dr. Greatbatch in his consulting-room voice.

"Everything has gone wrong at Willows this morning," explained Mary. "My godson Tony asked a beautiful strange girl to stay with us, for the tennis party at Crossgrove. Mercifully Sally Bates can give her a bed, for I have no room, but we waited lunch for her until half-past one, so I hadn't time to pack my tennis things, which means that I shall not be able to play. In the end I had to snatch some lunch, standing upright, and quite spoilt the look of the table. She drove up just as I drove off, and she was wearing men's white flannel cricketing trousers, and has saucer grey eyes and shoulder-long floss-silk hair. I told them to go on to Crossgrove by three, but I am quite sure they'll forget."

"Well," said Dr. Greatbatch, slamming the door of his car, "what if they do?"

"Ah!" continued Mary, "but you haven't heard the worst of it. Ted Squirl was up at Willows all morning, and he's lost his nerve, and doesn't know that he wants to get married after all."

"He'll turn up," said Dr. Greatbatch composedly.

"You didn't see him this morning," said Mary.

"No," said Dr. Greatbatch, "but I've seen four generations of Squirls."

They were approaching the self-appointed guard of honour from which was now arising a thunderous muttering. Mary thought it best to alter the topic of conversation.

"You can't say what someone will do, just because you've known his parents and grandparents," she objected. "Look at Shelley."

Dr. Greatbatch did not answer. Either he had been too busy for years to think of the poets, or he was thinking of something else.

In the porch, Syd Crippen from Croydon, with a crimson and a white rose in his buttonhole, was showing four brides-maids in buttercup satin how to take a photograph with the kind of camera which you hold up in front of your face and grimace behind. Doris and two companions were tittering excitedly. Ted Squirl's sister Amy, a heavy, pale girl, with the same furtive look and fishy eyes which distinguished her mother, was seated apart on cold stone, clutching her bridesmaid's bouquet with hands on which the knuckles stood out.

"Good afternoon, Amy," said Mary, bending down. "Aren't you feeling very well?"

"Amy's feeling sick, miss," said Doris, shrilly, deserting the fascinator from Croydon abruptly.

"Thank you very much, miss," said Amy, arising unsteadily. "I am feeling a little faint, miss," she added, casting a baleful glance at Doris, who tripped over her skirt in her retreat.

"Keep on sitting down then, and stick your head between your knees if necessary," advised Mary. "Could you suck a lozenge?"

"I don't think so, miss," said Amy, in a defeatist manner.

"Here's one, in case you feel you can, later," said Mary. "They're quite harmless. I always carry a tin in my bag in case I start coughing in church."

She nodded encouragingly at Amy, and passed into the heated dimness of the church. All seats with a prospect of the altar rails were already occupied, but Mary had, in any case, intended to sit in a side chapel. The Morrison chapel contained two fine fifteenth century brasses, which had nothing to do with the family, and a large window filled with glass of which the predominant colours were ham pink and butcher blue. An inscription at the base of the window proclaimed that it had been presented by the relict of Sir William Morrison, Bart., of Woodside, Anno Domini, 1860. Far the most noticeable objects in the Morrison chapel, however, were the enormous tombs of the two baronets who had flourished in the days of Queen Anne. There they lay—Sir Crosbie and his nephew, Sir Barnaby—mutely hallooing to one another, each with one arm upraised. Both had steamer rugs drawn up to their middles, and wore full-bottomed wigs pushed back from high marble foreheads, intricate lace cravats, and coats trimmed with many little buttons. They had evidently arisen in their bunks at a dramatic moment of ocean travel. "How are you, my poor fellow?" Sir Barnaby was calling to Sir Crosbie. But to Sir Crosbie, whose jaws were tightly compressed and whose lips had an unmistakable frilly appearance, speech was clearly impossible. Before she dropped on her knees, Mary cast an affectionate glance at the pair, always known at Woodside as "the seasick ancestors."

Her prayer for the future happiness of Ted and Florrie Squirl was about as successful as most prayers performed in a church packed with shifting and highly expectant persons. She received an unintended poke on the shoulder as she arose, and found that the dowager Lady Merle of Went and a granddaughter were attempting to pass along the pew.

"Ah! it is Mary," said her ladyship distinctly. "Do not move, Mary. Pamela and I can very well go behind."

Mary insisted upon moving, although this meant that she must now sit squeezed against the unyielding base of Sir Crosbie's monument.

"Granny's in a rage with me," confided Miss Pamela Wallis in a hoarse aside to her neighbour, when the Dowager was settled. "You see, in the churchyard just now, she saw what she thought was the married Harker girl, and she becked and bowed and said, 'I was glad to hear your news. Excellent! Excellent!' I suppose I ought to have left it, but I told her, as soon as I'd bustled her away, that it was Minnie, the unmarried one, for whom, of course, it's not excellent at all."

Mary stole a look at the Dowager's profile, which always resembled that of Queen Elizabeth in later life. Lady Merle was sitting very upright, with eyes closed and a handkerchief held to her nut-cracker nose and chin. But Mary could really think of only one thing at the moment. "I can't see Ted Squirl," she murmured uneasily.

Without scrambling past the ladies of Merle and leaving the pew, she could not decide beyond doubt whether he had adopted her advice to hide behind the pillar opposite. As far as she could see, the bridegroom was not present. Syd Crippen, who had promised so lavishly to stand by his doomed friend, was, she knew, acting as a candle to Doris and her fellow-moths in the porch.

"He's there all right," whispered Pamela.

"Where?" asked Mary.

"In the usual place, waiting," hissed Pamela.

With a start of incredulous relief, Mary recognized the back of a neck, always sunburnt, now almost crimson. Dr. Greatbatch had been right. Ted Squirl had come up to the scratch—more, he had actually taken up the position furiously described by him as standing like a stuckey. There he waited, in a parade attitude, with his arms straight by his sides and his legs planted firmly, staring with unwavering eyes straight ahead of him. Mary suddenly felt the shameful inclination to tears which often beset her at weddings.

Florrie, as Ted had prophesied, was late. The organ ceased to sound, and two o'clock tolled from the tower. Five minutes passed. The organist began to repeat himself. Mary calculated how many times the hired taxi, decorated with inch-wide satin ribbons, must be making the journey from Dead Woman's Lane to St. Nicholas' lych-gate. Before the bride and her brother could be allowed to embark, many relations would have to be collected and deposited. To her horror, the gentleman styled by Ted "the

Reverend Taylor" presently emerged from his vestry, looking remarkably sour, and inclining towards the rigid bridegroom, said quite audibly, "The bride is very late." Ted took no notice at all, but Syd Crippen, who was now masterfully escorting guests to pews, strode up just in time to suggest in a stage "aside," "Taken the lady's privilege and changed her mind, perhaps, sir."

At length came the familiar stir in the porch, and an increase of light as both south doors were opened wide. Many heads were screwed over shoulders. The first figures to appear, however, were those of the mother of the bride, attended by her widowed sister-in-law. The two Mrs. Potts scuttled up the aisle to the front pew on the bride's side of the church, with bowed heads. No stranger seeing them, would have guessed that they had only broken off a turbulent altercation as their taxi drew up at the door of the church. They looked like two meek little grey mice, and at a glance appeared identical, except that Florence's mother carried in both hands a cottage bunch of very fine mixed roses. Mary looked gloomily at the line of mouth which further distinguished Mrs. Potts senior, and told herself, "I shall have what Albert calls a tussle with her about Ted and the Territorials, I foresee."

The choir burst into a hymn, and the congregation rose. Mary, owing to Sir Crosbie's outstretched marble leg, terminating in a buckled shoe, could not stand perfectly straight and could see nothing at all of the advancing procession.

"Much better looking lot than last time I was here," said Miss Wallis gruffly.

"I've forgotten," breathed Mary.

"Puggy Blent. I was a bridesmaid. Seventh time. We all looked gaga in cellophane haloes," confided Miss Wallis.

The service proceeded. As far as Mary could judge, both bride and bridegroom were inarticulate. In the back of the church a child with whooping cough, was removed by a reluctant escort. The words which custom cannot stale were spoken, and the Reverend Taylor duly pronounced Florence Béthune Potts and

Edmund Squirl man and wife. The bride's age was about four and twenty. Inclining towards Pamela, Mary enquired in a very low voice, "Was Potts killed in the last war, do you know?"

"What Potts? Oh! Potts. No. Died of flu up in Cologne though. Territorial sergeant-major. Used to be a tailor in Went. Made Granny's habits, she was telling me in the car," whispered Pamela.

"She would go to him."

"Oh, dear!" sighed Mary, looking at Mrs. Potts thin line of mouth anew.

The bridal couple departed to the vestry, and a regrettable gust of whispering vied with the strains of the organ. Mary, who knew the possibilities of Pamela's whisper, sat as close to Sir Crosbie as she could, and tried to fix her mind on higher things. But she was distracted by the fact that she now had a perfect profile view of Amy Squirl, chief bridesmaid. Amy's jaws were working solidly. Presently, with the air of one who sees port looming, she stealthily, but not rapidly, consigned to a clean pocket handkerchief the remains of a highly odorous magenta lozenge.

At last came the moment which was Mary's favourite at country weddings. The solemn creak of heavy boots proceeding up the aisle, sounded loudly. Eight worthies slowly took off their coats and bestowed them, neatly folded, upon the altar tomb under which Abbot Wayne had slept in peace for four hundred years. The bell-ringers were not well matched for age or height or weight. The wrinkles on the back of little Mr. Sucksmith's old brown neck resembled a physical map of the Alps. James Macmichael, greengrocer, had a drayman's shoulders and a profusely oiled quiff. Young Terry, from the Bank, was pink-faced, with a shock of golden curls. They proceeded to their duty in perfect unison, and turned with military precision to face one another when they had reached the spot from which ropes, decorated for an interval with brilliantly coloured furry substance, dangled from an unseen height. Eight shirt-sleeves were laboriously rolled up, and eight arms, well provided with muscle, laid lovingly alongside the ropes. . . .

"I always feel exhausted from suppressed emotion after a wedding," shouted Mary to Lady Merle in the churchyard, five minutes later. "Didn't Florence look nice?"

"Good young man, Squirl, though no use except with chrysanthemums," replied the Dowager. "Also allergic to *Primula Obconica*. Head gardener tells me he daren't send him into the house with them. Boy comes out covered with spots. Not at all what a village wedding was in my young days. No artificial satin then, or photographs of London weddings in daily papers, to set country girls thinking. However, nice-looking girls, all of them. Wish it was my poor Pamela's turn. Ah! she's found the car. Good-bye, Mary dear. Wish that we saw more of you."

CHAPTER VI
WHIT-SATURDAY, MAY 27TH

(i)

THE DOWAGER Lady Merle of Went's wish that she saw more of Miss Morrison seemed to have been heard in heaven. Upon Westbury Hill Mary's progress was impeded by a large limousine. She followed it through narrow lanes to the gates of Crossgrove. Before she reached the second gate in the park, she hooted, and passed the vehicle containing the Dowager and Pamela. "May be best not to arrive in a bunch," she told herself.

There was a surprising number of cars already parked in the silent courtyard outside the perfect Georgian house. The front door stood open and the dark hall seemed full of flitting figures. Mary perceived Albert moving fast, carrying a tray laden with jugs of lemonade. She decided to walk through the house and find her own way to the tennis court. But as she passed the dining-room door Sir Daubeny came forth. He was wearing flannels and looked decidedly heated. "Hullo, Button!" said he, grasping her hand urgently. "I say! this party looks like being rather a flop. Unknown to me, Catha—bless her heart!—has asked everyone in the landscape to play tennis, and the grass courts turn out to be absolutely unplayable. I've bought seven acres of moss, as far as I can see. Mercifully the two hard courts, which Crispin made me put in, are all right, but there are about fifty people panting to perform upon them. I wish Crispin was here. Ah! there's the Bishop going. I must give him that book I promised. Where on earth did I lay it down? With my tennis racquet, I know."

"I believe it's in the billiard room, sir. I'll get it," said a voice from the entrance blocked by Sir Daubeny's agitated form.

"Who is that young man? I've seen him here before," asked Sir Daubeny, staring fiercely after the fleeing figure.

"His name's Cox. He stays with the Wilsons," said Mary. "A Gunner, I believe."

"Rather like the look of him," said Sir Daubeny. "Wonder if he would do for 'Ponto' Miller. 'Ponto' wrote to me yesterday, saying, 'Send me no more A.D.C.'s from your regiment. They all fall in love.'"

"He's in Australia, isn't he?" asked Mary.

Sir Daubeny did not answer. His attention had been attracted by a homily being delivered in his hall by an unknown female guest, to the venerable and somewhat shaky Bishop.

"Look here," Miss Pamela Wallis was saying, "if you're going down to see that little chap Taylor at Westbury now, I do wish you'd tell him not to spoil village weddings for everyone by sticking up a notice in the porch saying, 'No confetti or rice to be thrown.' Old Mrs. Gibbet and the Harker girls are perfectly capable of sweeping the stuff up, and he doesn't do it when anyone like Puggy Blent gets married there. It's simply spreading Bolshevism. Besides, it looks so rude, and it's not even clean."

"Rather an outspoken young lady!" commented Sir Daubeny, fixing his monocle.

"It's all right, or at any rate better than you know," explained Mary. "He married her parents and christened her and confirmed her. She's a Merle grandchild."

"All the same . . ." said Sir Daubeny, advancing with the book recovered by Mr. Cox.

Miss Wallis took leave of her august friend, saying in chastened accents, "I see. Still, I should have thought you could have got your Sec. to send him a tactful snorter."

As they paced together through the hall towards the terrace, Lady Merle asked, "Does Sir Daubeny play tennis?"

"He does indeed, and I believe was capable of wearing out any couple of aides-de-camp in India," reported Mary, her thoughts lingering on the problem of Mr. Cox.

"Our courts at Went were always considered good," said the Dowager with mournful dignity. "We used to have very pleasant tennis there, even when my dear husband was at his busiest. Good afternoon, Mrs. Mimms. Good afternoon, Miss Masquerier. I was just saying that we used to have very pleasant tennis at Went in the old days. We frequently could make up a set in which all players were in the Cabinet. I do not think that any recent Premier has been a keen player. I do not know whether my courts have been kept up. Since my daughter-in-law is, I regret to say, a vulgar-minded creature, I never go there nowadays."

"I wish," muttered Pamela, as her grandmother emerged on to the terrace, snapping open a parasol of white taffeta with black satin stripes, "I wish that Granny regretted Valerie sufficiently not to mention it."

A group consisting of the Dowager, her grand-daughter, Mary, Miss Masquerier, Mrs. Mimms and Rosemary Wright, were established by their hostess in chairs on the terrace. Their view was of beds bright with tulips and forget-me-nots, of chestnut trees with every white candle lit, and beyond that, fields which were this week a sheet of buttercups.

"I'm glad to see that you got here safely," said Mary to her connexion by marriage.

"Johanna made us be punctual," said Rosemary, looking wistful. "She wanted to play tennis. She's playing now. She's awfully good."

To the disappointment of most of her audience, the Dowager had evidently decided against any further family revelations. "And when," said she, turning graciously to Miss Masquerier, "shall you be giving us another of your charming studies?"

"I have a biography of the unfortunate Queen of Scots on the stocks at the moment," gabbled Miss Masquerier, clasping her hands, and staring fixedly at the pantry quarters of Crossgrove.

"Mary, Queen of Scots! How very interesting. But hasn't she been done already?" asked little Mrs. Mimms eagerly.

"I am sure," said the Dowager, lowering her sunshade, "that Miss Masquerier will be able to provide us with quite a New View." Resting both hands on the carved ivory crook of her long spindly parasol, she added, "My granddaughter here read your *Maria Theresa* aloud to us, at home, in the evenings, throughout last Christmas. I can assure you, we did not miss a word."

In the dead silence which ensued, everyone regarded with feverish interest the flight across the terrace of a cabbage butterfly.

"Granny means your *Maria Louisa*," explained Miss Wallis at length. "We really did all enjoy it tremendously. I do hope you sold lots of copies. Hasn't it gone into a cheap edition?"

"I am glad to say it has," affirmed Miss Masquerier, brightening.

"Now I am so interested to hear that you are pleased about that," said little Mrs. Mimms, to whom prolonged silence was an impossibility, whatever the circumstances. "I never know myself whether it is a good thing or a bad thing for an author when their books are sold off cheap. We had your book in the house over Christmas too. I ordered a copy to send to my old governess at Paignton. Poor thing, she is quite bed-ridden now, so has lots of time for reading. I often think that if only I could find the time, I should read all day. But with a husband and two growing children needing one's attention unceasingly. . . ." She flung up both hands.

"What is the matter with your husband and children?" enquired the Dowager, unimpressed. "Are they unhealthy? My dear late husband, during his busiest years of National Service, always made time to keep abreast of current literature. He used to read while changing for dinner. If a volume was missing, I always told our people to look in the bath."

"I think," said Mrs. Mimms, undaunted, "that the copy of your *Maria Louisa* which we got must have been the cheap edition. I remember it hadn't got the lovely photographs, which, to me, were half the charm of your previous book."

"One should not," said the Dowager, "expect an historical biography to be provided with photographs. One of the first photographs taken in England was of my great-uncle, on the Terrace at Windsor. Not a flattering likeness, but the boots were characteristic."

"What's historical biography, Auntie Bee?" enquired Rosemary in an undertone.

"You ought to know; but it's lives of people," said Mary. She was feeling slightly confused, for the Dowager had just inclined towards her to comment, "One always thinks that that pretty little woman is going to say something of interest, and she never does."

"All dead?" pursued Rosemary.

"Not necessarily," said Mary.

Overcoming mountains of shyness, Rosemary, whose gaze had long been fixed admiringly upon that lady, asked Miss Masquerier hoarsely, "Have you written a book?"

Before the authoress could reply, the Dowager took charge of the situation.

"Miss Masquerier," said she, "has written many, many books. Indeed, I do not think that I should be exaggerating in describing her as a famous woman writer. In Went," concluded the Dowager tremendously, "we are very proud of claiming Miss Rosanna Masquerier as a native of our cathedral city."

"How absolutely thrilling!" said Rosemary, with her sweetest smile. "Would you mind awfully telling me," she asked humbly of the authoress, "what name do you write under?"

"I think I am going to look at the tennis," announced Mary, who considered that the authoress had suffered enough. "Don't you think it is rather hot sitting here?"

But Miss Masquerier knew that the present Lord Merle was owner of a piece of jewellery believed by nobody except his family to have been presented on the scaffold to a faithful henchwoman by the unfortunate Queen of Scots. Determined not to miss the slenderest chance of gaining permission to view the dubious relic, she remained attached to the owner of the ivory-handled parasol.

Catha, who was seated amongst a row of sufferers in strong sun, watching tennis through wire netting, leapt up with alacrity when Mary approached. Sliding her arm through that of her friend, she wheeled her towards the kitchen-garden.

"This is rather an upsetting party, Button," she began. "You may have heard from Tim that the grass courts are unplayable. But what Tim doesn't know is that Dorothy Yarrow telephoned this morning to say might they bring a perfectly charming young German baron who is staying with them, and is a good player. And the Mimms have simply brought a broken-hearted exiled Austrian doctor, whom they knew we'd like. Of course, for all I know, the Baron may not be Nazi, and the Doctor may not be Non-Aryan. But I can't help feeling that it would be much wiser not to let them meet. Never before have I longed for an A.D.C. on the premises. If only Crispin could have got down!"

"Introduce whichever of them you can find to me, at once," said Mary. "I will do what I can."

"You are a darling," said Catha. "Elizabeth is doing her best, and being very good about not playing tennis, but she's too young to be a rock of strength. By the way, Tim doesn't know anything."

(ii)

When Lady Rollo and Miss Morrison returned to the vicinity of the courts, they beheld a spectacle devastating to the hostess of a tennis party. Both sets had apparently finished simultaneously. A muscular mob, for whom there were no seats, were hovering like unsatisfied birds of prey, above an audience, at least half of whom were obviously longing to occupy the vacated arena. At the sight of their hostess, the gentlemen who had just played began to wind scarves around their necks and assume coats. They soon looked ready for a trip to the Pole, whereas the ladies who had been their partners, nearly all of whom were wearing abbreviated shorts, suddenly appeared pitifully under-dressed.

"Sheep!" murmured Lady Rollo viciously. "For heaven's sake do something about this, Button. You know most of their names and faces, which is more than I do."

Mary stepped forward, and ran her eye along the row of occupied chairs. Unfortunately her eye was instantly arrested, for she did indeed know a great many of her fellow guests. Everyone who caught sight of her burst into greetings.

"Mary!" cried Mrs. Yarrow. "My dear, I do hope that you heard we've been in quarantine for mumps. When I met you in the train going up to London, weeks ago, I said I was going to telephone and suggest a day for lunch."

"Come and sit between us, Mary dear," invited Lady Wilson, firmly indicating the chair from which Tony Rollo had just risen.

"Mary! you're just the person I was wanting to see," said Sir James.

"Miss Morrison," said Major Albany Mimms, stepping forward, "I want to introduce Dr. Joachim Weiss."

"Just one moment," pleaded Mary. "I must help Catha to get the tennis started again, first. How do you do?" she added hastily to the stranger bowing before her. "I suppose you don't play?"

Major Mimms' protégé, who was wearing blue trousers, a white shirt and a grey checked blanket jacket, answered simply, "Thank you!"

"Mummy," breathed Elizabeth faintly, "some more people are arriving."

"One second, Mary," said Catha, darting a warning look at her assistant. Addressing a tall, thin young man with spectacles and straw-coloured hair, she said, "Baron, I want you to play in a mixed doubles now."

"He has just done that, Mummy," said Elizabeth, surprised.

"I know, dear," said Catha with dignity. "But I should like him to do it again. We have not," she announced, "enough players yet to make up a men's four."

This vile falsehood passed unnoticed, for at this moment the further guests espied by Elizabeth came up. That Catha had not the faintest idea of their identity was clear from her greeting to the Misses Hill.

"Hullo, Norah!—Sheilah! Aileen!" said Mary heartily. "You've come in the nick of time. Lady Rollo is just making up a mixed doubles, and a ladies' four."

Norah Hill, at her plainest and shyest, began to make semi-inaudible explanations to Catha.

"It was awfully kind of you, Lady Rollo, to say on the telephone that we might bring Sheilah's friend who's staying with us. We were so afraid that four girls might be too many. Here she is. She works in an Art School, and her name . . ."

But nobody heard the name of the composed little pallid flaxen-haired lady who had accompanied the Misses Hill.

Elizabeth had by now made up a peculiar set composed, inevitably, of the Baron, the Doctor, her brother Tony, who was growling that he would rather not play, and Rosemary Wright, who was clearly terrified by her situation.

"No, no! that won't do at all," interrupted Catha. "I want Mary's niece to play in the ladies' four, and—and—I want you," said she with great emphasis to Johanna Pratt, "to play with the Baron against—er—Captain Yarrow and Miss Hill."

Johanna, nothing loath to partner a more promising player than Tony, led the way to the further court promptly, saying in bell-like tones to the Baron as she did so, "Do you know Munich well?"

"Doctor Weiss," said Mary loudly, "I want to introduce you to Lady Wilson. Lady Wilson knows Vienna very well. She lived there for years."

"Oh, yes!" murmured the exile, looking piteous. "But I do not know Vienna very well. I am a Czech," he announced, as he seated himself next to Sheilah Hill.

This announcement reduced Sheilah to speechlessness, but her friend, who seemed to possess poise, began at once to talk to the Doctor.

A most uneven four—Aileen Hill, Mrs. Yarrow, Rosemary Wright and Pamela Wallis—had been despatched to the court in full view of the audience, amongst whom desultory conversation recommenced.

"How do you like your new home?" enquired Lady Wilson of Tony Rollo, who had gloomily re-seated himself next to her.

"I haven't seen much of it yet," muttered Tony, looking his surliest.

Lady Wilson preferred young men with good manners, but she was a wise old lady, and had known innumerable young men.

She told this one now, "Get up at once, then, and beginning at the ruined Chapel, go round the lake and stables. Look into the library and notice the ceiling. I want to talk to Mary Morrison."

"Is Jugo-Slavia a lovely country?" asked the voice of Sheilah Hill despairingly.

"Czechs do not come from Jugo-Slavia, Sheilah," corrected Sheilah's friend. Turning to the Doctor, she remarked, "It is quite extraordinary, is it not, how many people in England do not know the difference between Jugo-Slavia and Czecho-Slovakia?"

"I think," agreed Dr. Weiss politely, "that not all English young ladies do."

"But I am not English," explained Sheilah's friend, warming to her subject. "Though I have lived all my life in Golder's Green, I am a Russian! My poor father was a Colonel of the Imperial Guard. I was not six months old when my mother escaped in a sledge through the snow, with me in her arms and her diamonds sewn in her stays. We flung roubles to the peasants as we charged through. . . ."

Satisfied that Dr. Weiss was firmly held in conversation for some time, Mary sought out Catha and advised her, "Leave it all to me now, darling, and go up to the terrace and have your tea with your other guests. As soon as the mixed doubles finishes, I will bring the Baron up and you can introduce him to old Lady Merle, who likes meeting foreigners, and I can put Dr. Weiss on to play down here. By the way, if you need somebody to act as an A.D.C. there's a sensible young subaltern called Cox, up in the house with Tim now. He has lamb's-wool hair, and stays with the Wilsons."

But twenty minutes later, when Mary arrived on the terrace, Mr. David Cox was still lingering there, dutifully but not cheerfully employed, administering weak tea to Miss Rosanna Masquerier and Mrs. Mimms.

Mary asked him, "Have you seen Lady Rollo? I believe she was looking for you."

"Just as Lady Rollo was beginning to ask me to do something," said Mr. Cox, "a footman came out with a message. A young lady who had come with a Mrs. Jackson to call, had arrived ill, as she had driven here in an open car without a hat."

"Look here!" said Mary, "Elizabeth is in rather a muddle, trying to arrange sets of tennis. I wish you would go down and help her."

"I've been longing to," said Mr. Cox, looking startled, "but I was afraid of butting in, as somebody told me that her elder brother was here."

"He is, but he's not much of a player, and I believe he's show-ing people over the house," said Mary.

Half an hour later, as she ascended her limousine, the Dowa-ger Lady Merle of Went said to her grand-daughter, "Quite a comfortable afternoon, after all. An enjoyable tennis party. We must come again to Crossgrove, Pamela. Lady Rollo has inter-esting friends."

(iii)

Now the day was over, and Miss Morrison sat with her guests in her own parlour. Outside the skies were dark blue at last, and if the guests could have stopped babbling for one moment Miss Morrison believed that they might have heard a nightingale.

But she did not suggest this, for they were all obviously happy, maundering about their experiences at the tennis party. Everyone had obtained a bath and ample cold supper. Everyone, Miss Morrison believed, had taken sufficient violent exercise to be feeling benevolent. Even Rosemary's mother was temporarily exhausted, for she had succeeded in losing her train and arriv-ing at the wrong station, whence her hostess had been obliged to rescue her, at ten minutes past eight. They had not assembled to sup until after nine.

"Wasn't it extraordinary," said Rosemary, "finding an Austrian and a German and a Russian and a Frenchman all at one tennis party? Is your father fond of foreigners, Tony?"

"He wasn't an Austrian. He was a Czech," said Tony, evading the second question. "He's going to Chicago as soon as his rela-tions there forward his passage money. He chops up people's noses and throats. I had quite a long talk with him."

"He doesn't play tennis badly, considering he's a foreigner," said Rosemary.

"My dear child," said Rosemary's mother, in far from affectionate tones, "have you never happened to glance at the nationalities of the Wimbledon entrants?"

Mrs. Thomas Morrison was not unlike her child in outward appearance. She had what Mary thought of as "Bird's nesty" black hair, black eyes and a pale countenance. But she was smaller and far more energetic than Rosemary. She was wearing, this evening, a Paisley blouse covered with dejected frills, surmounted by a tiger's claw necklace, several jangling bracelets from which depended various charms, and a black satin skirt meant to fasten at the side, but not fastened. She sat by choice on the edge of her chair.

"I never saw any Frenchman," said Mary.

"He's staying with someone here while his people have their son in the south of France," explained Rosemary. "He wore a beret and had hair like patent-leather, and moved as if he was made of monkey nuts strung together. He said, 'I am a French boy,' although he looked at least twenty, and called me 'Miss Fright.' But he played awfully well, and had rather a jolly grin."

"You had quite a long talk with the young German, Johanna," said Mary. "What did you make of him?"

Johanna Pratt had, to Mary's surprise, appeared to sup in two converted seventeenth-century cottages, attired in a clinging garment of some lustrous shell-pink material, and blunt-toed silver sandals. Her dress reminded Mary at once of a Greek chiton and a nightdress, but it became its wearer's long limbs admirably. As she lay in the light of an alabaster lamp, backed by a bowl of white roses, with her floss-silk locks sprayed over a leaf-green cushion, Mary saw what Tony meant when he said that Johanna Pratt was startlingly beautiful.

"As a matter of fact," said Johanna, "he was rather a disappointment to me. Of course he is only nineteen, and doesn't quite realize himself as yet."

"He told me that his family was very ancient, and that when there was a Nazi rally in the nearest town, his father had to send tenants, and he was generally sent with them," said Rosemary, "but generally managed to get nose-bleed and slip out soon. I asked him if he wasn't afraid of being hounded to death by the Gestapo for doing that, and he looked very uncomfortable."

"Who shall blame him!" murmured Tony.

"You found the little Russian lady rather a disappointment too, didn't you, Tony?" enquired Johanna.

"Oh! a complete typical reactionary, you see," said Tony, spreading out his hands.

"Tony and I are thinking of going to Moscow this summer," announced Johanna.

To Mary's discomfort, her sister-in-law, looking her most intense, said, "Yes? Yes? That's how you young people are so wonderful nowadays. . . ."

"Actually," said Tony, fidgeting, "I believe we shan't be there at the same time. Johanna wants to go in July, and I can't manage that with a *viva* hanging over me. Still, I'm determined to see something of the Great Experiment before this year's out."

"Do you really think that you will like Moscow, Tony?" asked Rosemary. "A friend of Mummy's, an awfully clever woman, went there last summer, and she said . . ."

But Mrs. Morrison could not allow her child to poach on her preserves.

"Dr. Heap—Dr. Dorothea Mulvaney Heap," said she. "Perhaps you know some of her work?" Her feverish gaze scanned the faces of the company.

"Ah, well then—you all have a great pleasure to come. Dr. Heap is a quite outstanding authority on Child Education. Her own children have been brought up absolutely unrepressed."

"I do hope they never come here, then," murmured Mary, feeling frivolous amongst so many earnest thinkers.

"If I decide to settle here, dear," said her sister-in-law, "they are almost certain to do so. Dr. Heap would never allow a month to pass without coming to give me guidance."

"She told Mummy as a fact," said Rosemary, "that not a single hand-basin or bath in Moscow has a plug."

"Plugs!" ejaculated Tony scornfully.

"I've heard that before, Tony," said Johanna warningly. "Personally, I am going to take a selection of plugs with me, and some meat cubes and a tin of Keatings. Perhaps it's just as well that we shall not be there at the same time."

"I know I'm awfully stupid," said Rosemary, "but honestly I can't see why Tony and you should fight because you love Munich and he loves Moscow. I mean, they both have masses of spies and concentration camps and no religion. I never can see why they can't kiss and be friends."

Tony and Johanna smiled pityingly, and Mrs. Morrison returned to the subject of the infants Heap, in whose nursery the word "Don't" had never been uttered.

Outside in the hall the grandfather clock struck eleven.

"Alas!" said Johanna, arising, "I shall have to go. Do you know," she said, turning to Rosemary, "I'm certain now that the flowers that come in the last week of May are the pick of the bunch. Look at what we saw to-day."

"I didn't notice," faltered Rosemary.

Johanna began to tick off on her fingers. "Red horse-chestnut, honeysuckle, clematis, clove-pinks, columbines, sweet bill, sweet peas, dog-roses. Is that right, Miss Morrison?"

"Perfectly," said Mary, relinquishing her guest's proffered hand, and deciding against her will that Tony had been right about his idol.

"Well," said Johanna, "I'm not going to ruin a perfect day. Do you know what I'm going to do now? I'm simply going to get out my little car and run back to London by moonlight."

Mary's liking for Tony's idol died a sudden death.

"But you can't do that," she said blankly.

"Why not?" asked Johanna, opening wide her saucer eyes. "I often do. It's lovely motoring alone in the country at night in the summer. The trees hang down like bunches of grapes and the telegraph wires are all silver."

"Mrs. Bates," said Mary, steeling her heart, "has had your bed made, and would be bitterly disappointed."

The grandfather clock was striking midnight by the time that Mary Morrison turned out the electric light in her bedroom and opened the curtains. Johanna had needed persuasion before she consented to lie sleepless in a stuffy bedroom instead of caracoling up an arterial road. Her farewells had been protracted, considering that the company was due to meet again at nine-thirty.

The nightingale which Mary had promised her guests was singing. Mary ceased to hold her breath, hooked her windows open, wound her watch, shed her kimono and composed herself to rest. For several minutes her thoughts wandered drowsily. She thought of Florrie Squirl, at the seaside, hearing waves for the first time, and fat old Lord Merle, languidly dropping best-sellers into his bath, and Dr. Weiss operating on people's noses in Chicago, and last, just before she knew no more, beheld a distinct vision of Johanna Pratt, resolutely inserting bath plugs into the bawling open mouths of a hundred unrepressed children, all the offspring of that outstanding female, Dr. Dorothea Mulvaney Heap.

CHAPTER VII
JUNE 9TH—JUNE 10TH

(i)

"LADY ROLLO" said the invitation card, stuck crookedly into the Vauxhall mirror over the mantelpiece at Willows, "At Home, Friday, June 9th." In the corners of the card, printed in smaller italics, ran the legends, "Dancing 9.30," and "Crossgrove, Went." Along the top of the card Elizabeth had written, in firm, upright characters, using a broad nib and plenty of ink, "Miss Morrison and party." Miss Morrison's party consisted, rather unexpectedly, of herself, Lady Rollo's eldest son and two undergraduates on whom she had first set eyes an hour ago. The gentlemen were all upstairs at the moment.

Whether or not he could have helped it, Tony had behaved recently as coquettishly as a prima donna. On Tuesday he had sent a short, almost illegible note, saying that he was doubtful if he could get away from Oxford, and a telegram on Wednesday night had regretted Friday impossible. On Friday morning, a battered picture postcard, showing a gargoyle in the shape of a pig playing the bagpipes on the façade of Melrose Abbey, had announced, "Still trying to get away for E's dance." He had arrived at seven o'clock this evening, in no easy temper, bringing with him two large strange young men, whom he had introduced without explanation as Tony ffolliot and Derek Young. There had been a dispute about transport. Mary said that she refused to arrive looking like the Witch of Endor, and meant to leave directly after supper. She wished to go in her own closed car. Tony said he was very unlikely to stay as long as supper. His friends looked alarmed. Now both cars stood outside the garage, and through the parlour door came Tony himself, bearing a white tie in his hand. At the sight of him Mary's wrath died.

"Look here," began Tony, "would it be possible for you to do anything about this?"

"What's the matter with it?" asked Mary. "Can't you tie it?"

"I've tied it several times, but I've bled upon it," explained Tony. "Either the laundry or my scout had fastened up the sleeves of my shirt with large rusty pins."

"Dear me!" said Mary, receiving the tie. "It needs to be soaked and then washed, and probably ought to have a pinch of starch. . . . Tony! do you know you've bled all over your collar too? I suppose neither of your friends has got a spare tie and collar?"

"No," said Tony helplessly, "and anyway they've got necks like ferrets, and I've got a bull-dog's."

Mary rang the bell for Doris, who did not appear in answer, and was quite certainly using her brain and bringing in the soup.

Tony ffolliot, followed closely by Derek Young, came clattering down the stairs, and the parlour suddenly appeared very small.

"Ask Rose to soak these in cold water, and get ready some starch and the electric iron," said Mary, haughtily handing Tony's tie and collar to Doris.

Tony, who seemed to see himself as the labourer returned from toil, quite enjoyed the meal of which he partook innocent of collar or tie. He even condescended to explain that his namesake ffolliot was an expert on interior decoration, while Derek composed madrigals. "They're the result," said he, waving his hand at them, "of my mother's daily imperious but frantic letters commanding me to bring at least two men who can dance."

Mr. ffolliot, who did indeed remind Mary slightly of a ferret, since he had a narrow sleek head and a darting glance, was perfectly willing to discourse upon his hobby. As Mary had expected, the Empire period was his prey. Mr. Young had not so much to say for himself.

"I thought your musical niece was to have been with you," said Tony presently.

Mary answered with feeling, "It's quite sad. Your mother kindly asked me to bring both my sister-in-law and Rosemary, and I accepted for both of them, and now neither is here. Rosemary's leaving for South Africa with a touring company."

"Isn't that rather sudden?" asked Tony.

"It is," admitted Mary. "She went up on Monday last week as usual, and then she telephoned while I was out one day, saying that she was on the track of a job and wouldn't be coming down last week-end, and her mother took the next train up to London to see what she was about. I heard nothing from either of them until last night, when Rosemary telephoned again and said she was sailing for South Africa to-morrow. I'm going up by the eight-fifty to see her off."

"Is Mrs. Morrison still coming to live here if there's a war?" asked Tony, with a light in his eye.

"Well, she's toying with the idea," replied Mary. Doris and Rose, who evidently considered the prestige of Willows enhanced by the presence of three dancing men, did wonders with Tony's tie and collar in a wonderfully short time. Since Tony had pricked both his thumbs, his friends got him into his collar, and Mary tied the tie.

"And mind," she said, as she did so, "whatever you do, *don't* go into Mr. McGregor's garden."

But although it could not have been much more than a decade since all three dancing men had eagerly turned the pages of the masterpiece from which she quoted, two of them failed to respond.

After considerable prodding from their dinner hostess, the party set out at nine forty-five, somewhat officiously attended by Doris up to the last possible moment. Mary realized that, although to her Mr. ffolliot was mainly reminiscent of a ferret, to more experienced eyes, as he wound around his throat a tubular scarf bearing cut-out initials, he recalled glamorous memories of Hollywood as represented at the Went "Odeon." "I wish to goodness," she thought, as she seated herself in her car, "that my Cinderella was going to the ball, and I could stay behind in my nice kitchen."

"I'd better lead," she explained to Mr. Young, who was accompanying her, "for I'm far from sure that Tony knows the way."

Her cavalier, who was quite plain, with a good-humoured, freckled face, and noticeably long hands, said in his youthful pleasant voice, "That sounds bad. Still, his people haven't lived there long, have they? I wish Tony wouldn't be such an ass."

"Oh, so do we all," assented Mary, with fervour. "You can't do anything about it, I suppose?"

"I'm doing my best," said Mr. Young. "I've taken him up myself several times, and I've tried to get him keen, but he's not serious, I'm afraid."

"You've what?" asked Mary, quite at a loss.

"Well, he hasn't gone solo yet, but he ought to next week," continued Mr. Young. "I never saw anyone worse at landings. It can't be his sight, I shouldn't think," reflected Mr. Young cheerfully. "Still, several of our best pilots simply never learn to make a decent landing. But I know for a fact he's never even tried to pass his medical."

"Do you mean that you—that he—that you're both Learning to Fly?" asked Mary.

"He's learning. I've been in the Auxiliary Air Force for ten months now," said Mr. Young. "I don't really care for anything else, except music, which I can't afford."

"I've never known a young airman personally before," reflected Mary. Conscious that she seemed to be using journalese, she went on quickly, "Was flying in your family? Have you always been keen on it?"

"I haven't got any family," said Mr. Young confusedly. "You see, my father married again. Yes, I think I've always been keen on it. What I'd really like would be to go into the Regular Air Force."

"Then why on earth don't you?" asked Mary. "What are you going to do?"

"I've got to go into Paint," said Mr. Young. "Paint pays."

"Does pay matter, if you've got nobody but yourself to think of?" asked Mary.

"I see I've explained myself badly," said Mr.' Young, growing very red. "I live with my mother. She teaches tap-dancing in West Kensington. One of her few opulent clients is married to a man who makes paint. He's kindly offered to take me on appro. He wants some University men. I may end a millionaire."

"I see," said Mary. "I'm so sorry."

"It doesn't really matter. I'm one of thousands nowadays," said Mr. Young, scraping his feet, "but you see now why I think Tony Rollo's an ass—having a complete family longing to clasp him to their bosoms."

"Oh, look!" cried Mary. "They've floodlit the face of the house. We get out here. This is Crossgrove. Doesn't it look nice. But I ask myself, what will Tony's other friend say?"

(ii)

Up in Catha's bedroom, where the lights seemed dim after the glare in the hall, Ada and Albert's mother were taking the ladies' cloaks. "Hullo, Mary," said Pamela Wallis. "Isn't this a pretty room? Isn't it extraordinary how sordid coats look laid on beds with tickets pinned on them? See you later." Up here the thud of music sounded faintly. The room was crowded by chattering, bare-armed, curly-headed girls in filmy frocks. Many of them were unknown to Mary, and their looks rather alarmed her. She knew Catha's old maid very well, however, and as she prepared to leave the room, said to her in an aside, "Good evening, Ada. It's nice to see you again. I shall be coming up to have a chat with you later. Good evening, Mrs. Higgs. I hope you're happy in Lower Merle."

A single glance in a full-length mirror was all that Miss Morrison craved before she withdrew, but it was not easy to approach any mirror. A broad-backed figure, attired in a white crinoline gown, and wearing a large diamond bandeau on metallic golden locks, and many diamond bracelets, was seriously occupied on the stool in front of the dressing-table. "Isn't it absurd," she uttered in preoccupied accents, "that one should do all this just before one leaves one's house, and then begin all over again as soon as one arrives here?"

"I do what I can at home, in peace, and then hope for the best," said Mary, who recognized the voice.

"Mary!" ejaculated the character known in the neighbourhood as "young" Lady Merle. "What are you doing here?"

Mary, understanding afresh why this neighbour was not universally beloved, said meekly, "It's all right. I only mean to dance two or three times, and I shall be going home soon after supper."

Lady Merle pushed a powder-puff attached to an emerald green handkerchief into an elaborate bag, and began to apply lipstick to a Cupid's bow already overloaded. She said between gasps, "Don't be absurd, Mary. All the same, I wish I could follow your example. My dear! you've no idea what we mothers have to go through. Night after night. . . . I only wonder we don't all have nervous breakdowns. Doesn't it seem ridiculous to think of me with a débutante daughter?"

Since "young" Lady Merle was exactly her contemporary, Mary did not consider it at all remarkable that she should possess a grown-up child. "The mother of Henry VII was only thirteen when he was born," she said thoughtfully.

"How disgusting," said Lady Merle. "I'm so glad I didn't live in the eighteenth century."

"So am I, because of baths, principally," agreed Mary. "Is Lalage here?"

"She was a few minutes ago," said Lady Merle, snatching up a hand-mirror. "My dear, we've just had the most awful family reconciliation dinner." The reason why Lady Merle had not enjoyed her dinner was obvious to Mary when Pamela Wallis strode up and said in the undertone of an exasperated Sunday-school instructor, "Valerie, you're keeping Granny waiting."

Mary, despairing of approaching any mirror, picked her way downstairs between couples seated on the steps, and advanced slowly but surely in a procession of newly-arrived guests, towards the inner hall.

"Colonel Bloodshot," announced Catha's butler in a tremendous voice. "Dr. Greatbatch. Lady Norah Blent. Captain and Mrs. Yarrow." Bending confidentially, he enquired of the eldest Miss Hill, "What name if you please, miss?"

The three Hill girls, attended by a pink-cheeked boy in an enormous collar, who looked about sixteen, were delighted to see a familiar face.

"Miss Morrison," boomed the voice in full volume again. "Mr. Young."

Catha, dignified but harassed, backed by an insecure-looking trellis adorned with living roses and already-wilting greenery, had Elizabeth by her side. In the moment during which she passed in front of her old friend, Mary found time to say, "Many congratulations, dearest. The façade looks a dream."

"Oh! but you haven't heard," murmured Catha, wide-eyed. "The lights of the whole house fused as we got up from dinner. Tim's there still."

Elizabeth held upside down, in her left hand, a small bouquet of moss-roses and forget-me-nots, encircled by a stamped silver paper frill, and decorated with long silver ribbons. Her attitude was very much that of a six-year-old swinging a favourite doll by a single leg. Mary would not acknowledge, even to herself, that Elizabeth did not look her best in an Early Victorian picture dress. The poor child was evidently stiff with nerves. Her little curled black head was charming, but her vivid colouring had vanished, and her immature shoulders started out of a bodice which made her appear at once square and skinny.

"Many happy returns of the day, Elizabeth," said Mary, smiling encouragingly. "I want to introduce a friend whom Tony has brought from Oxford to your dance."

"I know," said Elizabeth, beginning to sparkle, "I've seen him—Tony ffolliot."

"No," said Mary, "one whom I think you don't know." Before she effected the introduction of Mr. Derek Young, she managed to declare in a murmur which reached nobody but the débutante, "Much nicer!"

Music was sounding again as Mary reached the crowded entrance to Catha's long white saloon. After a glance within she relinquished all hope of taking the floor herself to-night. She reflected with faint melancholy that in earlier days an entertainment to which twice the number of people who could do so in comfort had been invited to dance, would hardly have been deemed a success. "I see a great many people here whom I don't know," she confided to Mr. Young. "But I'd like to introduce you to some girls who arrived just before us, and who I know dance well."

Finding Mr. ffolliot at her elbow a few minutes later, she asked him, "Has my godson ratted? I feel his worst fears are being realized. Do you know many people here, or would you like me to introduce you to some I know?"

But Mr. ffolliot, after bowing with great *empressement* to "young" Lady Merle, at whom he had been glaring anxiously, said that he thought he saw a good many people he knew, thank you. This was evidently the truth, for whenever she noticed him later during the evening, Mary saw that he was happy in the company of those guests who were quite unknown to her, and whose looks particularly alarmed her. She guessed that they all came from London, and regretted having fed Mr. ffolliot on lobster and chicken in her humble abode. She suddenly realized that he was bound to die an old bachelor.

Nevertheless, Miss Morrison did take the floor at Miss Elizabeth Rollo's coming-out dance, for young Mr. Young reappeared and repeated the offer which he had made before she had delivered him to the Misses Hill. Mary remembered that his mother taught tapdancing, so hoped that he might be able to deal with a partner who had once been very fond of the sport, but now performed on an average twice a year. Her hopes were not disappointed, but she increasingly regretted that half the company present could not have been elsewhere.

In the library they met Sir Daubeny, looking deliberately festive. Down either side of his decent work-room ran trestle tables, covered with white damask, loaded by markedly unconvincing flamboyant plated ware displaying dainties.

"Ha! Button," said Sir Daubeny. "Now, what can I offer you—a damp sandwich cut in London this morning, or an impaled prawn to dip in a beaker of sweet cream? There are also some small sausages being kept really hot by a naked flame burning directly under my grandfather's oil portrait. Or perhaps you would like a few odds and ends of banana, an unstoned cherry and a squashed purple raspberry drowning in an amber liquid."

"How lovely!" said Mary. "But I fancy I saw a marquee on the tennis courts, as I arrived. I think I'll wait. Tim, I want to introduce a friend of Tony's who's staying with me."

Sir Daubeny, playing the host manfully, took his guests out on to the terrace, where balustrading and steps clothed with wavering foliage and flowers glimmered dimly, and the music sounded but faintly. Some individual trees in the park beyond had been floodlit. Unfortunately clouds were racing across the night sky above, and although there should have been a moon, not even a single star was visible. It seemed to Mary disobliging of Nature, considering that for the past three weeks the nights had been balmy.

"How lovely!" she repeated, controlling a shiver. Some shrub or plant growing close to the lighted windows was exhaling a strong fragrance.

"Like woodsmoke," said Mary, looking up and around. "What is it, I wonder? Oh! Tim, I don't know why, but this scene reminds me of Italy."

"It reminds me of the North Pole," grunted her host. "Come inside and dance with me, Button. I haven't danced yet. As you may have heard, our lights here fused as we rose from dinner. Ah! Elizabeth's dancing now. Looks happy, do you think?"

Mary looked, and saw, to her surprise, an Elizabeth whom she would not have recognized.

"Quite the prettiest thing here," she was truthfully able to assure the débutante's father.

(iii)

"Ah! there you are, Ada," said Mary. "I'm much later than I meant to be. You see, I'm enjoying myself so much."

"That's right, Miss Mary," said Catha's maid, emerging out of the shadows, beaming like the Cheshire Cat.

The ladies' cloak-room was deserted. "I've sent Mrs. Higgs down to get her bit of supper," explained Ada majestically. She removed from the dressing-table a duck-egg green paper sheet containing two and a half rows of pins, and three hair-slides. Having dusted the glass table-top and the triple mirror, she continued, ticking her tongue in her teeth. "There! That's all ready for you now to sit down to in peace, Miss Mary. Tut! tut! I was that annoyed at your having to go down to be announced without getting near a mirror. Mrs. Higgs and me both noticed I was just about to get you the hand-mirror, when her ladyship took up that too. But if there had been anything not right in the hang of your gown, Mrs. Higgs and me would never have let you go without a word."

"I'm sure you wouldn't," agreed Mary. Before seating herself, she said, "You've seen this dress before, Ada. I wore it the night I came to dine here. It's last year's really, but you see, my new one's black, and I thought I couldn't go to Miss Elizabeth's coming-out dance dressed in black."

"I'm sure you look very nice indeed, Miss Mary," said Ada comfortingly. "The pastel shades were always your favourites, I remember. How did you think Miss Elizabeth is looking, miss? Tut! tut! her ladyship and me was quite worried about her at four o'clock. Her temperature was up, of that I'm sure, though she wouldn't let us take it. She came in from her walk with the other young ladies, saying that she had a splitting headache and didn't want her tea. But I persuaded her to take off her things and just lie in her dressing-gown on the sofa in her room for half an hour. I slipped in a hot water-bottle when I brought up her cup of tea, and I covered her up with her ladyship's light cashmere rug. When I peeped in to get the tray, there she was, fast asleep, with her book topsy-turvy on the floor. She didn't wake until I turned on her bath."

"I've just been able to tell Sir Daubeny, with my hand on my heart," said Mary, "that I think his daughter's the prettiest thing in the room."

Ada looked relieved.

"She's enjoying herself, then. I'm sure I'm glad to hear it after all the trouble that's been taken." Ada sunk her voice. "She didn't want to have a white gown, you know, miss, and between you and me, I'm not sure that she wasn't right—being such a brunette. When she walked in to show herself to her father, I heard her saying, 'Well, here I am, Daddy, but I warn you, I'm looking my worst. I look exactly like a black fairy doll, off the top of a Christmas tree.'"

"She's got plenty of colour now, and she's having a grand time," said Mary. "Her ladyship does you credit to-night, Ada. I've never seen her look better."

"That blue matches her eyes, and did you notice the lovely fish-tail pleated train?" asked Ada eagerly.

"I wish you could see the gown her ladyship's ordered for the Court, though. She didn't want to order another. Everything's to be for Miss Elizabeth these days, as you'll understand, knowing her ladyship's nature. But Sir Daubeny put his foot down. Miss Elizabeth's got a peach-pink, very pretty. It doesn't seem to me quite the thing, for her to be having her dance so long before she really comes out, so to speak, but with Their Majesties away, I quite see it can't be helped, I shall be thankful when they're safe home again, shan't you, Miss Mary? Of course I don't know the Atlantic—rather full of icebergs from what I read in my paper—but I've been to India and back seven times with her ladyship now, so I think I may fairly say I know what Ocean Travel can be."

"Yes. I expect you're the most travelled woman ever born in Lower Merle, Ada," said Mary.

The look of gratification faded from Ada's face as she said, "It does seem sad neither of her brothers could get here for Miss Elizabeth's birthday ball. I did feel sorry for her ladyship when the telegrams came in."

"Mr. Tony's turned up, all right," said Mary, putting in a hair-pin. "He's staying with me, and has brought two Oxford friends."

"No, miss!" exclaimed Ada. "Well, I am pleased to hear that." After a pause, she continued wistfully, "I would like to catch a glimpse of Mr. Tony in his white tie and tails. You haven't happened to notice if he's dancing with any nice young ladies, Miss Mary? When all's said and done, I never can forget poor little Mr. Tony as he was when he had the mumps at six years old. He looks at himself in the glass—that trained nurse having let him have it—and he says to me in his gruff way, 'Shall I have to look like this for the rest of my life, Ada?' And then there was the time when he'd saved up to buy a present for his mother's birthday. I can see him at this moment coming round the door in his little dressing-gown with the 'Wilfred' by the ears."

"He was dancing with the prettiest girl in the room when I left," said Mary.

"With his sister!" nodded Ada. "There now! Won't her ladyship be pleased!"

"And absolutely between two old friends, Ada," added Mary, glancing round to see that the shadowy room was still empty, "he brought the most beautiful young lady down to stay with me the other day. She's here to-night, but there's nothing in it, I should say. They're just good friends."

"I've known the happiest marriages come that way, miss," began Ada wisely. Mrs. Higgs had come in to the dressing-room beyond, but was effacing herself.

"Come in, Mrs. Higgs," called Mary. "I'm just going. I've been asked by Sir Daubeny to sup with the family at their table, so I mustn't be late. How do you think the show's going?"

"After a sad start, miss," said Mrs. Higgs, who was wearing her abhorred teeth, "all seems to be going on as well as can be expected. You will have 'eard, miss, that all the lights fused just as the 'Ouse-Party rose from dinner. But there! my Albert 'as put that all right. 'Don't breathe a word of this, mother,' sez 'e to me, 'but there being no fuse wire in the 'ouse, I've done what I can with a piece of ordinary picture wire. It's to be 'opes that there won't be a fire,' sez 'e. 'Then Sir Daubeny would create.'"

Mary deemed it wisest to change the subject.

"Have either of you been inside the marquee?" she asked.

Both Ada and Mrs. Higgs had. Moreover, they were able to inform Mary that a troupe of artistes dressed in Mexican costume were going to entertain the guests on concertinas during supper.

"They go from table to table, miss," explained Mrs. Higgs, "asking the guests what tune they would like. They're all foreigners, I've 'eard from the young fellow wot fetched them from the station."

"That will be exciting!" said Mary, feeling slightly out of her depth. "I was just saying to Ada, Mrs. Higgs, how nice I thought Miss Elizabeth was looking—quite the prettiest girl in the room. And there are some pretty girls there to-night."

"And some lovely gowns, miss," nodded Ada, who seemed to think that she had been left out of the conversation long enough. "The young ladies' evening gowns are very pretty this season, I think, but some of their day clothes I can't fancy. There's a tall fair young lady staying in the house now. I don't know if you happen to have seen her, miss—Miss Pratt? The maid who unpacked for her told me that she's brought a pair of yellow leather trousers for all the world like a Dutchman's, and with bright scarlet patches on the knees. There's a navy fisherman's jersey to go with them."

"I've met her, but not in those trousers," said Mary, marvelling at Ada's cunning, but rising firmly.

"You haven't caught sight of anything that shouldn't, occurring downstairs to-night, I hope, miss?" asked Ada, as she detained Mary by operating on the back of her dress with a clothes brush. "I'm only asking, miss, because ever since the 'orrible idea was suggested to me, I haven't been able to put it out of my mind. It was at the dinner-table to-night, one of Miss Elizabeth's London friends, a young lady she doesn't really know well, I think, said to her that she wondered who'd have to be thrown out before this merry evening was over. Of course, miss, having been abroad so long, I don't know what habits may be nowadays, but by what one sees in the papers some of the younger set are very wild, and things happen, even in private houses. I haven't had an easy moment since, thinking of the possibility of anything happening in Sir Daubeny's house."

"Sir Daubeny's face set like a rock, when he heard what the young lady said," reported Mrs. Higgs with gusto. "You could almost see him putting on the Black Cap."

"Well, I hope he won't have to put on the Black Cap to-night," said Mary, "and from all I've seen it doesn't seem at all likely."

(iv)

Going up to London by the 8.50 in June was a comparatively easy business, and the morning after Elizabeth's coming-out dance was brilliant. After all, the weather did not seem likely to break yet awhile. Mary breakfasted alone, and stole out of her house, leaving her guests still sleeping. The Green was empty, as she turned out of the gates of Willows, and an undercurrent of faint buzzing, typical of a midsummer day of approaching heat, filled the air. She drove herself to the station between hedges, not yet dust-laden, screening fields in which buttercups and daisies were triumphing and cattle drowsing. The ditches were crowded with horse-parsley, ragged-robin and speedwell. As she paced the platform after parking her car, she could hear the voices of the mill-wheel at Merle End, and a collie seeing some of Giddy's cattle into the horseshoe-shaped pastures below Whiteladies. Only duty, she felt, could make anyone take a ticket for London on such a day.

She travelled up with Sheilah Hill, who was obsessed by the knowledge that she had a favourite bloodhound in the guard's van, destined for a purchaser from Northern Ireland. "I wouldn't have parted with her if it hadn't been for the European situation," explained Sheilah. "I meant to keep her for my Hengist in August. But since I'm liable to be called up, and anyway then, who'll be wanting bloodhound puppies, I've decided not to have any more litters this year. By the way, when your friend Lady Rollo came to call the other day, my new kennel boy, who let her in, said, 'Are you the Bloodhound's Mate?' I hope she wouldn't mind."

"Catha is devoted to dogs," said Mary. "How many have you at Bury Cottage now?"

"It's too depressing—only Hengist, for whom I've got a home in Yorkshire if I'm called up," said Sheilah, "and this lot expected next month, three of whom are bespoke. And of course there's always that unutterable sausage of Norah's. Norah is upstage with me at present because I got in first with the Yorkshire cousins, and they'll take Hengist, but no more."

"I daresay you're wise, but my Dutch bulb grower seems optimistic," said Mary, disclosing a glowing catalogue, labelled "Autumn 1939."

"I've suggested that Norah shall give the dachshund to Aileen as a wedding present," said Sheilah. "Neither of them seem keen."

"How is Aileen getting on with her trousseau?" asked Mary.

"She's going to ask Sally Bates in to see a display of it. I expect she'd ask you, if you'd like," said Sheilah. "Norah did most of the embroidery. She likes that sort of thing. I'm better inside a kennel or the bonnet of a car. Lord Merle's letting us practise driving vans in gas-masks with no lights, after dark, in his park. Rather decent of him."

"How are you managing?" asked Mary.

"Better than you might expect," said Sheilah. "Puggy Blent got into a corner of the garden, by mistake, the other night, and drove over Lady Merle's 'Friendship's Border,' including a lead Cupid. The really funny thing was that she mistook it for a human child, and being slightly flurried, put the van into reverse and went back over it again. Lady Merle was a bit unpatriotic on the telephone, and said it was late eighteenth century, and had been given her by a dear Italian nobleman. I really joined my corps because I had heard that in the event of an air raid, our duties included tethering loose horses to lamp-posts."

At the terminus Mary took a taxi to her club, where she deposited several odd-shaped parcels. She kept the taxi, and on her route to Waterloo dropped a basket of flowers at Marcelle's flat. Marcelle's maid, who was new to her, and had a brogue, said stormily that Mrs. Morrison was having her breakfast in her bed, and no wonder. Miss Rosemary had been called for by Miss String half an hour back. She had left her room a sight after the packing.

In London, tar was oozing from the streets. Mary's taxi was held up in a traffic block near Westminster Bridge for a full two minutes, and through its window she read mechanically the notice propped beside a pavement artist: "I am hurt inwardly." Seeing people off at stations did not agree with her; fortunately she had no time to consider her spirits. As she paid her taxi, her best umbrella, swinging from her arm, met, with disastrous results, a hand-saw being carried by another pedestrian. When she arrived on the platform from which the theatrical company was due to depart in seven minutes, she received an immediate impression that she had stepped into the middle of the third act. A guard was adjuring passengers to take their seats, please, and several members of the company had already done so. She hurried up the platform, scanning the windows, all partially obscured by long labels bearing the manager's name, and a press photographer stepped heavily back upon her, saying with a flourish, "Thank you very much, Miss Marvell."

Rosemary, unusually obedient or really eager to get off for South Africa, was amongst those who had taken their seats. Her appearance startled Mary, for she had had her wild locks permanently waved and her eyebrows plucked, and the nails with which she was rummaging in a newly opened box of chocolates on the seat beside her, were heather-coloured. Her costume for ocean travel consisted of a scarlet and white striped cotton frock made for an Austrian peasant, and an imitation leopard-skin jacket. She looked a curious mixture of childishness and sophistication, seemed touched that Mary should have come "all the way from Willows" to see her off, and introduced her to several other occupants of the carriage, one of whom turned out to be a Mrs. Thring.

"She's made puppets for eleven years in Sydenham. She's been divine to me," explained Rosemary in an aside.

Mrs. Thring, who was extraordinarily plain, but effectively attired, had two rows of absolutely regular black curls tied up in a petunia scarf, and a voice from which all individuality had been banished. She said with unaffected friendliness that Mary was Rosemary's aunt, and needn't worry a scrap. Since Rosemary had dismounted to watch the antics of the press photographer, Mary, seized the opportunity to answer, "That is very kind of you. I do feel a little nervous of her going so far and in such a hurry. She both looks, and is, particularly young for her age."

"Just a fresh young English girl," pronounced Mrs. Thring to the whole carriage-full. "That's why I'm sure your niece is going to be a success at the Cape, Miss Morrison."

"Do you really think she may be?" asked Mary, taking heart. "I've never seen her act since she was at school. I must say I once did think her very good as Apollyon."

"Somebody's sent Julia a gilt basket full of roses as tall as herself," said Rosemary, stepping back into the carriage. "She's in despair, for she says that when she reaches her state-room she knows it'll be like a funeral already."

"Tell me who some of the people are, please," asked Mary. "I've recognized Dame Sarah, of course. They all look famous and fashionable to my country eyes, but I suppose some of them are really dressers and stage hands."

"Oh, no!" said Rosemary, sounding shocked. "The stage hands and the electricians and dressers go with the dress-baskets and sets, and travel in a carriage by themselves."

"The company is nicely graded according to importance," nodded Mary.

"The tall, willowy girl, in the printed chiffon and silver foxes, who's getting such a send-off, with lots of bouquets, is Faith Foy," said Rosemary in a thrilled whisper. "She's broken-hearted at having to leave her Scotties. Her maid's brought them to the station to see her off. She's just been photographed with them. She's our leading lady, and gets a compartment to herself. So does the leading man, Maurice De Poitevin. That's really his name. He was President of the O.U.D.S. at Oxford, and is highbrow, and has written two brilliant modern novels. Julia is highbrow too. When she has to be Marie Antoinette or anything like that, she goes over to France and actually sees the places. She's got two daughters at boarding-school. You'd never guess it, would you? Some of the company don't like her, because she's married to a stockbroker and needn't take a part unless she likes, but personally I've always found her sweet. She's just given me these because she had got two copies. I've never had a shiny, unopened *Tatler* and *Sketch* of my own before. That's her husband, with the blue suit and no hair. The pale young man with lots of curly hair and a black and white spotted scarf, is Bruce, Maurice's cousin, the playwright. That's old Sir George standing beside him. He's got a beard at present because he's doing a film. He's not going, of course. The Arctic Blonde talking to the reporter is Pam—Pam Wayne. Isn't she marvellous? Do look! Nobody more surprised than the Star to discover that she's been photographed unawares."

"Now Rosemary!" began Mrs. Thring warningly.

"I think you had better get right into the carriage," suggested Mary. "I left some flowers at your mother's flat, and I shall be calling for the basket."

"Mummy staged a heart-attack last night, not very well done," said Rosemary, all the prettiness dying out of her face. "I must say, darling, I'm thankful to be going to South Africa, even if I wasn't going to act at last."

"I do hope you'll enjoy yourself," said Mary. "Here's a small present. It's just a cheque, as I couldn't think of anything else except a fur tippet, and I wasn't sure if that would be any good in Africa. I'd like you to keep the cheque for a rainy day, so to speak, if possible, but if ever you need anything you know you have only to cable."

"Thank you very much, Auntie Bee, I certainly will," said Rosemary with alarming alacrity.

"I wish I was going to see you—in Shakespeare, or something I should understand," said Mary, standing on tiptoe to pour her remarks over the carriage door. "If ever you have a photograph taken, please send me one—and anything from newspapers."

"I will, I will, Auntie," nodded Rosemary, her eyes growing large and lovely and slowly filling with tears.

At the very last moment, just as the train was about to draw out, a tall young man, beginning to put on weight, escorted the leading lady to her compartment, saying in unruffled tones, "Julia! those last photographs of yours—I only saw them this morning— positively intoxicating. . . ."

He tore his hat from his head, and stood, a commanding figure, quite eclipsing his inappropriate neighbour Miss Morrison, as the long train, plastered with labels, moved quicker towards daylight. A shaft of sunshine glancing through the arched glass roof of the blue and echoing terminus, obligingly outlined his form. Mary saw the frilled short sleeve of Rosemary's frock, and a bare and skinny young hand from which a handkerchief fluttered. She waited until the train ceased to describe a crescent, and the back of the last van grew small, and faded. Then, with many "Darlings," "Good-byes" and "Good Lucks" ringing in her ears, she turned thoughtfully towards Victoria.

The Irish maid at Marcelle's flat, who had now undergone a change of heart, asked avidly for news of Rosemary's departure, and said that the saints knew it would have been a black shame if the young innocent lamb had been allowed to sail without a kind word from a soul. Hearing that Mrs. Morrison had Dr. Dorothea Heap in attendance, Mary overcame her natural curiosity and refused to come in.

CHAPTER VIII
JUNE 13TH

(i)

MISS MORRISON sat at her desk in the parlour at Willows, opening letters. The hour was nine-thirty, and the day Tuesday, June 13th. She had already sucked the honey of her morning's post. The envelopes which remained unopened were both of oblong shape and flimsy texture. "Old Wookey and Millie Burst," she decided. "I suppose that, as usual, he's found something and she's lost something."

The sheet at which she was soon staring showed at a glance that her old friend Mr. Wookey was an original character. Its heading announced in Gothic capitals, "WILLIAM WOOKEY, Dealer In Antiques." Down the margin Mr. Wookey advertised some unusual amenities. "Taxis for Weddings," read Mary. "Outside Effects," "Perambulators." Dismissing speculations as to what "Outside Effects" might include, she applied herself to the manuscript portion of the letter, which was brief.

"Miss Morrison, Dear Madam," she read. "Hoping you will excuse the liberty, I have something nice which I would like you to see next time you are in, if you could spare the time, before any other lady. Yours respectfully, W. Wookey."

"Old fox!" commented Mary. "He doesn't throw out the least hint. Last time it was the weathercock off Slapham Church tower, weighing half a ton. However, I did get that spinet dressing-table from him, and the Chinese work-box I gave to the Yarrows as a wedding present."

The telephone rang. Lady Rollo was just leaving Crossgrove for Ascot.

"Look here, Button," she said, "you needn't answer now, but do turn over in your mind the possibility of coming with us one day. Elizabeth and I are going every day, but Tim has struck."

Mary said, "My dear! Impossible. I haven't been to Ascot for ten years at least. I haven't got any clothes. I haven't got an Enclosure Badge. Thursday's my only free day this week, and that's the Gold Cup."

"You've got the green you wore to the Merles' sherry party," said Catha, "and if you're only going one day it would hardly be worth your while having an Enclosure Badge, anyway. We shall be lunching in Tim's club tent. It would be the greatest kindness to me if you would come on Thursday."

"But," objected Mary, "everyone will be trailing about in lace dresses and picture hats."

"Nobody," said Catha decidedly, "will be trailing at all, on any day. I've got a short black with a pattern of spilt playing cards and a cap made of bits of silver fox to match my cape. That's what I shall be wearing on Thursday, even if we get a heat-wave, which doesn't seem at all likely. Come on, Button. Never say die. Crispin is driving us, and will get your badge when he gets his own at the gate of the Paddock. All you have to do is to be at Crossgrove by ten sharp, on Thursday. That's all settled, then. Splendid."

"It does make a difference having the Rollos at Crossgrove," meditated Mary, tapping her teeth with her pencil as she stared absently at the oval needlework picture above her desk. The picture represented a pastoral scene which appeared additionally peaceful since all the silks in which it was worked had faded to shades of straw colour. Its subject was a shepherdess, obviously of high rank, attired in a clinging muslin gown and a Leghorn hat, mildly herding three broken-spirited sheep whose contours did their owner no credit.

"Ascot. 10 sharp. Crossgrove," wrote Mary on her engagement block, in the space reserved for Thursday, June 15th. Before she had finished, the telephone rang again.

"Good morning, Mary dear," said the voice of Lady Wilson. "Are you likely to be able to call in here on your way to the

Hospital Committee? I should be very glad if you could. There are several small points which I wish to discuss with you."

"I could come in half an hour—soon after ten—if that is any good," said Mary, glancing at the clock ticking in the corner of the parlour. Miss Morrison was fond of her grandfather's grandfather clock, which had once stood in a hall of her old home. It was what Mr. Wookey called "a nice piece." Its long case was of shining mahogany; its pale steel face bore in its centre an engraving depicting an angler. Above its moonlike countenance arose a little scene painted in oils, showing a frigate nearing a fort. With every swing of the pendulum the courageous frigate rocked to and fro on tempestuous turquoise billows. A vermilion standard flew from the tower of the fort which it perpetually approached but never attained.

"That will be excellent," said Lady Wilson, sounding relieved. "I have had rather a vexing letter from Muriel Gidding by this morning's post. She is what she describes as 'Evacuation Queen' for this district, as no doubt you know. She writes that she has put us down to take half a dozen children from the Isle of Dogs. I do not think that we can. However, we may speak of that when you come."

Mary replaced the receiver and finished writing the word Crossgrove before asking the operator to give her the number of Hydden Hall.

"If it's Mrs. Yarrow you was wanting, Miss Mary," said the voice of Mrs. Crippen from the post office, "I know she's up in London for the week, not expected home till Friday night."

"That's exactly what I did want to know, thank you, Mrs. Crippen," said Mary, "though, as a matter of fact, it's Captain Yarrow I need. I think I'll try his London club. It's a Grosvenor number, I know. One second. . . ."

Three minutes later the comfortable tones of blond, solid Captain Rolfe Yarrow, Member of Parliament for the Went division, sounded in his old friend's ear.

"Hullo, Rolfe," said Mary. "Don't laugh, please, but I'm suddenly going to Ascot, on Thursday. I haven't been near a race-course for ten years, but I like to have my modest fling, and be no wet-blanket. What I want to know is, do you know of anything good?"

Captain Yarrow did not sound in the least inclined to laugh. He sounded very serious indeed as he answered in alarmed accents.

"My dear Mary! No! I'm very sorry, but as you know, we keep long hours in the Gas Works these days. I'm absolutely out of touch. In fact, I considerably doubt if I shall get down at all myself this week."

"I only thought," said Mary, persevering, "that your brother-in-law might have a horse running."

"Oh! he has," said Captain Yarrow, sounding positively funereal. "Poor old Gobbie. He's here now, having a kipper with me. Would you like to speak to him, perhaps?"

"Not at all, thank you," said Mary. "I've only met him once in my life, and I think he's perfectly terrifying. You pick his brains and send me a line to-night. There's a lamb."

"I wish I could say for certain that I could be there on Thursday," continued Rolfe in his painstaking polite way, "and that you could lunch with us. But I know that if I do go, we've got to lunch with those people from India who've taken Crossgrove."

"That's splendid," said Mary. "I'm going with them. Now you need not trouble to write. All you need to do is to remember what your brother-in-law says, and tell me at lunch on Thursday. Mind you come. *Au revoir.*"

"Hi!" shouted Rolfe, suddenly animated. "Look here! I won't answer for this, but I did happen to hear yesterday of a filly who might run well on Thursday. And for the last race. . . ."

Miss Morrison drew a half-sheet of notepaper towards her, and began to write rapidly from dictation. She glanced at the clock again in a somewhat guilty manner, before she asked Mrs. Crippen to get her another London number—a City number this time. "May as well make a clean job of it," she muttered, sounding the least bit uncertain.

The second old friend from whom Miss Morrison asked advice as to Thursday was a Merle grandchild. Mr. Christopher Hungerford, after an early career somewhat resembling that of Prince Hal, had, to his relatives' stupefaction, settled down to unremitting toil in an eminent firm of stockbrokers. Many years had passed since Mary had heard the highly characteristic voice which answered, after only a moment's pause, "Yes, Mary."

"Look here, Kit," said Mary, using an even firmer tone than she had employed when dealing with Captain Yarrow. "I know you always know. I'm going to Ascot on Thursday. Be quick, please, because I'm due at a committee at your grandmother's at eleven-thirty. What am I to do?"

But no Merle grandchild could ever hurry, least of all the one once affectionately known in the village as "Mr. Kit."

It was only after much pressing, and as if eager to avoid uttering an unpleasant truth, that he said, "If you really want my advice, Mary, you will keep right away from a Layer's Meeting."

"Don't attempt to impress me with your superior knowledge, Kit," said Mary. "I know you know a lot. I want you to tell me something good for Thursday."

"It will rain all day," proceeded the attractive voice from the City of London. "I can see from my window that it is raining already. You will get wet through, Mary. Yes, I know that you will take your mackintosh, but when the real cloudburst occurs you will be on the other side of the course, having just finished a large cold lunch. You will spend the afternoon miserably, huddled in a damp tent, when you might be comfortably at home in your picturesque house, no doubt garlanded with roses at this season."

"If you're really so concerned for my well-being," snapped Mary, "you might bring down an extra pair of goloshes. For I warn you, I'm going, Kit."

"I can hear from the fierceness of your accents that you are," said her melancholy acquaintance. "But you are wrong in imagining that I shall be amongst your fellow-sufferers."

"You can't mean to say that you're not going!" said Mary. "What nonsense! Of course you are. Well, if everything's so grim on the Stock Exchange, what can it matter that you're not there for one day to poke the dying embers? It's possibly the last Ascot any of us will ever see. Don't be defeatist, Kit."

Mr. Hungerford only escaped after trysting with his childhood's playmate for an early encounter in the paddock on the following Thursday.

Miss Morrison then opened the last letter of her morning's post.

"Dear Madam," she read,

"Thank you for P.C., unfortunately I shall not be able to attend on the 11th to pass through the Gas Waggon, as I am confined to the house with measles (G.).

"Unfortunately, last Saturday, I left my handbag in the Went Green Line. It had my Member's brassiere in it. I am hoping to get it at the bus office, but if I do not will it be difficult for you to get me another? It is most unfortunate, I know, madam, with the Camp coming on in August and your talk last meeting about correct uniform.

Yours faithfully,

MILDRED DORIS BURST."

(ii)

Every time that she arrived at the Old Mill House, Lower Merle, Mary Morrison wondered anew why an elderly couple, subject to rheumatism, should have chosen to settle there. On spring and autumn evenings, romantic wreaths of mist enveloped the house. With every hard frost, the two steep lanes leading down to it became toboggan runs. The nearest bus-stop was a mile and a quarter distant, even as the crow flies. Lady Wilson, who combined lofty standards of housekeeping with a dwindling income, was perpetually in the condition of banishing one inefficient staff to welcome another. On a mid-June morning, however, the place was decidedly at its best. As Mary approached it—in second gear—she became subconsciously aware of moss-green lawns and sap-green waters, of pergolas loaded with helpless-looking, old-fashioned roses, and of the cooing of many fluttering, snow-white pigeons. Lady Wilson kept tumblers who multiplied remorselessly, in spite of the fact that she employed male guests to shoot visiting mates of low degree. On one occasion, a young nephew had very nearly shot one of Mr. Wookey's step-daughters, who had ascended to the loft to destroy eggs. She had been engaged to perform the duties of housemaid, but found these uninteresting.

Mary turned the bad corner marked "Deep Ford" and the Old Mill House, much overshadowed by its Tudor barn, came into view. Somewhat to her surprise, almost before she had brought her car to a standstill, one of its doors was wrenched open by a strange figure, who bowed and beamed repeatedly.

"Good morning," said Miss Morrison, in the clear, loud accents often used by English ladies addressing foreigners of unknown nationality. "Thank you for opening that door, but only drivers in trousers can get out that side because of the gears and handbrakes." As she followed her bewildered and waddling guide towards the low-browed house, she told herself, "The Wilsons have got a curiosity this time. A refugee, I suppose."

Lady Wilson's new manservant had a complexion of warmer hue than was customary for one of his profession in this neighbourhood. He wore a grey alpaca jacket, which very nearly matched his greying hair, cut *en brosse*. He had small, dark brown eyes, pendulous rosy cheeks, reminiscent of nectarines, and a double chin. He was about five feet two inches in height, and had, apparently, not one word of English.

"What does he find to do in Lower Merle on his evenings out?" wondered Mary, as she followed him into a sitting-room remarkable for the number of gilt-framed engravings on its walls. The engravings all represented sunset or storm scenes in distant climes, inhabited by boneless but spotlessly clean peasants. Most of the furniture in the room was made of satinwood, inlaid with designs of doves and urns festooned with pale blue ribbon. A fine vase of mixed flowers masked the empty grate. It was rather a dark room even on a sunny day, and always filled with green reflections, for the lawn outside sloped upwards. Mary noted with approval that the two massive silver photograph frames which always stood in a place of honour on an occasional table in here, were burnished and glittering. They enclosed autographed likenesses of deceased crowned heads, and in the days when Mr. Wookey's step-daughters had been employed here they had too often exhibited brown thumbographs and peacock-blue tarnish. Irene and Evie Potts had recently departed to the factory near Went to spend their days making full-fashioned art. silk hose for a much larger wage than was obtainable at The Old Mill House.

"He's an Austrian," explained Lady Wilson to her guest, as the door closed behind her new servitor. "They arrived on Tuesday. It is rather pathetic. He owned quite a good little hotel and restaurant outside Vienna. My husband knew the place well when he was a young attaché. A connection—great-uncle, I believe—owned the business in those days. We discovered this almost at once, and had a most emotional first evening. The poor little man—he's fifty—served us with tears running down his cheeks. The wife— much younger—is distressed for her father, who is in a concentration camp, but cooks excellently. I am knowing comfort for the first time for years. Shall we go outside? I wish to lay my problem before you, but do not wish my husband to come in while we discuss it."

Lady Wilson led her guest out into the shimmering garden towards a seat beneath a spreading mulberry tree, well known and dreaded by her acquaintance. Since the month was June, however, there was no danger to-day of ripe fruit descending on a prized summer toilette. Mary seated herself, and waited for the promised revelation, but Lady Wilson's notions of good manners would not permit her to enter forthwith upon a recital of her own troubles. "How are your nurses?" she asked. "I was sorry to disturb you this morning at an hour when I knew you must be busy with your post."

Mary mentioned the prospect of the Gas Waggon, and said that her post had not been heavy this morning.

"I have often thought," said Lady Wilson, who really did think, "what an odd thing it is that we all develop without any training, an eagle eye, not only for a handwriting, but also for the type of notepaper and envelope used by a correspondent. My husband and I get fewer letters these days, yet if you were to spread in front of me five hundred envelopes, I could probably tell you without opening them from whom they all came. I don't mean only private letters. One gets to know the envelopes and typewriters used by shops and societies."

Mary, who had to be at Merle Dower House at eleven-thirty, agreed submissively.

"I can never pretend to judge character by handwriting, though," continued Lady Wilson. "I had a brother-in-law, a Senior Wrangler, who to the day of his death wrote like a backward child of nine. In fact, one might say he never learned to write."

"Tell me about Lady Muriel's letter," suggested Mary.

A pink colour crept into Lady Wilson's thin cheeks. For a moment she hesitated, looking away with faded blue eyes across the garden to the mill-stream. She was extremely spare and small, and when standing reached only to Mary's shoulder, but her decisive utterance and upright carriage always somehow suggested to her guest distant court and camp. She was wearing a red and white patterned silk blouse with a V neck, inside which arose a pleated net stand-up collar encircled by a necklace of silver coins. Several shreds of embroidery wool clung to her grey skirt. The skirt was provided with a sateen interior pocket, and when Lady Wilson had detached from a worn silver-mounted leather case a pair of gold-rimmed spectacles, she went through considerable further grabbings in a pocket before admitting—"Dear me, how vexing! After all, I must have left it in the house. Where can I have set it down? I know I was particularly careful not to leave it on my own desk by the inkpot, for when I place a letter there it means that I wish my husband to look at it, and that is just what I do not wish, in this case."

"I don't think that the Old Mill House would be at all a suitable home for six London children," said Mary briskly. "The nearest school is nearly three miles, even across the fields. Besides, you haven't room, have you?"

"Muriel says that she knows we have that splendid barn," explained Lady Wilson. "She does not know that it harbours rats, but actually there are more rooms in this little house than one might guess. My husband's study is really a double room. We close the curtains and sit in the inner half on chilly evenings. If it is true that they allot one room per head for residents, we have undoubtedly, at present, only four people living here, and eleven rooms, not counting the barn. But since we now exist in genteel poverty, we keep only two servants. I could not ask the Greenbaums to cook for six children in addition to ourselves, and I cannot afford to increase our staff. All these considerations are perhaps not insurmountable, but my husband is eighty-four and unaccustomed to children of any kind. What is your situation?"

"If there's a war, my widowed sister-in-law is coming from London," said Mary. "We're not in the Went district, luckily, and our difficulty, so far, has been to keep some of our village women from offering to take more children than they have rooms. They were attracted by the allowance."

"Everyone is being so patriotic, Muriel writes," said Lady Wilson. "Valerie Merle turning her house into a hospital for expectant mothers. Of course she has the space and means, still I agree that her example is admirable. I come of a Service family," said Lady Wilson, removing her spectacles with a hand which trembled. "My earliest recollection," she went on, gazing towards the river again, "is of bugles blowing across a barrack square. My dear eldest sister was born actually during the Mutiny. . . . My poor mother was scarcely seventeen, and even smaller than I. I have one of her gowns in a trunk upstairs. It is extraordinary, is it not, to think of an early Victorian bride in a crinoline and a bonnet, setting out from a Rectory in Somersetshire to sail round the Cape, and arrive in India for her first confinement and the Mutiny. For six weeks she knew not my father's fate, but I have old letters describing her as a model of female calm and dignity. I am sure I should not wish to fall below her standard."

"I am sure you never have," said Mary gruffly.

"I hope I never have," said Lady Wilson carefully. "But I cannot consider that I was ever called upon, as some of my forebears were. My twin uncles were born during an action against the French, in the Bay, prematurely, but both survived to become Admirals. Of course I had the earthquake in San Francisco—sad scenes. And in St. Petersburg my husband and I narrowly escaped a Nihilist bomb intended for the Grand Duke. Some fragments hit my muff. I never thought," concluded Lady Wilson mournfully, "that I should find such difficulty in my old age, in deciding as to my Duty."

"Well, that's because you've got to decide for Sir James too," said Mary. "That's what makes it so difficult. I really don't see. . . ."

"Exactly," interrupted Lady Wilson. "And he is, as you know, so utterly unfit. . . . Ah! we must speak of something else, for here he comes, on his way to the post."

Sir James, a stooping figure sloping across the lawn, happy in a faded suit built for him before he began to lose weight, bore in his hand a single postcard, which he was flapping to and fro to dry the ink.

"I can take that," said Mary. "I am going through the village. Honestly I ought to be through it already, for I've the Nursing Association Committee at eleven-thirty."

"That would be a most kind act," said Sir James. "I should like this to go as soon as possible. It is to Muriel Gidding," he explained airily. Lady Wilson laid a quick hand on Mary's wrist. "I found the letter which you left for me on my desk," went on Sir James, "and I have spoken to Greenbaum. His wife has a niece who eats nothing, I understand, and will be delighted to help us in a National Emergency in exchange for pin-money and a happy home. She is accustomed to looking after ten younger brothers and sisters, and desires to perfect her English. So I have sent our slightly heavy-handed neighbour our reply in a single sentence. My only fear is that she may not have sufficient intelligence to interpret it."

He handed the card to Mary.

"We feel as the first Lord Holland did about the destruction of his time-piece," read Mary.

"Well, my dear," said Lady Wilson in her sharpest accents, "I'm sorry, but I certainly have not sufficient intelligence to interpret that."

"Who would believe," appealed Sir James, "that she once had a learned uncle at Oxford—wrote tomes on the eighteenth century?"

Mary wrinkled her brow.

"It was when the infant Charles James Fox said that he felt he must smash his father's watch, wasn't it?" she asked. "Lord Holland's reply was, 'Well, if you must, I suppose you must.' I often thought that it was a wonder the child didn't turn out worse than he did, being brought up like that. Quite modern!"

"We shall soon feel quite modern, shall we not, my dear," said Sir James, taking his wife's arm under his own, "with six members of the younger generation under our roof?"

(iii)

From the Dowager Lady Merle of Went's large double drawing-room the committee was departing.

Mrs. Bates, whose tussore summer frocks always looked as if she slept in them, was accepting the offer of a lift home from bearded Miss Copper of the Dairy Farm. "Well, I must be off," said Dr. Greatbatch, lunging towards his hostess with outstretched hand, before flying from the roomful of females as if pursued by a wild beast. The figures of Mrs. Bracket and Miss Crouch, two of our firmest collectors, could be seen outlined against green distances, already half-way across the park, on their way to catch the twelve o'clock bus. But in a french window, shrouded by curtains of emerald silk and ivory net, Mrs. Gibson, a woman of many sterling qualities, was still completing the discomfiture of harmless little Mrs. Mimms. In a mad moment, Mrs. Mimms had offered that, since her neighbour reported sensational servant difficulties, the garden meeting might take place at her house this year.

"Come along then, good boys," chirped Miss Masquerier to the couple of snuffling and obviously cold-hearted King Charles spaniels who had been her companions since the outstanding success of her "Stuart Reverie."

"I am so glad to hear that my son was able to show you our Queen Mary jewel," said Lady Merle, advancing towards the authoress, after a glance at the couple in the window.

Miss Masquerier had been elected to the Executive Committee, three years ago at the instance of Lady Merle, President. She had never made a constructive suggestion, and often sat at meetings with her eyes closed, and a Buddha-like smile upon her face. However, she appeared to derive pleasure from lifting her hand to vote, and saying, in very clear accents, "I should like to second that proposal." Suspicions that she was collecting "copy" had died a lingering death.

Mary, who had been asked by Lady Merle to stay a moment after the committee had departed, looked around her resignedly. "Now I shan't catch Wookey before he goes to his dinner," she reflected. But she was comfortably certain that whatever Lady Merle might wish to confide, it had nothing to do with the misdemeanours of domestics.

The Dowager's drawing-room, this midsummer morning, exhibited its customary pyramids and banks of obediently grown flowers in season. Floods of sunshine lit several immovable-looking sofas and chairs marooned upon rugs and covered with crackling chintz. On the walls hung oil-paintings of Highland cattle, in frames so massive that you could lay down your hand-bag inside them and forget it. Every possible object in the room was polished to the nines. Mary had refused a murmured and somewhat surprising invitation to stay to luncheon. Pamela Wallis was away upon visits for six weeks. Luncheon alone with the Dowager and her secretary was, Mary knew, rather a trial, even when one knew what to expect. Overwhelmingly succulent dishes, created by a French chef, were served upon ornate Victorian silver by athletic footmen, at record speed. The dining-room had been remorselessly panelled in fumed oak by the last owner but one. Since Lady Merle herself eschewed nearly every delicacy, and expected intelligent comment on her observations, starvation or hiccups were the tyro's choice.

"The panelling in here is original. I should like to have a bonfire of the whole of the furniture," thought Mary, on whose spirits the hushed but ghoulish repetition of the word "illegitimate" by Mrs. Gibson and Mrs. Bracket had produced depressing effects.

Mrs. Gibson, having annihilated the presumptuous Mrs. Mimms, was now ready to take her leave, but her hostess appeared fully occupied hearing details of Miss Masquerier's recent visit to Merle Park.

"We were so much disappointed that you could not find room for my Diana amongst your members," said Mrs. Gibson, bearing down upon Mary with the light of battle still in her eye. "She is making enquiries about becoming an Ambulance driver. The uniform is much more up-to-date. I expect you agree."

Mary always felt uneasily that she would like to like this neighbour much more than she did. Mrs. Gibson was almost beautiful, in a noble, out-of-door manner that recalled to the memory statues of classic goddesses in the basements of museums, Indeed, so strong was this resemblance, that Mary often noticed with surprise that her friend had neither a head nor a hand knocked off.

Her voice echoes, she decided, as Mrs. Gibson continued, smiling resolutely, "You are still over-busy, I suppose?"

"I'm taking the day off on Thursday to go to Ascot," said Mary. "Shall we meet?" she enquired of Mrs. Mimms, who was lurking in the background with a heightened complexion.

Mrs. Gibson said playfully how worldly that sounded, and that she had never known Mary was an authority on the Turf, to which Mary replied with spirit that she was not, but she knew those that were.

"I'm meeting Kit Hungerford in the paddock at twelve sharp."

She regretted those words as soon as she found herself alone in the drawing-room, seated upon one of the crackling sofas opposite Kit's grandmother.

"I was relieved to hear that you are to see poor Christopher on Thursday," opened Lady Merle majestically. "Do you go down together?"

Mary explained hastily that she was going with a family party from Crossgrove.

"There is a pretty daughter there," commented Lady Merle, thinking aloud, "but Christopher is now forty-four. I never forget a descendant's age. I am afraid that he leads rather a melancholy life these days, poor fellow."

Mary, who considered this unlikely, said politely, "He works tremendously hard, I know."

"He does work," pronounced Lady Merle, looking down her Roman nose, "and with satisfactory results, I believe. Yet I often ask myself as I look at his face—is he truly happy? Christopher was such a sensitive young boy. You, as an old friend, will remember that."

"Well, I think he realizes now that he's a good deal happier than he might have been," said Mary boldly.

Lady Merle raised a hand, and paused impressively, before continuing, "Yes, indeed! If he had had to marry that Person, I think it would have been the end of his poor invalid mother."

"It would probably have been the end of him," said Mary, remembering that in real life invalids thrive upon family upheavals. "Poor old Kit!"

"But that is all finished and forgotten, years ago," said Lady Merle, fixing Mary with a glittering eye.

To her disgust, Mary found herself blushing, and could think of nothing more sensible to say than "Do you really think so?"

"I am positive of it," said Lady Merle, charging to the kill. "My poor daughter was here recently, you know. We had several talks. It would be the greatest relief to all of us to see Christopher settled. Naturally we dread that it may have to be some insipid young creature whom we none of us know—really Nobody. Christopher was always fatally susceptible to a pretty face. He is such an idealist."

"I'll ask him on Thursday if he realizes that it's high time he settled," said Mary, rising. "But I doubt if I get a success."

For the first time in her life, as she left the sun-flooded double drawing-room, Mary had the experience of seeing Lady Merle look baffled.

(iv)

Westbury church clock showed twenty minutes to one as Mary drew towards it. On the flat piece of road between Upper Merle and Westbury hill, she passed a picturesque countryside group. The sky had become overcast. Under the heavy green branches of a large oak on the outskirts of the village, an itinerant knife-grinder and china-mender had paused to shelter and dine. Several bullet-headed boys, who ought to have been home from school half an hour ago, clustered around the old man in the broken black hat, watching him intently. His machine, a rickety-looking affair on spindly wheels, surmounted by a worn little board bearing his name and trade painted in tipsy capitals, was perched at rest on the grass verge behind him. He had made himself a bright small fire of sticks and was cooking something in a tiny saucepan.

Mary deserted her car unconscientiously on the bad corner outside Mr. Wookey's shop, and passed into his show-room through a glass-panelled door, to which was attached a contrivance arranged to tweak an unmelodious bell in the yard behind. She could not, at a glance, see anything new to her amongst the objects displayed in here. Mr. Wookey had not yet disposed of the model of a Chinese junk, or the mermaid rum bottles, bought by him at the sale of the merchant captain's effects up on the Common last Easter. A thoroughly bitten Paisley shawl draped over a flaking lacquer screen came, Mary believed, from the same source. Eleven ruby Bohemian liqueur glasses, a royal blue witch ball and six reproduction bottle-green rummers were effectively set out on a shelf strung across the principal window. Mr. Wookey gave considerable thought to his window-dressing, and once at Christmas had staged a set piece consisting of ladder-backed chairs, drawn up around a refectory table, bearing a plaster roast turkey and a genuine cold plum pudding, guarded by a stuffed mastiff. Mary passed sideways between a chest of drawers lacking handles and a bookcase containing a few volumes, all of which fell down, making a startling noise. It was rather sad lingering amongst so many relics of dubious value, vocal of shattered homes, and she was thinking of trying the door again, when a shuffling step sounded behind her.

"Ah! good morning, miss," mouthed Mr. Wookey. "When I saw your car outside, I hurried across. That's right. I was going down after my dinner to give the bits to my birds, miss," explained Mr. Wookey amiably but falsely, as he returned to his pocket the turpentine cloth with which he had just dried his still working jaws.

Mr. Wookey's birds included a flotilla of ducks, imported to the village pond last summer by a film company taking shots of Westbury-on-the-Hill for inclusion in a sentimentalized version of the career of Dick Turpin. For several days the Went road had been enlivened by thundering coaches loaded with Regency belles and beaux. The company had disappeared from the landscape as suddenly as it had appeared. Those of Mary's friends who had viewed the resultant film had assured her variously that Westbury appeared only for two minutes, pitch black, and looking as if a thunder-storm was blowing up, and that you would have known Wookey's ducks anywhere.

Mr. Wookey had a shock of yellowing white hair, worn rather long, watery orbs, a pallid countenance and an empty sleeve. He reminded romantic lady purchasers of Nelson. Actually, he had lost an arm after falling from a hay-loft on to a hay-fork. He owned or leased lofts, sheds, barns and hutments all over Westbury village, and was the most accomplished potterer and mutterer in Mary's acquaintance. It appeared an impossibility for him to stick to any topic of conversation for more than two sentences, or to refrain from returning to it without warning. Mannerless interruption was the only means of getting even with him. According to local rumour, he had more than once, in perfect good faith, sold a piece of furniture left for repair by one valued customer, to another. Buying things at sales with an eye to a particular home in the neighbourhood was one of his hobbies—"Boy, don't kick that Early Wictoria hammock work-table. It's going up to The Old Mill House." "Does that belong to Lady Wilson?" "Well, her ladyship *will* be wanting it when she's seen it, miss."

Mary interrupted him now as he touched upon the tale of the nice old shutters made into a cupboard at Walnut Tree Farm, "which I'd like to take you to see, miss, next time you're up that way." He had already, without drawing breath, informed her of Miss Aileen Hill's desire for a peach-pink enamelled deal kidney dressing-table, "the spit of yours, miss," and the young lady staying with Mrs. Bates needing old swords to poke her fires.

"Was it about the shutters at Walnut Tree Farm that you wrote to me?" shouted Mary.

"No, miss," said Mr. Wookey, shaking his head pityingly. "Nor was it the oak staircase at the Dog and Fox on the lower road, though I fancy I shall be getting that soon. Arthritis. It's wunnerful the way one hears things from people passing through this village. Tinkers and tramps often put up at farms for the night where there's a dresser or a piece of china likely to be parted with. That's the way of it. You don't happen to know of any gentleman or lady needing a genuine refectory table twenty-eight feet long, with four fine stretchers, all complete, do you, miss?"

"No," said Mary.

"I was wondering if it might do for the hall at Crossgrove—the outer hall," mused Mr. Wookey. "I haven't the measurements of the outer hall at Crossgrove by me, I don't think. Looking lovely up there now, I hear. Going to have a dwarf wall round the new tennis courts, I hear. I bought the table without the stretchers. Next morning I goes back and has a look round, and there they is hid up in a stable."

"What is the thing that you want me to see?" shouted Mary.

"Ah! as soon as you sets eyes on them, you'll understand why I said to myself Willows!" chuckled Mr. Wookey maddeningly. "Colour of your drawing-room. Sad about the fire at Blackbridge, wasn't it, miss? If you don't mind stepping upstairs. I'm short-handed this week, or I would have had them down ready for you. That table's lost a leg, miss, don't trust her with your weight. The frost got that fuchsia at last."

Mary followed Mr. Wookey up a steep ladder into a loft smelling to heaven of turpentine, drew herself upright, dusted shavings from her palms and knees, and looked in the direction whence he had disappeared.

"There's three uprights and one easy," announced the voice of Mr. Wookey from behind a dusty tallboy. "I'm sorry my brother-in-law's at his dinner. Looks to me like Angelica Kauffmann. Came from a very nice house at Bournemouth."

The broken set of cane-seated painted chairs which Mr. Wookey dragged into the light of day for Mary's inspection, attracted her strongly. She saw at once that their faded lily-leaf green was not that of the walls at Willows, but she saw also that they were particularly suitable for the parlour of a lady whose windows looked out on grass and trees. They had elegant tapering legs, and their backs bore medallions decorated in sepia shades with Cupids and Graces.

"I could work a set of loose cushions to match those," she thought, as she tweaked them around one by one. "There's a loose rail or two," she commented aloud. "And of course there ought to be another of each kind. My walls are brighter."

"If there'd been the six, I'd have sent them straight up to London and got a London price," said Mr. Wookey. "As things are, I'm not going to ask more than the twenty guineas. Being an Air Warden takes up a lot of my brother-in-law's time. I bought them for Willows, as you might say. I never thought I'd live to see the 'Chime of Bells' in Went market come down, did you, miss? I got a couple of warming-pans, but the pewter was poor stuff. If you'll excuse me, I think I hear the telephone. That'll be the young gentleman rode over with Miss Elizabeth Rollo, asked me to keep the floral door-knobs and fingerplates she fancied."

After five minutes of wrestling with her conscience, Mary descended the ladder from Mr. Wookey's work-shop, and looked about her. The antique dealer himself was nowhere to be seen, but his married daughter appeared to invite her into the kitchen of a cottage from which issued a blare of mingled sound. From a wireless set in the window a gentleman was chanting that he was on a see-saw. A female child, imprisoned in a high chair, was battering the tray in front of her with a wooden spoon.

"He said I was not to let you go without your seeing that, miss," breathed Mrs. Herring, drooping over a table and nodding a listless head at the darkest corner of the room. Mrs. Herring was even paler than her parent, looked as if she might drop dead at any moment, and had the most depressing voice Mary knew.

From the high chair sounded a sudden battle cry.

"It's nice, but I don't want another grandfather clock," said Mary.

"Pardon, miss?" enquired Mrs. Herring.

"I don't really need another clock," repeated Mary, in vain. "Could you turn down that music for a moment?"

With the air of one inured to unreasonable requests, Mrs. Herring stepped towards her instrument and made it howl with pain. For a second only silence reigned, for on her way past the high chair she had nipped up the wooden spoon. The result was as might have been expected.

"I must be going now," yelled Mary, advancing to utter right into her companion's ear. "I said, I must be going now. Will you tell your father that I like those chairs very much, but I can't possibly spend twenty guineas on them? My house is packed with furniture, as he knows, and I don't feel that this is the moment to buy any more. But will you tell him that I'd like him to keep them for me until Thursday night? Yes. Will you tell him I'll telephone on Thursday night?" As she crossed the threshold, she asked, in some exasperation, "Is that your little girl?"

"Yes, miss," said Mrs. Herring, adding proudly, "she does it for attention, miss."

CHAPTER IX
JUNE 15TH

(i)

FROM THE MOMENT that she woke on the morning of Thursday, June 15th, Mary felt that Kit Hungerford had been right as far as the weather was concerned. This was not going to be the ideal Gold Cup Day. The sky was several shades of dirty white. Every tree in the garden was shuddering. Across the common, the pyjamas hung out by lazy Mrs. Harker yesterday, were signalling madly, with inflated legs and arms.

At nine forty-five Mary laid on the back seat of her car a green transparent mackintosh, a pair of sensible lace-up shoes with stockings stuck in their toes, and a crook-handled umbrella. Before she closed the front door of Willows, she cast a dubious glance at the quiet and comfortable home she was deserting. Not until she reached the courtyard of Crossgrove did her spirits begin to rise.

The young people, looking very spruce, were ready and waiting by their car, and Crispin, after transferring Mary's wet-weather outfit, drove her car to the garage. The party set out for Ascot half an hour later. Had Pamela Wallis been present, she would certainly have said that Catha Rollo was the kind of woman to spread Bolshevism.

On her parent's first arrival in the hall, Elizabeth interrupted her charming flow of greeting by a stern demand to see that Badge before we set out to-day. The hunt for Lady Rollo's Enclosure Badge, which was discovered marking the place in her bedside book, took only a few moments, but her decision to wear her little hat, after all, entailed a longer disappearance. As they descended the front steps together for the third time, a fatal remark by Mary caused Catha to realize that this was the day on which garden produce from neighbouring mansions was to be sold in aid of the Cottage Hospital at a stall on the by-pass. "The poor hospital! That must come before our pleasure!" From her interview with a hastily-summoned gardener, Catha failed to reappear, and gradually the dire rumour spread through the house that her ladyship had mislaid her pearls. Albert Higg's coat-tails streamed as he ran to the garage to search the little car in which Catha and Elizabeth had come down from London in the early hours of this morning, after a dance. Downstairs, under the disapproving eye of Symonds, rugs were taken up and chairs ransacked. Crispin, whistling gently, went through the pockets of every female coat hanging in the cloak-room. Elizabeth and

Mary, on receipt of a confused message from upstairs, turned out Catha's embroidery bag, sewing box, gardening apron and flower baskets. From the passages above came sounds of flying feet, slamming doors and worried murmurs.

"It's nearly twenty-five past. I think I'll go up and try to persuade her to wear her shams, and let them go on hunting here," said Elizabeth, pulling down a bodice which had arisen when she lay flat to look under a sofa, and recovering without comment a hat on which somebody had laid a cushion.

Crispin laid a hand on his sister's arm before she pattered off. "Don't upset her; but I think we ought to be moving. Tell her I go to sea on Monday." The Rollo children were genuinely good-humoured, Mary decided, for when Catha finally consented to embark, complaining in martyred tones that now they would be late, Crispin said, leading her on firmly, "I'm sorry about your poor beads, but I'm sure they'll turn up. Now you're off to enjoy yourself."

"After all, darling," Elizabeth reminded her parent, from the front seat, "they're insured, and it was only Daddy's old father, not Daddy, gave them to you."

"I richly deserved them," said Catha morbidly, shrinking in her corner, as Albert approached with a rug. She shrank and waved him away so dramatically that the next thing her companions heard was a pop, followed by the exclamation, "My one shoulder strap!"

"Drive on, Crispin," Elizabeth counselled her brother. "We'll get one of those helpful-faced women in the cloak-room to lend us a dagger and thread as soon as we arrive, darling," she promised over her shoulder.

"I shan't be able to get as far as any cloak-room," groaned Catha, who was going through extraordinary gymnastics in her efforts to insert a ringed hand inside the collar of a high-necked dress. Her voice changed to childlike wonder. "Good gracious! I've found them! They're round my neck inside. I was positive I'd worn them for breakfast in bed, and that Ada was talking nonsense when she said I might have dropped them down the waste as I washed my hands. Elizabeth, tell Crispin to stop."

Crispin, without a change of countenance, put the car into reverse and sent it spinning backwards, to draw up exactly alongside the startled Albert.

"Her ladyship's found her pearls," said Crispin softly.

"Tell Ada I found them round my neck," cried Catha, bowing and smiling.

"Very good, m'lady," said Albert, who was perspiring.

(ii)

Crispin Rollo drove his mother's large saloon car from the courtyard of Crossgrove to Went marketplace at a pace which surprised Mary. She was slightly breathless when they swept to a standstill outside a florist's shop, where they skilfully claimed the last feet of space available between an abandoned handcart, two bicycles and a lorry delivering fish-boxes. But she realized that Crispin, who did everything well, had a quick eye, plenty of imagination and nerves of steel. He was not likely to crash a party of ladies. He stuck his shining morning face in at the window nearest to her, and announced, "Here we buy buttonholes. A couple of white carnations for Miss Morrison, I think. I'm going to be pompous in crimson. What's your fancy, Mummy?"

"I don't think I'd like anything to-day," said Catha. "My dress has got a pattern already, and I don't care for flowers browsing in furs."

"I'm going to have a spray of actressy orchids," said Elizabeth, scrambling out of her seat and shaking herself like a puppy. "I piggied my bib with raspberry jam at breakfast this morning. Old Ada has done her stuff, but I've got a small place still."

"Oh! darling, and I let you get that frock because we thought that you could wear it for the Garden Party as well as Gold Cup Day," said Catha. "Why couldn't you have had breakfast in bed?"

"Because I had to go for a ride with Crispin before breakfast," explained Elizabeth, "and we got wet, and I couldn't face dressing three times before ten a.m. It's a very small Place, darling, and the petrolly smell is passing off fast."

She pattered off, swinging from her bare arm by long ribbons the headgear bitterly described by her as "my hurting hat." The violet of Miss Elizabeth Rollo's brief-skirted check gown was that of the indelible pencil. The remainder of her gala costume consisted of high-heeled sandals, fish-net stockings and gloves, and a handbag capable of swallowing all she wore with the exception of the cartwheel hat. Mary, watching her thread her way between through a press of flushed marketing women, towards a gay red-and-white striped awning shading a blaze of flowers, thought the débutante's choice of colour and accoutrements extraordinary, but could not deny that the effect was satisfactory.

Buxom Miss Cupp, of Cupp and Sons, Florists, Fruiterers and Fishmongers, thought that she detected in Crispin and Elizabeth the makings of a wedding. Her smile broadened when she perceived a familiar figure in the festal car halted outside her shop.

"The gentleman says only two carnations, both white, for the spray. I thought I'd bring it out for you to see if you wouldn't fancy a nice scarlet tucked sideways at the base, miss. Good morning, m'lady. I've got some lovely Butterfly roses fresh in this morning," spouted Miss Cupp, her fingers busy with wire and tinfoil.

"Where has Crispin disappeared to now?" asked Catha. "Now we shall be really late."

But Crispin reappeared as she spoke, to complete the conquest of Miss Cupp by finding her wire-cutters, which she had laid down beneath a roll of white satin ribbon stamped with the golden words "At Rest." The car stole down the steep, traffic-choked street leading to the cathedral close, and in its warm interior the smell of printer's ink warred with that of Malmaison carnations.

"Would either of you, behind, like a picture paper that comes off on one's fingers?" piped Elizabeth. "Crispin's bought me six, so that I can see all the pictures of yesterday at Ascot and all the prices for to-day." "No, thank you," said Catha. "Reading in the back of a car always makes me feel sick, and picture papers flurry me so, with their portraits of murdered women grinning like mad, and Ministers on their way to Downing Street with their soles turned up."

"Would you like some barley-sugar, darling?" inquired Elizabeth. "It's champion when one's feeling sick. As a matter of fact, I'm having some now. Ugh! there's a picture of the woman in zebra stripes. I saw her when I was in the Paddock with Tony ffolliot and Lalage, and Tony said she was the wife of somebody at one of the Legations, and he'd met her, and she was rather famous and fascinating. But the paper only says, 'Whipsnade lends inspiration.' Would you like to change places with me, darling, if you're feeling sick? I'm perfectly safe as long as I keep on with the barley-sugar."

"What Mary and I would really like to do now," said Catha, "would be to close our eyes until we have got off this utterly hideous by-pass."

"Hi!" exclaimed Crispin. "Before my mother begins one of her celebrated naps, I wonder if Mary would mind taking my hat?"

"I'm little likely to sleep while you drive on this death-trap road at fifty miles an hour," said Catha, wincing as her son removed one hand from the wheel.

Crispin, after he had passed his hat back to Mary, pointed silently with one finger at the speedometer. "I promise you, I won't crash you, old lady," he murmured indulgently.

"I shouldn't wonder if, some day, those were your last words," said Catha, closing her eyes.

Mary did not feel like sleeping. It was not every day that she drove at seventy miles an hour to a race-meeting, behind a young naval officer with yellow hair and a brick-red neck, and a débutante of undeniable chic, gorging barley-sugar and six illustrated papers.

She leant forward to touch Elizabeth and whisper, "When you've done with it, you might pass me the one that has a back sheet giving all the tipster's choices." But after a very short comparison of those columns with the half-sheet on which she had scribbled the suggestions of Kit Hungerford and Rolfe Yarrow, she too leant back in her seat and closed her eyes. Her thoughts wandered from her first Ascot to her plans for next week, which included the Gas Chamber, and from the painted chairs, grilling in Mr. Wookey's loft, to the pretty, door-knobs and finger-plates ordered by a young gentleman going abroad, for Miss Rollo at Crossgrove.

"Must you really leave on Monday morning, Cris?" asked Elizabeth in an undertone.

"Afraid so," answered Crispin, twitching the driving mirror to catch a glimpse of his other passengers.

"It's all right. They're both fast asleep, and Mummy won't wake until you draw up at a level crossing," Elizabeth advised him. "You see, I've got rather a specially nice dance on Tuesday night, and Mummy's asked four girls to dine with us, and we've still only got four men, so if you can't stay we shall have to ask someone I don't really like."

"In case you're going to say anything truly confidential, it is my duty to warn you that, as far as I am concerned, appearances are deceptive," murmured Mary.

"Oh!" exclaimed Elizabeth. "Well, it isn't confidential, but it's serious for me. Couldn't you stay, Cris?"

"I'm sorry," said Catha's younger son, sticking out his determined chin, "but if your choice is really between myself and someone you don't really like, why not give the show a miss, and try an evening at home, for a novelty?"

"Bah!" said Elizabeth, discarding her brother and her topic. "What are you thinking about, Auntie Bee?"

"I was remembering my first Ascot," said Mary. "My mother 'refused' at the last moment, and I was taken by old Lady Merle."

"How awful," said Elizabeth with deep feeling. "And did you have to wear a boned-up collar and a hat like a house?"

"No," said Mary, "because, owing to the war, I didn't go until I was nearly twenty-three. However, I was luckier than some. At the Garden Party—they didn't have any Courts that year—there were mothers shoving out two and even three dejected daughters, poor creatures. Clothes were quite sensible, but I recollect with some misgiving that I wore chestnut stockings and black patent leather shoes with a lace frock."

Elizabeth was so struck by this picture that she remained silent for ten minutes. During this time the car suddenly deserted the arterial road and fled into a countryside of water-meadows, where cows were gathered in the shade of heavy trees, and full-blown roses garlanded the faces of old inns and modern school houses.

"I've a feeling I shall remember this drive for years," thought Mary, "and probably under less happy circumstances."

Presently the landscape changed again, and she began to see sandy soil and conifers and heather. Catha woke up in the streets of Slough, which were extremely crowded and noisy. She re-entered the conversation with great dignity, saying, "Well, that was very nice. Now Button dear, I want to tell you about the other friends who are lunching with us."

"If there are any topics to be avoided," Mary advised her, "you had probably better not warn me. It only puts ideas in my head."

"Nonsense, dear," said Catha benevolently. "You know you are always tactful and kind."

"Far from it," declared Mary dismally. "Only yesterday I met a woman with a most unusual surname. I screeched at her, 'Ha! you must be my old school-friend Nesta's sister.' Her eyes grew like gas-balls, and I realized that of course she must be Nesta's sister's successor. Now that I come to think of it, I remember vaguely hearing that that marriage had dropped to pieces."

"Do you do awful things, Auntie Bee?" asked Elizabeth. "I am glad. Do you know, the other night one of my greatest friends absolutely disgraced Mummy and me? We took him to a house, to dine before a dance, and as we were announced he tripped, and went half across the room before we could stop him, and ended up flat at his hostess's feet, clutching an occasional table, with electric light flex wound round his legs, and one fist through a lampshade. You wouldn't have believed that he could have destroyed quite so much so quickly. He was absolutely overcome until we got to the fish, and then, imitating the Italian family with whom he's been living so as to get up another language, he flung up his hands and got one little finger inside the handle of the sauce-boat being offered to the girl next to him. Poor Derek's terribly unlucky." Mary remembered Tony's friend, whom she had taken to Elizabeth's coming-out dance, and wondered if Derek was a common name in the younger generation. But being rather drowsy and very cautious, she wondered in silence.

Not until they got into Windsor Park did the travellers find themselves in a line of traffic reduced to a sober pace.

"Now this is my idea of bliss," purred Catha, "to sail gently through a perfect English park on a June morning."

"Complete with distant historic castle and grazing deer," added Mary.

"And lovely comic picnic-parties feasting at the roadside," said Elizabeth, peeping at them.

"And every single bump rolled out," contributed Crispin, smiling, and sticking out his chin.

A few minutes later they began to experience frequent stoppages and short advances in first gear. The interior of the car became uncomfortably warm. It was a relief when all char-a-bancs were directed onto a fork road, and they began to move faster again. Their wheels softly took the turf of the Course, and Elizabeth, assuming her hated hat, piped, "Doesn't it look divine? Aren't you getting excited, Auntie Bee?"

Mary thought that the time had come for her to explain, "I've got a date in the Paddock before lunch, Catha, but as I see I'm already ten minutes late, I daresay nothing will come of it."

"Oh! Button, I am sorry," said Catha.

"It's all right. It's only a *beau* of my dancing-class days, one of the many Merle grandchildren—as a matter of fact, the Black Sheep of that family, I regret to say," said Mary.

"Mummy dear, oughtn't we to ask Auntie Bee's friend to lunch with us?" asked Elizabeth promptly.

"No, no," said poor Mary. "I mean it would be quite unnecessary. He has far too many friends already. Oh! dear, I should never have called poor Kit a Black Sheep. He was only rather wild when younger."

"What is he like now, Auntie Bee?" enquired Elizabeth, beginning to sparkle.

"Rather like a toad that's been run over by a steam-roller," said Mary graphically. "He's six feet four, and has a long, dark face of strongly marked features, and particularly black eyes and hair."

"He sounds exactly like Charles II, whom I adore," said Elizabeth.

"Well, all the Merles are descended from Charles II," admitted Mary.

"You might give this to that man, who's longing for it," said Crispin, patiently pressing a ten-shilling note into his sister's hand.

Fixing a parking ticket to their windscreen occupied Elizabeth while the car rocked slowly across the Heath, mounting and descending sandy inclines between gorse-bushes.

"This reminds me of taxi-ing in an aeroplane," shuddered Catha. Quite soon, however, Crispin brought the car to a standstill close behind a group of club tents. The party dismounted, and firmly refusing offers of late specials, lucky babies, white heather and race-cards, ascended to cross the Course again.

"I'd forgotten how like Frith's 'Derby Day' the crowd over this side still is," panted Mary, snatching at her hat as a gust of wind got beneath its brim.

"Not many people here yet, considering it's Thursday," pronounced Crispin, heavily loaded with mackintoshes, umbrellas and race-glasses, scanning the stands with the eye of one accustomed to wide horizons.

"Cris, don't lose me," bleated Elizabeth, clutching at an arm. "I don't want to catch that awful clown's eye again. Every day he's come up and bowed and bellowed at me, 'Cheerho! Here we are again!'"

Mary, squeezing past the flanks of a calmly-shifting police horse, said, with rising spirits, "Well, he's right."

(iii)

When Mary emerged from the cloak-room, which was full of women protesting, "My dear, I've got such a pretty frock at home which I'm not wearing to-day!" she saw at a glance that the worst had already happened.

The Paddock was far from full. A most unfestive wind was fluttering the garments of the stream of lunch-goers. At the spot appointed for her meeting with Kit, an unmistakable group was already assembled. It included Kit himself who, judging by the angle of his head-gear, was in the best of spirits, his cousins, "young" Lady Merle, her débutante daughter and Pamela Wallis, Catha and Elizabeth, Rolfe Yarrow, Violet Jackson and Mr. Tony ffolliot. Lady Merle, who was one of the few people present wearing "picture" skirts, which swept the depressingly damp turf, said in languid accents, "Mary! you are the last person I expected to see here," but Mrs. Jackson said with gusto, "Now, that's exactly what I come to Ascot for—to meet a lot of busy old friends whom I never can catch anywhere else. Everyone knows that I don't know a horse's head from its tail. Neither does my husband, but he refuses to come."

As the party straggled across the Course again, Mary found Kit striding by her side. She had heard him accept an invitation to lunch from Catha with great charm of manner. She began severely, darting a pronouncedly spinsterish glance at his dark profile, "I never knew that you knew Catha Rollo, Kit."

"There are still a few things about me that even my oldest and best friends don't know," mused Kit, looking, Mary realized, disturbingly like the Merry Monarch.

Their *tête-à-tête* was broken off by the arrival of Pamela, stumping and muttering, "I do wish Valerie would give up dressing as the Queen of the May, and devote five minutes to tidying up her unfortunate daughter. Have you seen the poor child to-day? Yesterday she was even worse. And she wouldn't be at all bad looking if anyone took the least trouble about her. You ought to speak to Valerie, Kit. She listens to you."

"If oughts are in question, I ought to be with five men in a box from which I'm now walking away as fast as I can," explained Kit, shaking his head.

Mary was glad to see that during the ten years that had passed since her last visit to Ascot, no new ideas as to the decoration of a club tent had vexed those responsible. The temporary flower garden, surrounded by walls of faded canvas, into which she now entered, was remarkable for its many small tables, surmounted by gently-rocking striped umbrellas, and many small ornamental beds boasting brilliant but recently transplanted rambler roses and heliotrope. The scene, lit by a burst of fitful sunshine and enlivened by a stream of chattering and cheerful people, was pretty enough.

Close inside the entrance Crispin was waiting with two older men, whom Mary wrote down instantly as brother officers of Tim's Indian days. She congratulated herself as a psychologist when Catha murmured to her, as they passed down into the tent itself, "Button, dear, I want to put you next to Colonel Bloodshot, because he's stone deaf in one ear, and I know you won't mind."

Violet Jackson had been right in saying that at Ascot one met unexpected old friends. Before she reached her seat, Mary had been greeted by a second cousin whom she believed to be in Java and a family from Ireland who, on their last Christmas card had announced themselves about to migrate to a boarding-house in West Kensington on the last of their overdraft. They were all knowledgable race-goers, and by the time that Mary joined her own party there was only one seat vacant at their table. She was doomed to feast between Mr. ffolliot, who had on his other side the dumb Merle débutante and Tim's old brother-in-arms, who opened the conversation by cupping an ear in gnarled fingers and saying, "Now this is just what suits me. When there's an undercurrent of row going on, I can hear every word that's said."

Mary would hardly have described the noise around them as an undercurrent, and although through a small window in the canvas walls she could see newspapers bowling over the Heath, the atmosphere within this crowded dimness was tropical. She nerved herself to the struggle, and began, "Did you know Tim well out in India?" to which her partner replied unpromisingly, "That's on the mainland, isn't it? Little place, Tingwall. No, only been to Shetland once in m'life. Know the Orkneys well, though. Hope to get up to Scotland in August."

One of the blessings of middle age, reflected Mary, is that one can appreciate unaccustomed pleasures of the table. While Colonel Bloodshot monologued on grouse prospects, she was able to enjoy some lobster mayonnaise and a stuffed quail with asparagus, followed by a little excellent cold curry. Opposite her, Elizabeth, who had piped, "Oh! no, please," as a saturnine waiter filled her tumbler with champagne, had already reached the haven of strawberries and cream, after a brief unsatisfactory tussle with two drumsticks and a spoonful of resilient green peas. Kit and Rolfe Yarrow were entertaining their hostess admirably, but Mr. ffolliot was making heavy weather with the Merle débutante, who did not care for dancing much, and loathed London, and was unable to explain that the only thing to which she was really looking forward this summer was going into Camp with her Guides in North Wales. Mary came to the rescue to the best of her ability, and Colonel Bloodshot raised an unexpected spark of interest in Mr. ffolliot, by a description of a bird-sanctuary, but Mary was not sorry when they adjourned for coffee to the bogus English garden, and the numbers for the first race were put up, and Kit and Tim's other friend fled suddenly with the countenances of those summoned to a death-bed.

Mary finished her coffee in the company of Violet Jackson, Catha and Colonel Bloodshot. She would much rather have seen the first race, but Violet, in spite of her tomato curls and chequered career, was an old school-friend and the mother of her godson, and Catha, as they seated themselves, had thanked her in a scurried aside for cheering up poor old Dick, who, she said, had really saved Tim's life once out East, when he had dengue fever.

"I'm going for a motoring tour in Germany, in August," said Mrs. Jackson, laughing heartily. "Everyone says I'm insane, but I say I've never seen Munich. I wish you'd come, Mary. I'd love you to join us, and we've still got room for two more. We're taking four cars, and coming back by Warsaw and Copenhagen. Everyone says Copenhagen's so gay. Little Elizabeth Rollo's coming. She's just accepted. She's sweet. Rinaldo won't come. He says he can't leave London. I'm awfully worried about Rinaldo, these days, Mary."

"Oh, dear," said Mary. "I'm so sorry."

"It's his new secretary," pursued Violet, searching Mary's face with over-bright, once-lovely blue eyes. "Quite a pretty girl, nineteen, engaged to a dentist. But I'm afraid she's broken that off. I like her, you know, Mary, and I do try to be decent to her."

"I'm sure you do," said Mary, "and I'm sure she's not prettier than you were, when you and I were nineteen. Look here, Violet, why not give up this German tour, and come down quietly to me for August, bringing my godson? I could put up Rinaldo for week-ends, if he really can't leave London."

"That's just like you, Mary," said Violet, producing out of her handbag, to Mary's relief, a jewelled lipstick. "And I do appreciate your kind heart. But it's all settled, and can't be altered. The boy's going to Frinton with his nurse, and Rinaldo's going up to the City every day from Sussex. I'd love you to see my new home, Mary. It's a period house, Jacobean. I bought it for our honeymoon. It's mine. It's got a chapel and a Maze, though I never go into them. Rinaldo says that as long as I'm allowed to paint the bathrooms peach, I'm perfectly happy. But I'm not at all happy, Mary. He's so sarcastic, these days. And it's no use being sarcastic with me, is it?"

"No use at all, and most unkind," said Mary, adding to a hovering waiter, "No, no more coffee, thank you. I'd like to lunch with you in London, one day, Violet," she went on, "and I'd like it to be on a day when Rinaldo's coming home for lunch."

"That would be lovely," said Violet, sounding absent-minded, "but what I'd really like, if you can spare the time, would be to show you my country home. I'm giving a dance on Midsummer's Night—fancy dress. . . . There's cheering. That must be the horses going down. I do love a race-meeting."

(iv)

The first race was over by the time that Mary reached the Paddock again, so she spent a peaceful half-hour seated under a chestnut tree with Catha, and when horses began to appear in the top ring, persuaded her friend to walk up there with her. Catha, as a companion at a race-meeting, was one stage more satisfactory than Violet, as she did not turn her back on a race and talk throughout it, but she showed an instinctive admiration for all greys, and said that she could not be sufficiently thankful that Elizabeth was now of an age to accompany her father, and fearless on horseback. She had left the race-card with which Crispin had presented her, on the luncheon table, and seemed surprised when Mary insisted on buying her another. She was irritated that Violet should have invited Elizabeth to go for a motor tour in Germany: "Luckily, Tim will never allow it." At an interesting moment, when the horses were leaving the paddock, she began, "What a fascinating creature your old friend Christopher Hungerford is, Button. So responsive."

"The male Merle grandchildren are all notorious for their elegant carriage and ineradicable eccentricity," said Mary. "Both come through the Dowager. I never knew you knew Kit."

"Oh! Elizabeth and I have met him several times this summer," said Catha calmly. "Lady Merle brought him to our dance."

"Good gracious!" said Mary.

Mary saw the finish of the second race from the Paddock with her hostess, and then delivering her firmly to Rolfe Yarrow for return to the Enclosure, explained, "Now I'm going to spend ten minutes more in here before strolling slowly in front of your railings while policemen say, 'Keep moving, please.' You see, Mrs. Bates, in our village, reads all the Ascot fashion notes, and gets terribly distressed when one paper tells her that a Royal Duchess was wearing the new cornflower and another says palest turquoise. She was so sorry for me; coming on a year when there's no Royal Procession, and I promised her to notice the hats particularly, as she is waiting to order her new one. Considering that she is practically immobile from rheumatism and never moves five miles from the Green anyway, it sounds rather odd, but this is the sort of thing that makes life so interesting."

Mary found standing-room from which to watch the horses entering the ring. She was not very comfortable, because she was on the top row of the white-painted wooden laths, and her heels kept slipping through, which made her collapse towards a hot gentleman in a mackintosh, reading a damp newspaper. Her heart missed a beat when she turned the pages of her race-card giving the runners for the Gold Cup, and found pencil ticks against two names. She remembered that the card had been presented to her by Kit before he made his hurried exit. She hung on in the paddock, goggling at the horses, until the last possible moment, before deciding that it would be puerile to let a preference for a name influence one's judgment. At length, with a fast beating heart, she stalked past the crowded row of windows advertising tickets at 2s. and 10s. and, halting in front of one of those labelled £1, unfolded two beautiful-looking clean pound notes, and said in the cheep of a mouse, "Flyon, both ways, please."

There was an anti-climax when the clerk within laid his head sideways and asked, "Wot number, miss?" which meant that she had to disinter her race-card from her handbag again. Nevertheless, Miss Morrison was safely on the top of the stand, pressed tight against the rock-like form of Crispin Rollo, in good time to see the horses for the big race go down.

(v)

Crispin said that they ought to celebrate Mary's having won twenty pounds. On their way to do so, they met Rolfe Yarrow, who had so far backed three seconds to win only. Elizabeth came in sight as they set down their glasses, and Mary was amused by the skill with which Crispin disengaged his sister from her companion, Mr. ffolliot.

Left alone with Rolfe, who was looking his most stolid and a trifle disconsolate, Mary suggested that they should get onto the Paddock rails early. It was while they were watching a single horse being led round and round, that she received the second extraordinary confidence made to her by an old friend to-day.

"Dorothy was awfully sorry to have to fail to-day," said Rolfe, staring at the horse in a hypnotized manner. "She's going up to her mother in Scotland for a month. Dorothy's just had rather a shock, I'm sorry to say," said Rolfe, turning his stare upon Mary.

"Oh!" exclaimed Mary, staring back. She had known Rolfe since he went to preparatory school, and as far as character went, he had not altered much since, so she added bluntly, "What?"

"Dorothy's got to spend the rest of the summer quietly," announced Rolfe, tilting back his hat from a heated brow.

After a pause, Mary exclaimed again, "You don't say so! Well, this a surprise!"

"It is a surprise for all," said Rolfe heavily, fetching a pair of horn-rimmed spectacles out of a pocket, "but you only know half of it yet. It'll be in October, if not earlier," he explained, flicking over the pages of his race-card, "for we know now that it's twins. And in the opinion of a good many people, a European War will open on August 4th, and I am Reserve of Officers," he ended with gloomy relish.

"Oh dear!" said Mary. "Poor Dorothy. How is she?"

"Well, she's naturally rather under the weather at the moment," said Rolfe, putting on the spectacles and glaring at Mary. "I mean, she's all right, and the doctors are satisfied with her, and she insisted on my coming here to enjoy myself. But it is the very devil, you know, Mary," he burst out. "Nobody can say I haven't done my best to be peace-minded. I've had a perfectly strange Pomeranian to stay for a month. Hang it all, I even promised to speak at a meeting for promoting Anglo-German *Brüderschaft*. That fell on the day they occupied Prague! Last September, when we thought we were in for a war, we fixed everything up. We got the children settled at schools that would move to Scotland, and we offered the house as a hospital. Dorothy was going to run that, and the children were going to her mother for the holidays. She was to slip up north to see them when she could. Now what we are to do, we simply don't know. I forgot to add that we heard yesterday that the house has been accepted as a Maternity Hospital for evacuated East London cases. And there," concluded Captain Yarrow, nodding viciously at one of the string now parading the ring, "is another horse that I'm going to back, who will not win a race to-day."

"I'm not going to do anything this race, I fancy," said Mary thoughtfully. "Yarrow twins will be rather sweet, Rolfe."

"If they're boys, I'm ruined. Dorothy was glad I was going to see you to-day," said Rolfe, beginning to speak with unusual speed. "As you know, she's an only child and I've got one brother-in-law, a widower. I was to ask you if you would consent to be guardian. Five children, all under ten," ended Rolfe, as if he was quoting from an auctioneer's catalogue.

(vi)

The Merle débutante was hanging over the rail opposite to Mary and Rolfe. She had two first-class reasons for feeling despondent. Her hat was tight, and her feet ached. In addition to this, for the past three days, she had made a tiring journey in company of an irritable mother, to a scene crowded by strangers gathered to watch unrecognizable horses flash past a winning post at irregular intervals.

She gathered courage and, turning to Elizabeth Rollo, who had invited her in a friendly way, "Let's go and look at the horses," breathed in an agonized whisper, "Aren't you bored? Don't you wish you could go home?"

Elizabeth, who was screwing up her eyes to watch an electric sign at work aloft, suspended the pencil with which she was ticking off numbers on her card, and said in surprise, "My dear, no! I was just glooming that it's the second last race and Thursday. That means only eight more races this Ascot. Are you coming to-morrow?"

"Oh, yes," groaned her companion. "No hopes of getting out of that. And the worst of it is that I'm supposed to be enjoying myself."

Elizabeth Rollo regarded her contemporary in a judicial manner, before saying, "If you'll promise not to do what my father calls opposing one's intellect to the idea, I know I could make you mad keen to come here. I could make you so keen that you'd lie awake at nights wondering who's going to win what."

"Oh, no, you couldn't," said her victim listlessly. "I'm different."

Elizabeth gave vent to her favourite "Bah!" before opening, much in the manner of a specialist interviewing a patient, "Now look here, Lalage, let's get this quite clear. I suppose you've never been to a race-meeting before."

"I've been taken to several bitterly cold Point to Points, when I'd sooner have been reading a book at home," said Lalage, looking more than usually like a Bronte sister.

"I shall be buying you a very interesting book here in the Paddock presently," said Elizabeth. "It tells you all about horses' relations and what races they've won. It will be your home-work. It will take you ages to get abreast of all the interesting information it contains, and the best of it is that it's a serial story that never ends. What I meant to ask was, I suppose you don't know a single thing about any of the horses you see here?"

"They all look alike to me, except that of course I can see they're different colours," affirmed Lalage.

"And their jockeys are wearing different colours," suggested Elizabeth. "Quite bright ones, too."

"But I don't know why," said Lalage.

"Can you do sums at all?" inquired Elizabeth patiently.

"Yes, I can do sums a bit," said Lalage. "That was why I wanted to go to Newnham or Girton instead of coming out."

"I must say," said Elizabeth with the courage of youth, "that I think somebody is very much to blame for letting you come here without telling you a single thing. Before I went to my first race-meeting my daddy coached me for it in the study after dinner every evening for a week. He discussed with me what we were going to back, and why, exactly as if I was another grown-up. I mean it was ages ago. I was only seventeen, or something."

"My mother wants me to marry as soon as possible, so that she can play Bridge and try on clothes all day in comfort," muttered Lalage, "and my father spends his evenings drinking, mostly."

"If I didn't know you, I should think you must be a horrid girl, saying things like that," said Elizabeth, with very bright eyes and a lovely spot of colour in either cheek. "Don't you want to be a Success?"

"That's all right, I know I'm not!" sighed Lalage.

"You can't possibly know yet, and of course you want to be. What beats me is, when you've got an expert in your own family, why you don't go to headquarters for information about racing," said Elizabeth.

"You mean Kit Hungerford. But I'm absolutely terrified of him, and Mummy says he's lost two fortunes on the turf already," said Lalage, round-eyed.

"As a matter of fact, I meant your other cousin, Miss Wallis," said Elizabeth. "She's terrifying, I grant you, but she hasn't missed an Ascot since she was our age, and she's very nice to the young. I don't find Mr. Hungerford at all alarming. He reminds me of Rupert of Hentzau and Sir Percy Blakeney."

"I don't read that kind of book," said Lalage, setting her lips.

"Oh! very well, then, Rupert of the Rhine and Charles Surface," said Elizabeth. "He's over there, talking to Button Morrison now, but I don't think we'll call him in yet. He's what I call Advanced Course, and you're a complete beginner. Now look here, Lalage, some of the finest horses in the world are being paraded before your eyes at this moment. Within the next ten minutes you're going to choose and back one of them. I'll lend you the two bob this time, as it's really not quite fair, but to-morrow you shall play your own hand, entirely unaided. And there's another thing. I'm never going to let you back a horse that you haven't seen. My daddy made me promise that when he coached me."

"Has your father coached you for other things as well as racing?" asked Lalage, with a spark of interest in her mournful chestnut eyes.

"Of course," said Elizabeth promptly. "He's taught me a whole pack of things, so that I shan't be a bore to myself and everyone else, supposing I get a broken heart or nose or something, and end up a single old lady in a bath chair at Torquay." Much to the surprise of an elderly gentleman close beside her, a note of nursery boasting entered the débutante's voice, as she ticked off her triumphs on her fingers. "Golf, Tennis, Bridge, Billiards, Racing, and oh! a whole pack of other little things, such as picking up pennies in one's mouth from the bottom of the swimming bath. What are you laughing at, Lalage?"

(vii)

Mr. Christopher Hungerford said to Miss Mary Morrison in a manner that took her consent for granted, "Let's walk up to the top. There's nothing in here yet."

"Just a moment," objected Mary. "I want to see what they paid for a place in the last race."

The distant strains of a band playing behind the Enclosure Stand, amongst temporary azaleas, floated to Mary's ears as she jotted down figures and did some amateurish sums on the blank page at the end of her race-card. Presently she was strolling in the direction that Kit had indicated, under green trees beneath which sat people whose faces she could not see clearly.

"I hear from Crispin Rollo that I may congratulate you," said Kit, smiling the smile that had aroused romantic comparisons in the heart of Elizabeth Rollo.

After the stolidity of Rolfe Yarrow, Kit's lively play of facial expression seemed remarkable. Mary could not help feeling that her companion had ordered the whole scene around them, or at any rate foreseen and calculated its possibilities.

"I thank you," she said, looking straight ahead. "It was kind of you to mark my card. If I'd noticed before that you'd marked the second race too, I might now be even more affluent. Unfortunately I lent it to Catha, who had already managed to lose hers. But it was fiendish of you to lunch with my friends and leave me stranded between that awful boy and the poor deaf Colonel."

"I couldn't exactly choose, you know," suggested Kit.

"No, you couldn't choose at all, since you're a man," said Mary, "but you're forty-four, and perfectly able to fiddle about at the hat rack until I came along, if you'd really wanted to."

"I did want to," said Kit, "but to tell you the truth, I was afraid of getting my nose bitten off."

"You were always a genius at putting other people in the wrong," recollected Mary. "Still, since I shall now be able to telephone to Wookey to-night and say that I'll have the painted chairs, I'll forgive you."

"Tell me about Wookey's painted chairs," begged Kit.

Mary did that, and Kit said, sounding reminiscent, "And you'll put them in your green room at Willows under the grandfather clock from Woodside, with the little ship that moves through angry waters with every tick, but never reaches harbour. Do you know, I thought I could hear it ticking when you spoke to me on the telephone the other day?"

"You've only seen Willows once," said Mary. "I never knew you'd taken in so much."

"Indeed yes," said Kit. "The grandfather clock, of course, I knew of old. In the hollow under the stairs behind it, was my favourite place when we played hide and seek at Woodside. I used to call it 'my ship.' Your mother did give the most marvellous children's parties, Mary. They are amongst the happiest memories of my life."

"I always rather hated them myself, because I had to let the other children smash my toys, and smile to boot," reflected Mary.

"To return to Willows, I perfectly remember being shown every plant in your herbaceous border in light rain," continued Kit. "Do you still grow Fair Maids of France?"

"Yes, but not in my herbaceous border," said Mary. "Why do you remember them with such painful clarity?"

"I sent in my papers that day, and three months later sailed for Buenos Ayres, poor but honest, to attempt to earn a modest competence," said Kit. "I often thought of your garden when I was in Buenos Ayres, and in Sydney, and at the Cape and in Montreal. You ought to see the gardens at Vancouver, Mary. You'd like them."

"Very likely," said Mary. "Aileen Hill, from Lower Merle, is marrying a man and going out there. I might ask her to send me some postcards. I wish I'd known that you were coming down to Went for the dance at Crossgrove, Kit. I never knew you were there."

"You looked straight through me twice," said Kit. "In spite of the fact that you never failed to send me a Christmas card at the appropriate date for the past ten years, I did not feel emboldened to ask for more."

"It only proves what I said before, that there were far too many people at Elizabeth's dance," said Mary. "Do you come down to your grandmother often?"

"The dance at Crossgrove was the first occasion," said Kit. "We had a grand family reconciliation dinner. My grandmother and Valerie sat down together without a single mutter, for the first time in local history, I believe."

"Valerie was muttering like anything in the cloak room at Crossgrove afterwards," remembered Mary.

It seemed to her ominous that when they reached the top of the Paddock Kit turned round and began to lead her down its other side. Horses were evidently far from his thoughts. She felt more embarrassed than she had felt for years when he began slowly, "There's something I'd like to ask you, Mary, only I'm afraid of hurting your feelings."

"By the time one's thirty, they say," said Mary, "one's heart is either broken or steeled. Neither of us will see forty again. Ask away, Kit."

"Is it true that Woodside is in the market again?" asked Kit unexpectedly.

"I haven't heard that," said Mary, looking full in his dark face in her surprise. "I sold it to a girls' school, you know." As cheerfully as possible she added, "The last I heard was that in the event of war it was to be turned into a Mental Hospital."

"Valerie told me the other day that she'd definitely seen a photograph of it in *Country Life*, up for sale again," mentioned Kit. "I was thinking of making an offer, if you've no objection."

"I can't possibly object, for it's nothing to do with me now," said Mary. "But do you mean to settle there yourself? Kit, that would be lovely!"

"I'm glad you approve of the idea," said Kit. "The girls' school, I understand, is moving to the West Country, in view of what the more cautious of my acquaintance describe as a National Emergency."

"Do you know at all what will happen to you, yourself, in the case of a National Emergency?" wondered Mary suddenly. "I mean, you're not Reserve of Officers still, are you?"

"Alas, no!" said Kit, sounding very thoughtful. In lighter tones, after a pause, he explained, "This time, Mary, I fear I shall have to be The Man Who Stayed at Home."

"Oh!" said Mary, sounding rather flat. "Well, let's hope nothing of the kind happens."

"You never were a great theatre-goer, were you, Mary?" asked Kit, stopping to hitch around a leathern case, from which he abstracted a fearsome-looking pair of race-glasses.

"Never," agreed Mary, "though I love going to the Play when I get a chance. Do you remember the Merle theatricals in the Christmas holidays? You used to be a marvellous amateur actor, Kit."

"I still am, I still am," murmured Mr. Hungerford, raising the glasses and focusing them on the top of the Grand Stand.

"Oh! where?" asked Mary startled. "I mean, when?"

"Most days and nearly all the time," said her companion softly.

"The trouble about you, Kit," said Mary boldly, "is that you're unsettled. You ought to settle. Buy Woodside by all means, though you'll have to put in at least six bathrooms, or nobody will ever come again. When your grandmother, who was charmed to hear that I was going to see you to-day, was talking to me about you, after the Nursing Committee last Tuesday, we agreed that it was high time that you settled. We mean really settle, Kit—get married."

"All my grandmother's ideas are sound," said Kit, putting away the glasses quickly, and bestowing overfull attention on his companion. He sounded delighted as he asked, "What do you think of the idea yourself? Shall we say, presuming that Woodside is still in the market, for I realize naturally, that the sacrifice will be great. Still, I am told that there are amenities. You are fond of foreign travel, for instance. I have done scarcely anything else for the past ten years. We could travel tremendously, or else I could be constantly from home, whichever you prefer. I'm told that even nowadays foreign travel for a single English lady presents some difficulties."

"You've been told wrong. We've trained the natives marvellously," snapped Mary, hardly able to believe her ears. Pulling herself together, she asked in uncertain tones, "Are you speaking seriously?"

"Absolutely," nodded Kit, smiling his maddening smile.

"I'm sorry," said Mary, having great difficulty with her breathing, "but I can tell you straight away that it would never work. After all, as you said yourself before lunch, there are a great many things about you that your oldest and best friends don't know. It's ten years since I lost sight of you. I've settled long ago, and I've got accustomed to having my own way."

"I said a few things," corrected Kit with emphasis, "and, believe me, you need never know them."

"It's beginning to rain, and I've left my umbrella in the cloakroom. I must go," said Mary desperately. "Look here, Kit, I hope you'll buy Woodside, and I'd like to come and see it sometimes, and I hope you'll be awfully happy there, but as far as I'm concerned, I'm much best in the green room at Willows, watching my little ship rock away the minutes."

"But that has always been my ship," Kit reminded her, as he took his leave with his accustomed elegance and speed.

Chapter X
JUNE 24TH—JULY 24TH

(i)

Everybody in and around Westbury-on-the-Green was deeply interested to hear that Mr. Christopher Hungerford had bought Woodside. Even in 1939, the advent of a wealthy and handsome bachelor, to whose name clung the glamour of a misspent youth, was not a matter of indifference to country hostesses. The landscape around Went was noticeably deficient in unattached males. Two seasons past, when it became known that a new Adjutant of Territorials had taken a lease of Little Kingscote, with a view to hunting, hopes had run high. But they had soon been dashed by the news, characteristically expressed by Miss Pamela Wallis—"A total loss. The beast's engaged." It would be false to say that any of the ladies who took such friendly interest in Mr. Hungerford's purchase considered him as a future Romeo, or even sympathetic son-in-law. The unromantic fact was that a bachelor was often and desperately needed by those who gave dinner parties. Even to Sunday lunches and sherry parties—staple forms of local entertainment an extra man lent an air of careless affluence. When Miss Wallis reported that her cousin played Bridge—although she added his own comment, "To save me from worse things"—many ladies heaved a sigh of relief. Their husbands were reconciled by Lord Merle's muttered pronouncement that, whatever people might say, Kit had always been the best shot in the family.

Several people, of course, discussed in decent privacy, the possibility of Mr. Hungerford's inviting the late owner of Woodside to return to her old home as a bride. It was well known that the couple had been friends in childhood. A tolerably well-informed circle declared that they had actually been engaged to be married in the spring of 1914. But Mrs. Bates, who was never wrong, pointed out that at that date Mary could only have been sixteen and three-quarters. "If anything of the kind ever happened," said Mrs. Bates, who had paused in her totter around the Green to watch Norah Hill clipping her hedge, "it must have been later. And I don't see how that could have been, for poor Mary was a nurse in the hospital here until she went out to France, and Miss Wallis has told me that Mr. Hungerford was with a cavalry regiment in Palestine throughout the late war, and lost a rib and got the M.C."

"Still," pointed out Norah, clipping vigorously, "he must have got leave and come down here."

"I don't believe he ever did," said Mrs. Bates, helpfully sweeping clippings together with the ferrule of her parasol. "Mary told me that she had only met him once or twice in London, since she grew up, until the other day, when he gave her the winner for the Gold Cup at Ascot. She's not having those painted chairs from Wookey's, all the same. She's given the money to the Red Cross. I don't think she'll ever marry now. Such a pity for a girl. Did you hear that Sam Barker came home drunk on Friday night, and poor Mrs. Harker had such a black eye she wasn't able to come in to help Mary's cook wash up after Sunday supper? Imphm!" Mrs. Bates nodded hard, making the affirmative grunt with which she always accompanied her choicest pieces of information.

"I expect it'll end in his being run over on the hill, like the Mimms' handy-man," said Norah morbidly. She had finished the hedge now, and was waiting to trundle her wicker basket on wheels to her rubbish heap. "Is it true that Mr. Hungerford was once mixed up in a divorce?" she paused to ask.

Mrs. Bates nodded so fast that the ribbon rose on the front of her last year's hat seemed in danger of becoming detached, and joining the clippings. But she said nothing, and Norah had to ask, "What happened?"

"It was many years ago, my dear, and Mary has told me that Corisande, Lady Merle, says it is all past and forgotten." Mrs. Bates threw a stern look of the Dowager into her air for a second before adding, "After all, he's putting six bathrooms into Woodside, and going to let the Legion use the old Moot Hall."

"But he's never been married," said Norah.

"There were a lot of letters published in all the papers," confided Mrs. Bates, unbending, "and pictures. Imphm! So good-looking. 'On His Way to the Court.' She was eight years older, but always signed herself 'your Tootsie Chickie.' I simply don't understand such things. She said that her husband beat her, but he got rid of her, and Corisande, Lady Merle, shut up Went and spent the whole season at a place called Bad Gastein, with a waterfall, in Austria. But she didn't marry Mr. Hungerford, I mean the Lady in the Case. She married somebody quite else, with a Jewish name, very well off, I believe. Mr. Hungerford turned out to have no money at all at that moment, and Corisande, Lady Merle, sold the Gainsborough of her ancestress with the pug in blue satin, and made him go out to South America. It was the second time that she'd had to come to the rescue in two years. But as she says, all this is past and quite forgotten now. I have heard, but you'd better not repeat this, that he's been in the Secret Service for years. Imphm!"

(ii)

In spite of all that she had said against them in February, by June Catha Rollo was thankful to become a member of a ladies' club. Stronger mothers whose homes were nearer London, spoke doggedly of doing the Season from the country. "It may be all right for them," said Catha. "Some of their daughters weigh fourteen stone. But as far as Elizabeth and I are concerned, it's a physical impossibility. By the time I've motored back to Crossgrove after a dance, I'm fit for nothing next day, except to snap people's heads off, and Elizabeth's getting rings round her eyes."

Sir Daubeny, who did not care for a home in which the mistress arose from bed after tea, or a daughter with rings round her eyes, urged his wife to join a club. "Button will help you." But after Mary had taken considerable trouble to get Catha's name advanced for election at her own club, her friend announced that she had joined another, in the same street.

"It was very kind of you, dear, to give me lunch, and get that secretary person to show me all over, but you see, at this one I've joined, I can have Elizabeth to stay as my guest, and always get a room for Ada. Besides, if you'll forgive me mentioning this, I was deeply impressed by a notice in your cloak-room, saying one was requested not to smoke in it, and another upstairs about not letting one's maid bag a bathroom for one. I'm positive I should never have been able to remember, and should only have become a source of disgrace to you, by breaking the rules."

On a warm, wet evening of midsummer week, Mary approached Catha's club on weary feet. She had spent a virtuous but not rewarding day, visiting her old School Mission, in Kennington. She noticed with satisfaction that the club upon which Catha's choice had fallen had a dressmaker's establishment on either side. Between the hours of ten and six it must be almost impossible of access by car or taxi. Over London, which had been filled all day by heavy traffic proceeding through gusts of rain, a grey level light now reigned. In some of the emptying streets and squares close by, awnings and tunnels of striped canvas announced revelry to take place later. The night on which Miss Elizabeth Rollo was to be presented at Court had arrived.

The head porter who spent his days in an electric-lighted, glass-walled hutch close within the entrance of Catha's club, looked to Mary pallid. While they waited for a reply by telephone from Lady Rollo's room, Mary drew from him the history of his varicose veins, which had put him out of the army. By the time that Miss Morrison was directed to Room 14, she had learnt other interesting details of a hall porter's life.

Room 14 was said to be on the third floor, but when they reached the first floor, the page working the lift brought it to a standstill in answer to frantic signals made by a small lady dressed in nun-like garments, surmounted by a battered straw hat tied on under the chin by a black lace scarf. She said to Mary in fluttered accents, "Oh! were you going up? Well, then, I'll just go up with you and down again. You see I'm terrified of going in a lift alone, in case it sticks. This lift often sticks, doesn't it, Lionel?"

Lionel replied in dispassionate accents that the lift hadn't stuck since last Tuesday, and the fourth passenger, who had a heavily powdered countenance and chestnut curls, said triumphantly that she had no fear of lifts, because her medium had told her that she would die in her bed, probably in Italy.

"The members here are even worse than in my club," thought Mary with growing satisfaction, as she entered Number 14.

Catha, clutching around her a Chinese robe embroidered with storks, appeared at first sight to be paddling knee-deep in a sea of tissue-paper. She gave her friend greeting in a preoccupied manner, before announcing in a tight voice, "Elizabeth is ill in bed next door, and Ada's out, trying to get my dress from the dressmaker's."

"Tut! tut!" said Mary. "This doesn't sound very good. What is the matter with Elizabeth?"

"At four o'clock," detailed Catha, "I thought I should have to get a doctor for her. She hasn't had any lunch or tea, and she says she feels unutterably sick. However, Ada put her to bed after lunch, and we've given her two aspirins and a hot water-bottle, and she's sleeping now. It was just the same on the day of her dance, and she perked up perfectly then. She's hopelessly temperamental, I'm afraid, poor child. I've telephoned to the hairdresser, and told him he needn't come."

"When did you order your dress, Catha?" asked Mary, beginning to fold up tissue-paper.

"It was ordered in April, dear," answered Catha coldly. "I knew that you would ask that, and I know that Tim will ask that too. The facts are that he will be arriving in the car, blazing in uniform, in forty minutes from now, and his daughter is still in bed and his wife has no clothes in London."

"Exactly what do you mean when you say, 'No clothes'?" asked Mary, beginning to look serious.

"Exactly what I say," snapped Catha. "We're up for this night only, and my entire wardrobe, except for this dressing-gown, consists of a knee-length green pleated silk day frock."

"I'm taking Marcelle to a cinema to-night, to cheer her up, so I've not brought up anything either," pondered Mary. "There are dressmakers on either side of this club, I noticed, but of course it's long past closing time."

"Ada's out now, hammering in vain, I expect, at the doors of the beastly place where they've got my dress," said Catha. "And it was going to be lovely, Button! It is all Tim's fault. He made me order it. Oh! isn't it absurd to think that we're in the very heart of London, and there are hundreds of women with dozens of dresses hanging up in their cupboards, who are not due to take a daughter who's feeling unutterably sick to Buckingham Palace in forty minutes' time."

"What about Elizabeth? Are her things on the premises?" asked Mary.

"Oh! yes. I had hers sent home a fortnight ago, and we brought them up," said Catha. "You see, she got hers at a much smaller place, which specializes for débutantes. I wasn't quite correct when I said that I had no clothes in London. I've got my lace train, which I merely made them do up, and my veil and feathers, and a feather cape and fan, and my shoes and gloves and my stars."

"Look here," said Mary, "we have now thirty-five minutes in hand. Will you go in next door and get Elizabeth out of bed, while I telephone to Dorothy Yarrow and ask her to lend you what you need? I know she's in London, and I know she's been to Court earlier this year. It's just a chance. The only drawback is that she's at least three inches shorter than you. If I can get anything for you, will you, for Elizabeth's sake, consent to set out looking, possibly, far from your best?"

"Dear Button, I think of nobody but my child at this moment," said Catha grandly. "Just touch the bell that you're nearly sitting on, will you, and get a maid to help me? Without Ada I am practically helpless." While the maid formed an appreciative audience for Lady Rollo's tale of woe, Mary learnt that Mrs. Yarrow's telephone number was engaged. Dismissing the maid and Catha to the next room, she telephoned to Sir Daubeny's club, and left a message, asking him to defer his arrival for three-quarters of an hour. She then tried Mrs. Yarrow's number twice more, left the room, took the lift to the hall, and asked for the secretary. The secretary of Catha's club was a white-haired lady, seated at a crowded desk in a small sitting-room on the first floor, much darkened by a near-growing plane tree. She seemed rather pleased than otherwise at being asked by an entire stranger if she would lend the mother of a débutante an evening dress. She said, "Oh! poor Lady Rollo. Of course! Dear me!" But when she arose from her desk, at which she appeared a commanding figure, she proved to be one of the shortest-legged women upon whom Mary had ever set eyes. After pointing out this fact to her, with all possible delicacy, Mary asked if any tall member could help. The secretary said that one, whom she knew to be a friend of Lady Rollo, was, she believed, staying here to-night. She would see. She applied herself to the telephone, and Mary returned to Catha's bedroom.

The scene there was now full of movement. A quantity of the tissue-paper which Mary had folded up had got loose again, and in the midst of it stood Elizabeth, with arms upraised, biting her lip, and looking very much as if she would like to cry. The maid attending her was also biting her lip, as she struggled with fastenings which were evidently intricate. A second maid was getting silver shoes out of boxes, and attempting to insinuate them towards Elizabeth's feet. In a bedroom jug, surrounded by a pool of spilt water, and decorated with an absurd design of blue ribbon bows, stood a bouquet of Emma Wright roses. A burst of late sunshine had struggled through the heavy greyness outside, and illuminated much billowing shell-pink satin and lace with becoming effect. On the bed, still attired in her copper-coloured Oriental dressing-gown, Catha was telephoning dictatorially. "Yes," Mary heard her say, "any evening dress, so long as it's not black, and as soon as Mrs. Hunter comes in, ask her to send it round instantly by taxi."

"Good evening, Elizabeth. That's the very prettiest débutante's get-up I've ever seen," said Mary, advancing to bestow a pecking kiss.

"Do you really think so, Auntie Bee," breathed Elizabeth. "I still feel awfully sick."

"Have you any barley-sugar up here?" inquired Mary.

"Oh, yes, I have, Auntie Bee, in my dressing-case. But that's next door, and in a terrible muddle." Mary told the maid with the shoes to find the barley sugar, and proceeded encouragingly, "Now don't wriggle, Elizabeth. Everything is going to be all right. The secretary is looking out a dress for your mother, and I've telephoned to your father's club to tell him not to come for three-quarters of an hour."

"Daddy will be delighted," said Elizabeth, brightening. "He loathed the idea of driving round and round, only everyone told me that we must if we wanted to see. Mummy's got three friends sending round dresses with maids in taxis."

"One is almost certainly rose-pink," announced Catha, rising from her telephoning. "However I now feel that if we can get there at all and get the deed done, that is the great thing. How did Tim sound, Button?"

"I sent a message. But men's clubs are good," said Mary. "Ah! thank you. Here is your barley-sugar, Elizabeth. I'll sponge your fingers when I've teed-up your hair. Sit down now, and wrap this face-towel round your shoulders."

A cry of "Ada!" from the lips of Catha caused Elizabeth to turn violently, oversetting the maid crouching behind her. Ada had returned from the faithless dressmaker's, bringing as captive a frigid-looking member of that establishment, carrying at arms' length a large cardboard box, embellished with several coats of arms and much flowing gilt lettering. It had been understood, said Ada, looking volumes, that her ladyship's gown was required for to-morrow night. It had no fastenings, but the fitter had brought along her needle and thread. The sea of tissue-paper arose knee-high again, and the entrance of three more maids, all carrying cardboard boxes, completed an effective crowd scene.

In the end, since they had been assisted by six maids and a devoted friend, the ladies of the Rollo family had to wait for eleven minutes, fully garbed, before the large car with the Crossgrove chauffeur at the wheel, and Albert by his side, drew up at the doors of the ladies' club just off Bond Street.

"Tim, you do look magnificent," said Mary, in the hall.

"Thank you for your message, Button. I always said you had a kind heart," said Tim, screwing his eyeglass into his eye, the better to behold with possessive pride, two particularly cool and elegant-looking females, with trains folded over their arms, being shepherded by the club porter, Lionel and Albert, across two feet of dampish pavement. "Everything all right, eh?" added Tim, his glance returning to the noticeably disordered complexion of his old friend with a kind heart.

"Everything perfectly all right," smiled Mary.

(iii)

On July 6th Mary took Catha to Wimbledon. Dorothy Yarrow had posted a generous bunch of tickets to Willows so Mary was able to return much hospitality. She gave tickets for the following Saturday to Tim, who was reported by the people occupying the next seats to have brought a very handsome foreign officer. Elizabeth went on the Tuesday with another débutante, and on the Friday with an unknown cavalier.

Catha at Wimbledon was almost as uninterested in first-class tennis as Catha at Ascot had been in first-class horses. However, she apparently enjoyed her day, for the weather was perfection and she looked exceedingly calm and fair in a most becoming white and aquamarine *ensemble*. In the echoing passages of the big stand she met several other mothers who professed themselves worn to shadows, but appeared to be fighting fit. "I think," said Mary, as the friends sat side by side in the packed stand, "that if I were to be dropped here blindfold from an aeroplane, I should be able to guess where I had arrived. The sound of the ball being smacked to and fro, and the sighs and yells from the spectators, not to speak of the umpire's voice, are unmistakable."

Over strawberries and cream in a sun-bathed tea-tent, although they were obliged to share a table with four strangers, Catha detailed all the latest news from Crossgrove. She was thankful to say that Elizabeth was not going to tour Germany with Violet Jackson. Elizabeth's great friend Lalage, who was devoted to racing, had wheedled an invitation for both of them to stay with a Merle cousin for Doncaster week. Tony had gone off to Moscow as soon as he had finished Schools, and a post-card depicting Lenin's tomb had informed his mother that he thought he had probably secured a third class. Crispin had been last heard of, happy at Malta, and Tim, who was being worried by an ingrowing toe-nail and visiting Russian officers, wished heartily that his eldest son might have chosen another date for his first visit to the U.S.S.R. One of the Dalmatians which Catha had got from Lady Merle had turned out to be stone-deaf, and Albert had most nobly offered to take it to the vet. to-day during Catha's absence. Altogether the Rollos seemed to be behaving characteristically.

When Catha asked for Mary's news, Mary was obliged to confess, "Except that I'm taking my members into a concentration of Tear Gas on the Friday, I can't think of any act that I'm due to perform next week that could possibly be called interesting."

"My poor one!" said Catha, opening wide her blue eyes. "But I thought you'd done all that months ago."

"Well, I haven't," explained Mary, "because I kept on trying to get a Gas Waggon for us, as we're a country district, and every day that I fixed for it, something happened to prevent it. On the last occasion Valerie Merle literally stole it from me. If only I'd had my classes last autumn, before everyone got so worked up! However, I've got on to the Mayor of Went and the County Anti-Gas Officer, and it turns out that one of the new factories outside Went has got an air-tight penthouse on its roof, and the members are meeting me at the factory gates at six-thirty next Friday."

"I'm so glad that you're not asking me," said Catha, "because going into a penthouse full of gas is one of the things I could never do. I can't stand heights and the smell of rubber makes me ill. Tim was frightfully angry with me, Button, really angry, because he found out that on the morning that the Air Warden came to fit the gas masks for Crossgrove I had breakfast in bed. I had mine sent up on the tray with my grapefruit. Apparently Tim had told Symonds that the entire staff must be mustered in the hall, and. her ladyship would take command. The Air Warden turned out to be only little Pettit, that retired school-master person, but unluckily he chose the kitchen-maid as his first victim, and as he advanced towards her, holding out her mask, before he even touched her, she rolled off her chair in a dead faint. Wasn't it ridiculous?"

"Highly ridiculous," agreed Mary, "and probably would not have happened if her ladyship had been present to take command."

"You said that just like Tim," affirmed Catha. "You don't want me to become one of your members, do you, Button darling? I've been meaning to ask for some time, because, as a matter of fact, Valerie Merle has offered that if I join her lot she'll give me a splendid job in her office, and I need never go into a hospital ward. Indeed, it would be quite useless for me to do so, as I know that I simply hate people in bed. The only thing against it is that Miss Wallis, who is Valerie's second in command, says that I must take two exams., and I must turn up for at least six lectures out of eight, or I can't enter for the exams. For the mother of a débutante, as I told her on the telephone, that is a total impossibility. Miss Wallis is not a great favourite with me. I don't care for her abrupt manner. I do hope that nice cousin of hers is not going to ask her to marry him. I couldn't fancy her queening it in your old home, and we should have to meet on every committee."

"I think Pamela Wallis is a splendid woman, a perfect rock of strength," said Mary, stooping to pick up her programme and handbag. "But who says that she's going to marry Kit Hungerford?"

"I can't remember," decided Catha. "Several people, I know. I should like to join Valerie's lot, because, as she says, they are all so nice. She hasn't got a single girl from the factories, or from a really poor home. They're all the wives and daughters of tenants."

"I've got all sorts," said Mary shortly.

She realized the truth of this when she drew up at the gates of the factory in a blaze of evening sunlight at six-forty on July 14th. She had told the members not to wear uniform, as many of them would have to come direct from office and shop. In uniform they looked much better. She was feeling hot and dejected. When she had returned to Willows at lunch-time, after arranging difficult flowers in the church, she had found a telephone message in Doris's script. "Mr. Christopher Hungerford rang up from London, saying he was coming down to Woodside this evening. Would Miss Morrison care to meet him and Miss Wallis there at six-fifteen?"

"I told the gentleman's secretary that I knew you couldn't, miss, because of the Gas Chamber," explained Doris proudly. "I hope that I did right!"

"Quite right," said Mary.

A call to the residence of the Dowager had brought the answer that her ladyship was not expecting Mr. Hungerford to-night. Miss Wallis was in London for the day. A call to Woodside at six-fifteen had produced "No reply."

To Mary's relief, a goodly number of her members had turned up at the factory gates. She thought as she looked at stout

Mrs. Dudman, who kept the Art Needle-work shop on Went market-place, and little Carrie Window, laundress, who rode on a tandem bike in shorts with her Intended on Sundays, that something must be shockingly wrong in the world since she was now engaged to lead such innocent characters into a concentration of gas. The younger members chattered like starlings, as they waited outside the two lifts which shot them by twenties up to the penthouse, but Mary was fully occupied dealing with a character in overalls, who said had everyone arrived yet, and at what hour exactly could he expect to lock up, as he was in charge

Like her friend, Lady Rollo, Miss Morrison particularly disliked the smell of rubber, and had no head for heights. Moreover, when she emerged from the lift, she discovered that it would be her fate to walk in slow procession along an iron fire-escape stairway towards the Chamber of Horrors. Although she tried not to do so, she could not help catching a glimpse of a parking place so far below that the figures reclaiming cars and driving away, looked about the size of mice entering matchboxes. As they squeezed uneasily forwards, Carrie Window, obviously in the mood described by her fellow workers as "inclined to be goosey" announced suddenly in a high voice that she didn't like her gas mask. But Miss Marriner from the Bank said icily, "It's not a question of what you like, Miss Window, dear. This is your duty," whereupon the voice of Carrie was heard no more.

An orderly in navy blue was waiting on the platform at the end of the stairway. His quick eye lit on Mary's uniform, and he called out, "Will you please give the order for all your members to assume their masks as they reach this spot, madam?" He had been stationed to test the fit of every mask as the grotesque troupe filed past him. Mary had intended to enter the chamber with the first batch, but they had already disappeared by the time she got upstairs. She had to wait for a very long five minutes on the platform ready masked and staring at a closed door. The orderly said that this was a good thing, as "it got people accustomed to the feel of the Gas Mask and quite comfortable." Mary accepted this theory in silence. At length the door in front of her opened, and a goggled male monster stuck out a head and said in appropriately bloodthirsty tones, "Another twenty, please."

Already in the passage leading to the chamber, Mary, whose sense of smell was highly developed, detected a strong odour of furniture polish. A voice behind her said, "Oh dear! I can smell it!" The Male Monster pointed an awful finger and said, "You keep right over by the door, please." He saw the last of his victims in, and closed the door. "I want you to make conversation with one another," he opened calmly.

Mary turned to her nearest neighbour and heard a burlesque of her own voice saying, "It's not as warm as it was yesterday, is it, Mrs. Hemingway?" to which she received the heavy answer, "No, miss, it was yesterday, though." Two figures whom Mary could not identify said to one another simultaneously, "My dear! I never knew it was you!" and got the giggles. The Anti-Gas Officer raised a hand for silence, asked the group to gather around him, and announced that he was going to give them a short talk. "You are now in a concentration of Gas. . . ."

The penthouse was low in the roof and possessed many windows filled with shiny glass and pale blue sky. In one of them, an accomplice was performing what appeared at first sight to be unsuccessful amateur cookery on a small scale. He was breaking capsules and applying matches to their contents. "Ethel!" hissed another figure unknown to Mary, "doesn't he remind you for all the world of Aunt P. on that cruise, trying to heat her curling tongs in the cabin?"

Miss Morrison heard very little of the Anti-Gas Officer's few words. She soon realized that he was not saying anything startlingly novel, and her thoughts wandered. She thought, "I suppose Kit only wanted to ask my advice about his alterations at Woodside," and "If it wasn't for that group of trees, one could see the lower road leading to Woodside from up here. I'd no idea this factory had such a fine view." An aeroplane was climbing slowly across the pale blue sky, but in here she could hear no sound of its progress. . . .

In a blessedly short time the Anti-Gas Officer asked his listeners to walk out this way, please, and wait on the platform in the open air before going back to the main building, where he would meet them in twenty minutes. When the party took off their hated headgear in approved fashion, only a couple were coughing fastidiously. Miss Moote from the Stores had red patches on her throat, but appeared to be rather pleased about this, as it gave her the opportunity of repeating again and again that her skin was so delicate.

"Well, that's over," thought Mary, half an hour later, as she offered a lift to the bus stop to anyone wanting to catch the 7.30 for Westbury North.

(iv)

On Saturday, July 15th, Mary went by Elizabeth's invitation to watch polo at Hurlingham. She was much touched, and thought it particularly nice-mannered of Elizabeth to attempt to entertain her. After the polo, three young men attired for tennis met them, and took tea with them under green trees, to the strains of a string orchestra. Tim, who had been at the War Office, joined them at six-thirty, and they played tennis until dusk, after which they dined *al fresco* and motored home by moonlight.

Tim, while sitting out with Mary during the tennis, screwed his eye-glass into his eye, and said with ferocity which must have terrified a stranger, "Who's that young man?"

"There are three present, but I've no doubt that you mean Derek Young," said Mary.

"The carroty one, with freckles," said Tim.

"Yes, that's Derek, and he's rather on my conscience," said Mary. "For, as you can see, of the three present, he's by far the most hopelessly enamoured of your fascinating daughter."

"Very likely," said Tim, "but who is he?"

"He's in the Auxiliary Air Force, and very keen. He's just down from Oxford, where I understand he's likely to have done well," said Mary, marshalling her facts tactfully. "His parents are divorced, and he lives with his mother in a suburb where she teaches tapdancing. He hopes to make a fortune in paint, but I am the guilty party who took him to Elizabeth's coming-out dance, and I wish now that I had not, because I like him."

Tim said "Humph!"

On Monday morning Mary waited carefully until half-past ten, before telephoning to Mr. Christopher Hungerford's London office. There she learnt that Mr. Hungerford had left by air on Saturday to see a client in Roumania. The Hotel Adlon, Berlin, was his address after July 21st.

Next day Mary went up to London again. Dr. Greatbatch wanted Miss Taylor, the Rector of Westbury's sister, to see a specialist in Wimpole Street. Mary had known Miss Taylor for fifteen years, but had never got to know her, so she was a little taken aback when her companion announced in the train, *à propos* of nothing, that she had once been engaged to be married to a Divinity student, who had died of tuberculosis. She soon reverted to normal, and said that Westbury was not an easy parish in which to do good. The villagers were an independent lot. "That's what I like," said Mary, but immediately regretted her words, because Miss Taylor was going to see a specialist and anyway could not help being like that.

Miss Taylor was so fussing, trying to pay for their first taxi, that Mary decided, in spite of the heat and pressure of time, to do the remainder of their travelling by Underground. She much regretted that they had not gone up by road, but in preparation for motoring to Scotland on Friday, she had sent her car in to Went to be decarbonized. Miss Taylor knew London hardly at all, and was, apparently, far more nervous of the moving staircases at Piccadilly Circus and the possibility of losing her way in the London streets, than of the results of the appointment made for her at three o'clock. In a large Oxford Street store she bought a holland dressing-table set, to be worked in orange and pink lustrenes. She obviously enjoyed an hour spent in the largest Woolworth's she had ever seen choosing prizes for the Church School sports. At Mary's club she watched with fascinated eyes, Dame Sarah Lys lunching with Miss Rosanna Masquerier, of whose works she was a faithful reader. When the specialist in Wimpole Street said, as Dr. Greatbatch had warned Mary that he probably would, that he would like to operate, Miss Taylor seemed rather relieved than otherwise.

The nursing home which the specialist wished her to enter was in Manchester Street, so the ladies from Westbury walked round there together and chose a room. After that Mary delivered Miss Taylor at a private hotel near the Victoria and Albert Museum, where she had trysted with an old school friend about to return to Kenya. Mary was in no spirits for further trials when she arrived at Violet Jackson's flat, to fulfil her promise of seeing Rinaldo and attempting to make him see sense.

Violet's flat was a large one, in a street off Park Lane, but although the sun was shining brilliantly outside, electric light was necessary even in the drawing-room. To Mary's mingled relief and annoyance, Violet was in the best of spirits and at her worst. Since her last urgent telephone call to Mary, all was altered. The party to tour Germany in high-powered cars throughout August had finally dropped to pieces. Rinaldo had come home in a jitter, telling her to sail at once for Buenos Ayres, taking their child. He was going to follow them, and had promised that they should spend Christmas together, "alone in the Bahamas."

"A second honeymoon!" said Violet, with ready tears in her restless eyes.

Mary asked with the licence of an old-school friend, "What's happened to the pretty secretary?" and Violet said, "My dear, she's gone off to become a Wren, or a Rat, or something. I always liked the girl. Come upstairs and see the things I've been buying."

Violet's dressing-room was a revelation to Mary, and would have delighted anyone with a low opinion of the idle rich. Its walls were entirely covered with mirrors, its furniture was upholstered in white fur, and on the dressing-table stood not less than fifty bottles of beautifying lotions, scents and creams. Mary never saw the trousseau which Violet had bought for her second honeymoon, because, before they had got beyond the dressing-room, a telephone message told Mrs. Jackson that fifteen friends had arrived. Mary would have given much for a cup of weak China tea, but all she got, before taking the omnibus back to South Kensington, was a blue cocktail, a Russian cigarette and a hideously thirst-provoking cheese biscuit smeared with caviare.

Next morning at an early hour she telephoned to Pamela Wallis, and said, "Look here, Pamela, would you like to do someone a good turn?"

"Probably not, dear, but I expect I shall," answered Miss Wallis, with manly resignation.

"It's like this," explained Mary. "You know the Taylors at Westbury? Yes, I know he's rather a frightful little chap, and she's a bit of a dud. But you see, she's going into a nursing home on Sunday for an operation. Dr. Greatbatch asked me to take her up to London yesterday to arrange about it, and I can assure you it was necessary. I mean, my taking her by the hand. Now I'm due to set off for Scotland on Friday. I could put it off, but I've promised the servants their holidays, and arranged to have several things done in the house. What I want to ask is, could you keep an eye on the Taylors? She's astonishingly brave, in a way I couldn't hope to imitate, and only says that she's so glad it is not her brother who's to have the operation, and that the only thing she dreads is the expense for him."

"Why does she dread that?" interrupted Pamela's voice. "He's well able to afford her an operation or two."

"I know," agreed Mary. "But she's like that, and I was really sorry for him last night. We walked round and round the

Rectory shrubbery together, being bitten by midges, and he beat his brow, and said that he had never been good enough to Aggie, and that if he was to lose her now he would never forgive himself. Yes, it was awful, but you could see he meant it. I never knew, did you, that she was eight years older than him, and had brought him up single-handed since he was eleven? Somehow one never thinks of Miss Taylor being eighteen and engaged to a Divinity student dying of tuberculosis. They don't seem to have a relation alive."

"Right-ho!" said Pamela's voice. "I'll go and see old Great-batch and little Taylor, and volunteer for service. To tell the truth, I've never minded little Taylor. He's not a pincher, and he was once quite a good fast bowler. He only needs taking in hand, and being told a few things firmly. But I must say, Mary, you do find the most absorbing jobs for your friends." Mary had intended, when she spoke to Pamela, to ask her how the altera-tions at Woodside were going on, and if Kit had seemed to like the place when he came down on Monday. But with the pictures of little Taylor beating his brow, and Miss Taylor only dreading the expense, still fresh in her eye, she closed the conversation without making these enquiries so deeply interesting to her.

CHAPTER XI
AUGUST 5TH—SEPTEMBER 3RD

(i)

MISS MORRISON lay full-length on a most uncomfortable sofa, which included amongst its adjuncts a mahogany rail and a cush-ion the shape of a sausage roll. Her writing-pad was balanced on her knee, and she gazed at Scottish scenery.

Her bedroom possessed two windows, one of the large round-headed variety, known as "Venetian," the other a mere slit, deep sunk in a particularly grey and crumbling outer wall. Both windows were curtained with white repp, patterned with pale La France roses, and on the satin-striped wallpaper, in this large and light spare-room, hung water-colours, in gilt mounts and frames, depicting blue lakes in Switzerland, and narrow dark streets and palaces above canal waters. On the mantelpiece stood a pottery bust of the Czar Alexander I, a vase of crimson rambler roses, and a mug containing local flora picked by Miss Morrison on outings. She had put her collection in a toothglass, but a severe red-haired maid had swiftly replaced the tooth-glass by a brown mug bearing a doggerel couplet in praise of North Britain. The collection included one bog orchid, two sprigs of white ling and one of white bell-heather, and a spreading spray of heliotrope. The view out of the window on Mary's left-hand was of khaki-coloured moor, scarred and wrinkled, a white streak of road attended by a tangle of telegraph poles and wires, and beneath these, grassy lower slopes, and then tree tops. From the window opposite her she could see a sinister-looking sheet of black water, reflecting rhododendrons and silver patches of sky, and silver birch trunks amongst green leaves.

The Scottish country house in which Miss Morrison was a favoured guest for a visit of not less than three weeks every year, belonged to a distant cousin. Like most of its kind, it had been added to by successive owners. It had begun life as a fortress. In the eighteenth century, a colonel who had raised a regiment for Queen Anne (and been rewarded by a more-than-life-size portrait of Her Majesty, still presiding over the shallow-stepped main staircase) had planned gigantic schemes of re-building, something in the Blenheim style. His money had run out, and he had died. According to local rumour, he had never left the house of his unrealized dreams, and his little figure was still to be seen, shivering in a many-caped overcoat in the study, totting up architects' estimates. Maids imported for the shooting season complained that they had been unable to "do" the lovely little room panelled in fraying yellow brocade, because

Mary's cousin—also a small retired colonel—had been already at his desk when they had peeped in, armed with broom and duster at 6 a.m.

At present Mary's cousin entertained her every evening by treading the floors of his library (another exquisite room, hallowed by quite another ghost-story dealing with a fatal duel between local gentry), and telling her that if there was to be war now, he would be too old and out of it.

At about the date that Queen Victoria's Journal brought popularity to Scotland, a gentleman of the correct name, who had made a fortune in Glasgow, struck by the beauty of its situation, had purchased this property, which he had declared unhesitatingly to be the cradle of his race. He had added a forest of pepper-pot turrets, a baronial hall panelled in pitch-pine, five glass-houses, a cavernous double drawing-room, and the word "Castle" to the notepaper.

At the Castle the London letters did not come in till tea-time, and Miss Morrison had formed the habit of taking this meal, not much regarded in a widower's establishment, up in her own room. After tea she always descended to play games for an hour before their bedtime with the children of her cousin's married daughters. The adult members of the party, which was almost entirely a family party, usually met for the first time in full force punctually at eight p.m. And while they dined by slanting golden sunlight, it was no uncommon thing for the roe deer, leading her two calves, to pick her way delicately up the drive, and standing with her twins grouped around her, stare in at the feasters. At a sound or a movement she would bound back into the greenery from which she had emerged, and from which at intervals appeared also the hen pheasant with chicks and a quantity of black rabbits, firmly believed by those in the Castle nursery to be fairy princes in captivity.

Mary always told her cousin, with sincerity, that she thought her weeks under his roof set her up again for the year. On her Scottish holiday, days sped past like hours. She could tell Saturday, because on that morning she awoke to the sound of the drive being raked. Sunday could be known because the evening before it was made hideous with complicated plans for transport to church. Otherwise the days were indistinguishable, and the possibilities of occupation altered not from year to year. You could shoot and bathe, and go out in a boat, either on sea or loch, and fish, either in river or loch, and motor to the country town to buy tweeds and sheepskins. There was a tennis court, but it had never, in Mary's memory, been the scene of a tennis party. Nobody came to dine without coming also for the night, for the nearest neighbour was seventeen miles distant. The lawn at the back of the Castle stretched to a sea-view, and watching the isles was another constant entertainment. On sunny mornings Mary could clearly distinguish tall red cliffs haunted by birds. On doubtful days the isles retreated into a romantic distance, and appeared to be carved out of mother-of-pearl. Rain and mist removed them altogether. In stormy weather they drew closest, and became theatrically blue and inviting. The children from London and Edinburgh grew brown and contented, solemnly sporting all day on the silver sands. They built a hidey-hole, roofed with heather, and played at being Prince Charlie and Flora Macdonald, and Captain Hook, and the Vikings. There were only seven children here at present, but the colonel had promised to harbour eleven more if things got worse in the South.

Except when the post brought her letters, Mary could scarcely believe that her real life centred around a place called Westbury-on-the-Green. She had been up here for a fortnight now, and had done all the usual things. On the two Sundays she had driven away over the moor to the creaking, primitive little church. Sunday mornings, obviously owing to the machinations of the Evil One, were invariably fine, and the scene as she approached the white-washed building with a black shingled steeple, rising in the midst of nowhere against azure heavens, always reminded her of Scandinavia. In the kirkyard, where the turf was springy and sweet-scented, sharp-eyed and slow-spoken people, many of whom came from afar and had such an opportunity but once a week, gathered in groups for conversation. They returned with eager interest the greeting of the minister—a visitor—as he strode through their midst. Mary sat in a pitch-pine pew and watched strong seaward light shining on the minister's braided black gown, and through the clear glass windows behind his swooping figure, cattle moving on the hills, and the reflections of clouds.

She spent several peaceful hours in the walled garden three-quarters of a mile from the Castle, where foxes' brushes of purple buddleia, populated by bees, over-hung nets guarding glistening cherries. She had picnicked on the moor, in the heat of midday, and heard distant gunfire from His Majesty's ships, and the clatter of a hay-rake being drawn uphill by heavy horses, and the liquid tinkle of unseen peaty water, and the swish of a car passing on the road along the skyline, and a never-ceasing wa-ing of sheep. This morning she had driven eight miles along a highway and three more along an obscurer road ending in a succession of gates leading down to woods and a loch. Across the moor, which was a sour green and vivid lilac at this season, lay a range of mountains as blue as Wedgwood ware. When first she had burst upon this scene, Mary had instantly nicknamed it "Set for Act III, 'The Immortal Hour.'" She had spent five and a half hours in a boat this morning upon loch waters, alternately black and shiny as oilskins, and crystalline, splashing the boat's sides. The rain had come down in sheets upon her bowed head, and the sun had come out and made her eyes run. She had landed to eat hard-boiled eggs and plum cake at the far end of the loch, where white suds fringed a bay the shape and colour of a slice of melon.

Miss Morrison, drowsy after her happy day, drew her writing-pad towards her, scratched unromantically at a knee which had been well bitten by midges, and unscrewed her fountain pen. "Dear Kit," she wrote.

"It seems incredible that this letter should ever reach you, for I know that its first stage on its journey will be to a small faded box attached to a creosoted post standing up like a sentry at a particularly bleak moorland crossroads. My reason for troubling you with it is that last night, in the library here (which is a room you would appreciate) I discovered that I have been very stupid again.

"My cousin Charles, who cannot think why he does not get a sensible answer from the War Office, since he is a mere sixty-eight, announced last night in a burst of gloom that this time he supposed he would have to be The Man Who Stayed at Home. He might as well, he said bitterly, start training carrier pigeons at once. When I asked him what on earth he meant, he told me that he was alluding to a capital play which he had seen when he was on leave in 1915. My thoughts flew to a conversation which I had with you in the Paddock at Ascot. I think I have got it correctly.

"'This time, Mary, I fear I shall have to be The Man Who Stayed at Home. . . . You never were a great theatre-goer, were you, Mary?'

"'Never, though I love going to the Play when I get a chance. You used to be a marvellous actor, Kit.'

"'I still am, I still am.'

"'Oh! when? I mean, where?'

"'Most days, and nearly all the time, Mary.'

"If I have been as stupid as I fear, I apologize, Kit, and since the remainder of the conversation was carried on by me under a misapprehension, I think we had better consider it cancelled. . . .'"

The maid with red hair was tapping at the door. She had a justifiably low opinion of ladies from the South who bought lengths of tweed up here and paid their London tailors just as much for making up the suits as if the man had supplied the material. But she was inured to this guest, and a wintry smile lit her features as she announced,

"There's just the two letters for you the day, Miss Mary."

As she partook of drop scones and honey from the comb, Mary read her correspondence.

"Dear Mary," wrote Pamela Wallis, whose script was large and untidy,

"I have been meaning for days to send you a line about the Taylors. As you will see, I'm staying at my Club, so that I can go round to Manchester Street every morning and afternoon. They operated on Aggie as arranged, or rather didn't operate because as soon as they got to work they found it was too late. She knows, and is looking forward to going home on Saturday by ambulance. She is not in pain, and sits or lies all day working at a perfectly unbelievable dressing-table set which she designs for you. Yesterday she told me that she did hope she might be given time to finish it, as, all her life, she had longed to embroider 'something just pretty.' I don't think there is anything else to say, except that little Taylor is being a brick.

"Yrs. ever,

"Pamela."

Mary's second letter bore South African stamps. "Darling Auntie Bee," wrote Rosemary Wright in her round schoolgirl hand,

"I want you to be the first to know that by the time this arrives I may be Rosemary Something Else! In fact a Missis. Doesn't it seem ridiculous? My career as a Siddons nipped in the bud! He has been married before, and was frightfully smashed in the war, so came out here to farm, and we met first at a sherry party last month and settled everything up last night. I can scarcely believe it still. I have never been so happy in my life. I have told him all about you, and he is longing to meet what he calls my 'fairy godmother,' but as times are not good at present, we can't hope to come home for our honeymoon. Do cable me your blessing."

On second thoughts, Rosemary had added in a postscript, the name of her future husband, and an airy comment, "The papers said I was quite good as Miranda, but the Stage is now a Thing of the Past."

When Miss Morrison looked up again she was not surprised to see that the sun had gone in and the Scottish scene looked grim. Before she descended to play with the children she wrote out a cable addressed to an old friend—indeed an old flame—long settled in South Africa. She printed the name of Rosemary's fiancé, prefaced by the words "Do you know," and after considerable pencil biting, added the not strictly truthful explanation, "engaged to be married to my niece, Rosemary Wright, now touring with a theatrical company."

The answer to Mary's cable was awaiting her in the baronial hall next evening, when she returned from a long day on the moors with a painful blister on her heel. It ran, "Advise you summon your niece home immediately. Letter follows." But of course Rosemary, who was so young for her age, had given her darling Auntie Bee no address.

(ii)

Miss Morrison had one of the most uncomfortable journeys in her life getting home from Camp on Thursday, August 31st. Although the official evacuation of children was not scheduled to begin until the following morning, already along all roads leading west proceeded an incessant and fast-moving stream of cars containing nursery parties. Many limousines had perambulators bobbing on their roofs, and several bird cages. Mary's bad day began early. She was over-tired before she began to meet the heavy traffic. Her car pulled badly all morning. She hoped at first that this was merely due to its being overloaded with luggage, but as she neared Leicester the unwelcome sound of water boiling in the radiator became unmistakable. She had left North Wales at five-thirty a.m. Not until dusk did she draw near Went. She was turned off the Went road a couple of miles north of the aerodrome, and had to approach Westbury by Highbridge and Upper Merle. The staring sunshine, which was to make so unsympathetic a background for the days to come, had set in. When at last she drew on her handbrake in front of her home, she knew that she had almost reached the end of her tether. Her legs, as she stumped stiffly into the house, ached as if she had walked a score of miles. Her ears buzzed so that she could scarcely hear what Doris and Rose had to report. Rose wanted to say at once that the Air Warden had come thundering at the door last night to say that the bathroom Black Out was inefficient. Doris announced with gusto that the telephone had been on the go all this morning, but now, according to Mrs. Crippen, there was indefinite delay on all lines.

"It's not quite dark yet. Perhaps I'd better have a bath before I do anything else," considered Mary. "No, on the whole, I think I'll just have a cup of tea and some sandwiches, and go straight to bed."

"Some of the calls was very urgent, I was to tell you, Miss," suggested Doris, making an unwilling exit.

With her dust-laden overcoat still buttoned and hooked, and her hard hat pushed up unbecomingly from a brow on which the fair hair was plastered in unmeant curls, Miss Morrison focused her painful gaze on the following collection of telephone messages. All were written in Doris's best copper-plate, and occupied separate slips of paper.

"Corisande, Lady Merle, would like to see Miss Morrison as early as possible to-morrow."

"The County Medical Officer of Health will ring again."

"Can Miss. Morrison provide Went Park Maternity Home with six helpers at once?"

"Mrs. Garment will call in to-morrow early to tell Miss Morrison about the Trouble at the F.A. Post."

"Mrs. Thomas Morrison will arrive in time for lunch to-day, bringing the children."

"The Misses Hill called to say good-bye. Miss Aileen is leaving for Canada to get married."

"Lady Rollo's footman has rung three times to ask if Miss Morrison is home yet. Miss Elizabeth was operated on for appendicitis late last night. Her condition is very serious."

(iii)

When Mary alighted from Wookey's taxi at the doors of Crossgrove, Symonds looked so awful that she feared for a moment that the worst must already have happened. She asked, "How is Miss Elizabeth?" as she followed him through the two panelled halls, now illuminated by a single blue bulb and a standard lamp with its head wrapped up in brown paper. She supposed he did not hear her question, for his answer was that her ladyship was in the ballroom, which sounded quite mad.

There was nobody in the long formal saloon, which had been decorated in chalk-white for a débutante's coming-out dance, but Mary saw at a glance why Catha was occupying this room. Its many windows were all equipped with full-length wooden shutters. Lights were sparkling in two of the cut-glass chandeliers hanging from the ceiling. The ivory brocade chesterfield beside one of the fireplaces showed signs of having been sat upon. One of its cushions was lying on the floor, and by its side stood an occasional table bearing an ash-tray containing several spent matches and carelessly extinguished half-smoked cigarettes. The air in the shuttered room was close, and smelt strongly of flowers and nicotine. Symonds cast a cold look at the disorder, but made no attempt to repair it. After snapping on the lights in a couple more chandeliers, he withdrew unhelpfully.

"I never liked this room," thought Mary uneasily, as she listened to noises of stumbling and whispering on the staircase, and the slam of a door somewhere upstairs, followed by an angry murmur. Catha, who entered the glaring saloon from the dark library a moment later, was wearing her Chinese robe over the tumbled summer frock decorated with a pattern of spilt playing cards. The back curls of her hair were ruffled, and she looked pale, but in this room, Mary knew, everyone always looked much aged.

Catha's greeting seemed as inappropriate as her costume.

"Button dear," said she, forcing a smile. "So nice to see you again after all these weeks. I never did anything about Black Out, you know. That is why we are having to camp in here in such discomfort. I've been trying to snatch a few minutes' peace on the sofa next door, where we can't use a light at all."

She helped herself to a cigarette and sat down stiffly upon the chesterfield. Mary, seating herself beside her, repeated the question she had put to Symonds.

"I don't know," answered Catha, her countenance beginning to work. "I still can't believe it."

"Tell me everything from the beginning," suggested Mary.

"I've had the most awful time since you left," said Catha jerkily. "Ada went away on her holiday a fortnight ago, and you know how helpless I am without her. She's back now, and acting as second nurse until Dr. Greatbatch can get us another. Doesn't it seem a little strange," she asked, her voice rising, "considering the way that her father and I have poured forth subscriptions to local hospitals, that when our only daughter is at death's door nobody will raise a finger to help us?"

Mary, looking away from Catha's face at the elaborate room, equipped with eight radiators, six chandeliers and a telephone enclosed in a sedan chair, but seven and a half miles from the nearest town, said thoughtfully, "I suppose there's considerable congestion and dislocation everywhere, at the moment."

"I thought that I should go mad last night, waiting to get through to Dr. Greatbatch on the telephone," said Catha. "In the end, Albert had to go in a car and fetch him. A girl called Harker was having a complicated illegitimate child in a cottage somewhere beyond the railway line. I hardly know him, and he's such an odd-looking little man, with that mop of white hair and fierce black eyes. Picture my feelings when he said to me last night, after standing silent in the window for several minutes, all hunched and fiddling with a silver pencil case, 'Lady Rollo, I am going to operate.' He was quite rude when I said that I was sorry, but that in that case I must insist upon the best specialist in London. He said that expense was indeed not in question."

"But he operated successfully," said Mary, "and in time."

"Oh! I don't know," said Catha restlessly. "He says she's unusually low vitality, or something, for her age. Of course, she's tiny, but she's always been wiry, as I told him. He says that this may have been coming on for ages, and was quite angry when I told him that she always ran a temperature and felt sick when anything important was going to happen. We naturally thought it was just nerves. . . . Didn't we?"

"I suppose so. I ought to have thought . . ." muttered Mary.

"To begin at the beginning," said Catha. "On Tuesday I went down to Surrey to reclaim my four darling bull-terriers, who've been in quarantine since we got back from India. One of them has bitten Symonds in the leg."

"So that's what's the matter with Symonds!" exclaimed Mary.

"Oh, no!" said Catha. "Did you notice, though? He's being quite insufferable and refusing to speak to anyone, even me. It's all because Tim, before he left, said that he thought two of the under-gardeners ought to join up at once. It's so inexplicable, because Symonds is an old soldier, and was Tim's batman for years, and it isn't as if Tim had said that he must join up. There's no question of that, because he's over fifty and sixty per cent, disabled since Passchendaele, when Tim and he were hit by the same shell."

"I should tell him straight out," advised Mary, "that times are going to be hard, and that if he can't behave himself he'd better go now."

"Oh! would you?" asked Catha uncertainly. "Well, then, I spent the night in London on Tuesday, but as I was dead tired

I let Elizabeth go out alone to dine and dance with some young people. Next morning, on our way down here, she was very bright-eyed and pink-cheeked and began to cry, in the back of the car, and it turned out that she'd had an upsetting scene, coming back to the club in a taxi, the night before. I couldn't get much sense out of her, but she kept on saying that she was afraid she'd been horrid to Derek, and he might think she'd led him on, and that now he would be sure to be killed, since he's an Auxiliary Air Pilot, but that until it came to the point she didn't realize that he wasn't what she called the Right Person."

"How well we know . . ." murmured Mary.

"I tried to comfort her," said Catha. "I said, 'Of course, darling, there can be no question of your wanting to marry anyone for years,' and 'You're much too young.' She didn't like that, and said no more. I scarcely saw her yesterday, as I was feeling exhausted. In the middle of the night she woke me up, coming into my room, in tears again. I thought at first that she was still fussing about the young pilot, and I was inclined to be annoyed, but this time it was that she had a pain. Sim kept on clutching her tummy and saying, 'A terrible pain, Mummy.' I've never seen my child since. I mean, that from that moment she's been snatched away from me, and turned into quite a different person. As you know, I've a perfect horror of people in bed. . . . My natural instinct when little Greatbatch said that she had peritonitis, was to put my fingers in my ears and run away."

"What help have you got upstairs?" asked Mary, staring at her friend.

"Ada came back from her holiday this morning," said Catha. "Albert telegraphed to her, and she couldn't get a train from Went, and arrived on a man's bicycle. I nearly had hysterics when I saw her coming up the drive. The doctor who came to give the anaesthetic picked up a nurse from the Cottage Hospital on his way here. There's supposed to be another coming from the Went Infirmary for to-night, but it's past midnight now, and no sign of her. I've sent Albert in a car to Went, and told him not to return without someone responsible-looking. The one we've got doesn't impress me. The doctor who came to give the anaesthetic wasn't the one Dr. Greatbatch expected, and looked to me like a medical student. They used the kitchen table. It has all been an utter nightmare, and Tim still doesn't know."

"Where is Tim?" asked Mary.

"I don't know," said Catha, stubbing out her cigarette and lighting another. "I haven't seen him since he came in on Monday night, and glared at me as if I was made of wood, and said, 'I shall be able to keep you on here for the present. You will wait for instructions.' He gave me a mass of instructions then and there, in his worst barrack-square manner, about getting the house properly blacked out, about which he was perfectly furious, although I've had the stuff lying in the house for nine weeks. Then he went off again as suddenly as he had come, leaving me feeling like pulp, and with Symonds thoroughly poked up, and all these unspeakable things have happened, and nobody helps me. I've telephoned to his club, and he's not there. Anyway, I feel as if I never wanted to see him again."

"Nonsense," said Mary.

"I'm not talking nonsense," said Catha, laying down her cigarette, and beginning to tremble. "I can see now that if I'm to lose my only daughter, my life is at an end. Nobody else in the world cares for me. Tony thinks of nobody but himself, and Crispin never has belonged to me since he went to sea. Often when I've been talking to him, I've seen him looking as if he was miles away, and I've known he was thinking of submarines really. I used to think that it didn't matter being unhappily married so long as the children were on your side. If Elizabeth dies, I shall have to get a separation."

"Catha, darling!" exclaimed Mary, taking her friend's hand.

"I don't know how I've borne it for so many years," said Catha, snatching away her hand. "His temper has always been intolerable, and it's getting worse. I can't bear it! I won't bear it!"

"You well knew, before ever you married him," said Mary steadily, "that Tim Rollo had a sterling character and a fiery temper. I remember your telling me so while we watched cricket at Lord's in the summer after the war."

But Lady Rollo was beyond hearing words of comfort.

"My marriage has been a failure from the first," she sobbed, choosing an Italian silk cushion on which to sink her ravaged countenance. "And now if I'm to lose my favourite child, and there's to be a war and everything is going to be horrible, I shall simply give up. Nobody feels for me! Nobody cares for me!"

Ten minutes later, facing Ada in the dim stillness of an upper chamber, Mary said in a flat voice, "Her ladyship has had a good cry, Ada, so I hope that she may be able to sleep now. I want you to put her to bed, and I want you to go to bed yourself. I've got plenty of caps and aprons in my luggage, as I've just come from Camp, and I'm already dressed for the part, as you can see. Has the nurse had any supper or any rest since she came?"

Mary's words were confident, but as she laid her hand on the rose-painted doorknob presented to a débutante by an admirer banished to Australia, she looked dubious. She entered the sick room so quietly that the nurse seated by a frilled muslin-skirted dressing table beyond the bed, did not for a moment realize her presence. For a moment also Mary felt that there was nobody else in the room. Elizabeth was, as her mother had said, so tiny. In any case, the waif lying sunk in an attitude of complete exhaustion in the pretty, frivolous shell-pink bed, was no longer recognizable as Elizabeth.

The patient's face, which might have belonged to a woman of any age, was anxious, pinched and drawn. Her respirations were quick and shallow. Mary forgot that she was looking at Catha's favourite child. A blessed feeling of complete calm and resolution came to her, as the nurse whom she had arrived to relieve rose to her feet.

(iv)

The three children brought by Mrs. Thomas Morrison to Willows, "for the duration," were those of Dr. Dorothea Mulvaney Heap. They arrived in time for lunch on Saturday, September 2nd, and after lunch, Priscilla-Ann, seating herself on the sofa in the parlour, and looking around her, commented, "What a pokey little room. I shouldn't think anything ever happened here."

"Now, Mary!" said Marcelle, holding up a finger, and looking roguish, "you see what you'll have to expect!"

The Heaps had been brought up absolutely unrepressed. That is to say, their parents never attempted to correct them, but as soon as Theodore-John had reached the age to snatch a toy belonging to his elder sister, she had bitten him, and Theodore-John, in his turn, had discovered his spectacled younger brother Augustine, an ideal object to thump. Mary had to admit, however, that the two elder Heaps were some of the finest children she had ever seen. They had enormous rosy cheeks, flashing eyes, glossy natural ringlets and unbounded vitality. She quite saw that even if the price exacted was to be her sanity, they could not be left to perish in London. She said now, lifting Augustine onto her lap, "That's all you know! This little room has seen men in jerkins and hose like Shakespeare heroes."

"Has a baby ever been born in this room?" asked Priscilla-Ann, who had been told everything by her enlightened mother when she was four years old.

"I shouldn't think so, as it's not a bedroom," said Mary.

"Your cat scratched me yesterday," announced Augustine, wriggling.

"I expect you squeezed him," said Mary.

"Can we have a Big Dog, as it's so dull here?" enquired all the Heaps, in chorus, clawing Mary's knees.

Wookey's taxi was at the door. Mary disengaged herself, and after assuring the Heaps that she was only going to see two First Aid Posts and one old lady, mounted into her hired equipage.

At the Westbury Hill Post all was going well. The premises hastily allotted to Mary's members was the old Infant School, a late Victorian building. The members were busy scrubbing floors and furniture, erecting stretchers and filling cupboards with bandages, splints, bottles, enamel bowls and trays and surgical instruments. In the entrance, Dr. Greatbatch was turning admiringly in his long, dry hands an operating knife of the most recent manufacture. Except that very little conversation was going on, and one or two faces somewhat resembled in colour the pile of oilskin suits dumped outside a door labelled "Decontamination," the meeting might have been an ordinary weekly practice. All the windows, which were of the lancet variety, had been thoroughly blacked out, with the result that it took Mary several minutes to realize who was present. The company was indeed representative. Amongst those on their knees, clad in sacking aprons and sloshing soapy water over bare boards, were Norah Hill, Amy Squirl, the married Harker girl, Wookey's daughter, Miss Stone, the retired schoolmistress, Millie Burst, and, to Mary's surprise, Miss Rosanna Masquerier and Lalage Merle. The well-known authoress, arising from her bucket, said in thrilling tones:

"Well, Miss Morrison, here I am! I know I haven't been a regular attendant so far, but from henceforth you may count upon me." In less ecstatic accents she explained, "All the Original Documents which I require for my studies are, I understand, at the bottom of Tube Stations. However, if it is true that the Germans have raided Warsaw, a little article on the Walewska is a tempting project."

Lalage said, blushing like a rose, that she knew she ought not to be here really, and of course it was frightfully late to ask, but might she come along to see Miss Morrison about joining up, as soon as possible, and—in pleading accents—might she go on working here so long as there were things needing to be done? Granny had said she thought Miss Morrison might let her, and but for her Guides, whom she couldn't totally desert, she could work all day and every day.

At the Lower Merle Post, which was an efficient wooden hut erected for the purpose in March, the spirit of self-effacement was not so noticeable. Since the hut had been fully equipped and manned, day and night, for many weeks, no sudden rush of work was in progress. Mary s heart sank when Mrs. Garment, after a request for a word alone with you, Ma'am, led her into a fastness between sand-bags, piled behind the back of the structure, and began, "We had a Spot of Trouble down here last night, Ma'am. The medical officer said he would be reporting us to you, so we would like to have your ruling on the point. I am sure we all only want to do what is correct at this Post."

(v)

The old lady with whom Mary was to have tea was Corisande, Lady Merle, and as she sat on her crackling, outsize settee, behind an equipage of massive silver and a service of richly gleaming Crown Derby, the Dowager had never looked older, or more like Queen Elizabeth. She snorted with satisfaction and scorn when she heard that by the time that Mary had arranged transport for the six helpers demanded by Went Park Maternity Home, a further telephone message from "young" Lady Merle's secretary had announced that the helpers were no longer required. Mary said that she would be glad to enrol Lalage, so long as "young" Lady Merle would not consider that she had "poached" in doing so, and the Dowager said, "I told the child to come to you. She's quite a good physical specimen, and will be the better of steady occupation. No nerves, and almost as stupid as her father. I hope she may be useful to you. I said to her, when she came to ask my advice, 'My dear, if you want to flourish about in a uniform and see your likeness in illustrated papers, join something run by your mother. If you want to work, I'll speak a word to Mary Morrison, who will make you go down on your knees and scrub floors.'"

"Yes, she was doing that when I saw her," nodded Mary.

The Dowager was gratified to hear that Miss Masquerier, of whom she had always approved, was also scrubbing floors to the confounding of her country's enemies. Mary explained that she had been unable to visit her Posts before, as she had been at Crossgrove since her return from Camp. Two trained nurses were now established there, so although Elizabeth Rollo could not yet be termed out of danger, Mary's presence in the sick room was no longer a necessity, and she could not consider that her first duty now was to support poor Lady Rollo.

"A pleasant but futile woman," pronounced the Dowager. "One saw that at one's first glance. The husband I liked. No nonsense about him. He ought to beat her."

Mary remembered Kit saying that all his grandmother's ideas were sound. In her wonder, she nearly asked, "Did you really see that at a glance? It took me a quarter of a century." After a pause, she answered, "I am very fond of Catha Rollo, and always shall be. She has shown me many kindnesses, and we were at school together." After another pause she added, "But I begin to think that sometimes one loves people for no other reason than that one has known them for a very long while. This is certainly a time for disclosing character."

When she looked up, she received the impression that she had unwittingly hit some nail on the head. The Dowager, with her handkerchief pressed to her lips, and little of her wonted firmness in her mien, was breathing the unexpected word "Macnaughton! . . ." She drew herself upright, and continued faintly, "My maid Macnaughton has been with me since my marriage. She is a Highlander, and has temperament. I have always made allowances. I see now that I have been weak."

Mary very nearly said, "Impossible!"

"Macnaughton," declared the Dowager, "is, I am sorry to say, mutinously opposed to my intention of offering shelter in my house to twelve Expectant Mothers."

Mary asked, "Does that matter?"

"It cannot matter," agreed the Dowager, "but meanwhile the situation is upsetting. I feel quite shaken, as if anything might happen." She proceeded unhappily, "Went, as you know, has been offered by my son as a Maternity Hospital. I agreed on Sunday to take under my roof such cases as were not imminent. There was never any question of our having the actual accoutrements here. Macnaughton, who does not seem to realize what has come upon us, refuses to recognize my intention. She has told Wilkins, my butler, that no woman in that condition will enter this house while she remains in it."

"Well, it's twelve to one against her," suggested Mary, unable to believe her ears.

"Macnaughton," said the Dowager, dwindling visibly, "seems to have taken leave of her senses. She said to me yesterday that she could not believe that I was 'going in,' as she expressed it, for another war. I have seen five reigns, and lost the closest of relatives in three wars . . ."

"Can't you sack her?" asked Mary, blinking at an orderly prospect of massed pompom dahlias and asters, backed by park landscape in westering sunshine.

"I have sent her a message that I shall not require her services to-day, and that she may begin her holiday from to-morrow," said the Dowager. "It is most inconvenient, and means explanations and arrangements which should never be necessary, but it will show her my displeasure. I do not wish to see her again. Her inimical presence frets me."

"Is Pamela at home?" wondered Mary.

"Pamela is at home," said the Dowager in stronger tones. "But I do not wish to trouble her at present."

Silence fell, and Mary had just opened her mouth to ask, "Did you happen to hear from Pamela how Kit liked Woodside?" when the Dowager forestalled her.

"To a very old friend," she said, "and since I believe that she has to thank you, in a sense, for bringing them together, I may confide that I have great hopes that dear Pamela is going to settle at last. The match is not what I would have chosen for her twenty years ago, but as I said to her last night, 'Beggars can't be choosers,' and a long acquaintance is a sure foundation for a marriage, when the habits and tastes of both parties are fixed. To have her so close will be a decided advantage. . . ."

When Mary got home—with a very bad headache— she read through carefully the letter which she had written to Kit from her Scottish bedroom. Disturbed by the news of Rosemary Wright's sudden engagement, she had pushed the letter into her travelling writing-case, and failed to finish it. She read it through twice now, and after reflection did not tear it into tiny pieces. Instead, she transferred it to the pigeon-hole in her desk labelled "Difficult."

(vi)

"Miss Hill," announced Doris.

Mary detached her thoughts from the incredible vision of terrifying old Lady Merle, terrified of her own Scottish maid, and rose from the writing-desk, into which she had just confided her unfinished love-letter. She stared at her visitor as if at a being from another continent, and her visitor stared back as blankly.

Norah Hill, clad in a nurse's outdoor uniform, and lugging a pith suit-case which she set down just inside the door, was further encumbered by the object described by her sister Aileen as "that unutterable sausage." Alone of the company, the dachshund, attired in an amber patent-leather collar with lead to match, looked as pleased as Punch.

"I'm so glad you're in," said Norah, sounding anything but jubilant. "Aileen left yesterday for Canada. I expect you heard. She was awfully sorry not to see you, to say good-bye. Her fiancé cabled last week, telling her to come out at once, so we took her down by car to Southampton yesterday, and she sailed."

"I'm sure she'll be happy," said Mary, rallying.

"Sheilah was called up on Tuesday—only to go to East Anglia, though," went on Norah, "so she didn't come back with me. When I got home from Westbury this afternoon, I found that I'd been posted to a hospital in the West Country. I expect, as I belong to you, that they let you know."

"They doubtless have, but as I have been solidly at Crossgrove since I returned from Camp, I've never got abreast of anything typewritten," explained Mary. "It's what you wanted, I know. Can I do anything to help, in the way of shutting up Bury Cottage?"

"No, thank you," said Norah. "Thank you very much, but that's all settled. That's not it."

"What is it?" asked Mary, thinking what a pity it was that Norah was so noticeably drained of life and spirit. The poor girl really had not one good feature, and to-night, in her nurse's overcoat, with wisps of rain-straight hair straggling beneath her unbecoming hat, and every pale feature shining, she looked her worst.

"Miss Morrison," asked Norah suddenly, "do you hate dogs? I know you haven't got one."

The little ship above the face of the grandfather clock in the quiet parlour rocked to and fro several times before its owner answered, "I haven't had a dog since I left Woodside. My old 'Patch' died in my bedroom there, the night before I left. I think I had let myself get too fond of him. I travelled for a year before settling here. I'm afraid I've rather hardened my heart. I decided that night not to replace 'Patch' and I never have."

"Everything has been such a rush in the end," said Norah. "I've tried everyone I can think of, but, as you may have noticed, I've not got many friends. I can't think of anyone who cares enough for me to want to take him for almost nothing, and I can't pay enough to send him to a first-class kennels, even if I were sure they'd be kind to him. He's been spoilt, you see."

"Do you mean your little dog? What's his name?" asked Mary.

"Otto," said Norah listlessly.

Otto, hearing his name spoken, rose on his short legs and began to frisk. He believed that this very dull interview was drawing to a close, and that the most wonderful woman in the world was about to take him for a long scamper off the lead in magical though familiar woods.

"I've thought and thought," said Norah, clasping her brow, "but I don't seem to be able to think. In the end, after tea, I decided that the best thing I could do was to take him to the vet. on my way to the train. I've rung up and made an appointment for us. But just in hope of meeting somebody I started half an hour too early, and as I was walking round and round the Green, I saw your car come in, and realized that of course you're back."

(vii)

Mary rang the bell for Doris, and said, "In the garage you will find an old motoring rug which will have to do for the week-end, until I can run into Went and buy a dog basket. This is Miss Hill's little dog, Otto, whom she's leaving with us for the present. He doesn't get on with cats, and is accustomed to sleeping on his mistress's bed, so we shall have to be careful."

"Has Miss Hill gone to nurse the wounded, miss?" asked Doris. "If you please, miss, could you find time to slip up to my bedroom for a minute to look at something?"

"What?" asked Mary.

"I've seen something queer from my window," said Doris, round-eyed.

Doris's attic bedroom commanded the finest view obtainable from Willows. It looked far over the Green and Giddy's fifteen-acre field, to Lower Merle woods, and in spring, when the wild cherry was out, Mary heartily envied Doris. Beyond the woods, the hangars at Went Aerodrome could be clearly see on fine days. Went Abbey spire nestled against a further range of hills. Pamela Wallis had said unromantically on the day that she had helped Mary to move in, that the prospect only reminded her of a very good *Times* photograph.

"Look, miss," breathed Dons now.

With her sixteen-year-old henchwoman pressed tight against her, and Otto standing on his hind legs glaring eagerly, not at the view, but at Doris pointing, Mary craned out of the topmost window of Willows. Months afterwards, when dining out on this story, she always had to confess that she could not explain why the words Balloon Barrage had never penetrated to her brain.

"Is it the German Fleet—Zeppelins?" asked Doris.

Mary looked and saw, rising in the furthest distance, amongst the particularly fine arrangement of billowing cloud and evening blue, a string of large silver tadpole-shaped objects. They were unquestionably air-borne, and moving slowly towards her. For a second, she honestly believed that her last hour had come. A moment later, she heard her own voice saying in rousing accents—

"Do you know what that is, Doris? It's the Outer Defences of London—Things going up to protect us."

(viii)

Since her car was not yet ready for use, Mary walked to church on the hot morning of Sunday, September 3rd.

In her orchard she encountered a strange child, remorselessly dogging the footsteps of one of her bantams. She stopped and said, "Do you come from London?"

"Never seen an 'en lay a hegg, miss," replied the beady-eyed child.

On the kitchen-garden walls the greengages and peaches and nectarines were ripening. In the lanes, blackberries were turning from rose madder to maroon. The days of poppies and convolvulus and cracks in the soil were here. The two fields across which Mary walked to church were as hot as an oven.

Outside the small classic temple built by the Lord Merle who had been a friend of Fox, Mr. Mallet, Rector of Lower Merle, was wandering to and fro in the sunshine, as was his pleasant custom, shaking hands with his parishioners, and welcoming them to worship. Sometimes since he was very absent-minded he continued his perambulations after the five-minute bell had ceased tolling, and a churchwarden had to remind him that his congregation awaited his ministrations. This morning he did not smile, as he took Mary's hand, and said "Better news, I hope?"

Mary had such a lump in her throat that she could only mop and mow in reply.

On her way back from church, in the narrowest and leafiest part of the lane, she was overtaken by a car driven by Mrs. Gibson.

Mrs. Gibson stopped to ask if Willows could accommodate four of the forty mothers who had arrived at Went Junction by mistake, and told Mary that war had been declared at eleven a.m.

PART TWO
1940

CHAPTER XII
MIDSUMMER, 1940

"THERE HAS recently," read Miss Morrison, "been a marked revival of interest in Cacti and other Succulents."

Throughout the months which she had spent in a Naval Hospital on the south coast, where the noise of gunfire was constantly audible, Miss Morrison had chosen as her bedside book a gardening magazine. In vain her fellow nurses offered to lend her the most recently published revelations by those who had intimate knowledge of the Enemy Leaders. Miss Morrison found her gardening magazine ideal escape literature.

As she dressed to catch the early train to Went Junction, this midsummer morning, she studied mechanically the two large printed notices set up on the mantelpiece of her London Club bedroom.

"A.R.P.", she read. "In case of an attack, full arrangements have been made in consultation with the nearest Air Warden. Organization of the Staff has been arranged. A Shelter in the Basement is equipped according to official regulations."

The second notice announced in smaller type:

"In order to economize fuel, and that the Staff may get home early while the Black Out continues, Dinners are not served after 8 p.m. Hot soup and a cold meal can always be served to any Member arriving from a distance after that hour."

Miss Morrison had enjoyed hot soup at ten-thirty last night, and had slept soundly for eight hours, despite the sound of friendly aircraft overhead.

The club was almost empty. The porter said, as he put her luggage on a taxi ordered overnight, "Going home, miss?"

"For the first time since the Glazed Frost," smiled Mary.

She could not help smiling as the dolefully humbled express threaded its way through a countryside which seemed, determined to display in perfect weather every advantage in its possession. Outside the station at Went junction, a strange, elderly chauffeur was standing beside a twelve horse-power car. He asked, "For the Dower House, miss? Her ladyship," he mentioned, as he bestowed Mary's suit-case in a back seat of the small saloon model, "has put the Rolls up on blocks for the duration."

Although the Dowager Lady Merle's new chauffeur was a stranger, Mary chose to sit beside him on their eight miles' journey, and draw from him as much local information as possible. She thus learnt that Went Park Maternity Home was still functioning, and that Dick Harker, Tom Herring and Syd Crippen were all safe back from Dunkirk, but no news yet of Ted Squirl. It was a sad thing for Went, losing her Member, Captain Yarrow, a very nice gentleman, all said. Sir James Wilson had been much disappointed that he wasn't the age for the Local Defence Volunteers, but attended every meeting in the Village Hall just the same. Mrs. Taylor had been to see the Bishop about the Reverend Taylor joining, and he had been the first at the police station when we got the Yellow Warning, Tuesday.

Mary had gathered, from the infrequent letters of her old neighbours, that the sudden and quiet marriage of Miss Pamela Wallis to the bereaved Rector of Westbury-on-the-Hill had caused much amazement in the district. She hoped against hope that Pamela, who had an excellent memory, had forgotten her own description of "little Taylor" as "rather a frightful little chap."

"I wonder," thought Mary, as the car came to a standstill to allow Cupp, the fishmonger's van to pass between two sand-bag barricades at the corner of the Highridge road, "I wonder whether Pamela has made him take down that notice about not throwing rice and confetti at weddings."

In her sun-flooded double drawing-room, the Dowager was enthroned in front of a superb massed effect of innocent-hued Canterbury bells, which, she hastened to assure her guest, had been raised entirely without heat. She embraced Mary warmly, and said, holding her at arm's length, "Mary, dear! You look very nice in your uniform."

"I'm afraid not," said Mary truthfully.

"And how," asked the Dowager, "is the throat?"

"Quite well, thank you. Indeed I feel a fraud, taking a holiday just now," said Mary. "But our medical officer said that until things got worse, as we must expect, he wanted us to carry on with leave as arranged."

The athletic footmen had vanished, but the meal of which Mary presently partook was still served at record speed. The French *chef* had presumably also vanished, for the two courses were a plain roast chicken, with new potatoes and green peas, followed by strawberries and cream. On the other hand, the table still bore glittering Victorian silver and crystal, and not a detail in the decoration of this truly hideous room had been altered.

"It's an odd thing how fond one becomes of familiar objects," thought Mary, recognizing with pleasure the white silk, lace-edged mat, hand-painted with the likeness of a plover, reposing beneath her finger-bowl. It was extraordinarily soothing to be seated once more at the table of this commanding, shaky, hook-nosed old lady, faced by an enormous picture of Loch Maree, and with a docile spaniel rubbing against one's legs.

After luncheon the ladies adjourned for coffee to garden seats, placed in the shade of a beautiful copper beech, but with a prospect of nothing but staring yellow gravel, ruby and purple petunias, and pink geraniums in hanging baskets.

"Now let me see," said the Dowager. "Pamela and her husband are coming to dine to-night."

"Lovely! How are they?" asked Mary.

"To tell you the truth," said the Dowager, sipping her unsweetened coffee with a wry mouth, "I am beginning to lose patience with my grand-daughters and their families."

"Families!" echoed Mary.

"Pamela, who is having one in September, is disgusted with herself," said the Dowager. "She says it is what everyone will expect of a clergyman's wife, and she only hopes she may not repeat her success annually. However, as I pointed out to her last night, by the time that I was her age I was already a grand-mother. Her husband is concerned for her safety, and keeps on begging me to order her not to over-exert herself. They still have fifteen evacuated children at the Rectory, and as Pamela says she has quite enough to do running the parish and looking after the refugees, without opening a nursery of her own at this unsuitable time. They are happy. An excellent arrangement. Not the least of poor John's many good qualities is that he has abso-lutely no relations. Pamela is going in to Valerie's Maternity Home for the Event. The matron, my daughter-in-law assures me, is a fiend. I believe they fight day and night, and Valerie always loses. It will be nice for the child to be born at Went.

"My other granddaughter, Lalage," continued the Dowager, "is an even worse case at present, coming down to breakfast with swollen eyes and sniffing about the house, looking like a ferret. Her trouble is that she is not having a family. Since she is just nineteen, and has been married for six months to a particularly fine young husband who has been on leave once, I suggest that she need not give up hope yet. I can't have her in the room at night, when I listen to the nine o'clock bulletin, though. I listen once a day only. The least that old people like myself can do is to keep quiet and try not to worry the workers. This jersey is for a Merchant Marine. I have completed eleven. Lalage still goes to your First Aid Post every day, and was on duty during our raid on Tuesday, with Mrs. Bates."

"You can't mean Sally Bates, from the Green!" exclaimed Mary. "She's crippled with rheumatism."

"Her rheumatism has entirely gone," explained the Dowager. "She says now that she has discovered it was a Subconscious Protest against a life of inactivity. As soon as everybody had no petrol, and couldn't take her into Went to shop, she recovered the use of her legs and bought a bicycle."

"Tell me about the Rollos. I'm to go to Crossgrove to-morrow afternoon, you said," said Mary.

"To Crispin I have become quite attached," declared the Dowager. "In fact, I think of all my grandsons-in-law he is my favourite. I wish that you had been able to get down for the wedding. Lalage looked really well, and I gave her My Pearls, which infuriated Valerie, who had always hoped for them. But it was a whirlwind affair, a real sailor's wooing—only ten days' engagement, and all arranged at the last by telegram. I had to take a car and go to his headquarters to make my son see reason. Lalage has very thick legs, and is his only child. As you know, my son has been with his unit since the outbreak of war. He has lost weight, and I believe is knowing peace of mind for the first time since he married. He gave Lalage away, and Sir Daubeny was able to be present too, so we had a good array of medal ribbons on both sides of the family. They had a small gathering at Cross-grove afterwards, as Went was unobtainable, and I still had the school-teachers here then. One of Lady Rollo's many under-exercised dogs bit that stodgy woman, Mary Ogilvy, and the elder Rollo son arrived late, dressed in an oil-stained khaki linen mechanic's costume. Elizabeth Rollo was not well enough yet then to be a bridesmaid. She lay on a brocade sofa in that theatrical white room, and held quite a little court, with her poor foolish mother fussing around her. I hear she's blooming again now."

"How do her parents like Elizabeth's engagement to somebody old enough to be her father?" enquired Mary.

"He's Crispin's Captain, and scarcely looks his age, especially with his cap on," said the Dowager defensively. "Her own father says that if she had considered his feelings, she would have made it an Admiral while she was about it. Lady Rollo, I hear, is pleased that her only daughter is marrying a sailor, because they are proverbially absent. There is no question of the wedding taking place for some time, one is told, but I have heard that story too often, nowadays. Now, my dear, I am sure that you would like a rest after your journey. Only a few people, whom you like, are coming to tea. Poor Dorothy Yarrow will be dropping in later. She has long since taken up her normal round, as far as duties are concerned, but does not go out much. With so many young children and only one nurse, I daresay she has no opportunity. Did I tell you that the girl twin received my Christian name? A handsome child. I have told Macnaughton to put Miss Masquerier's new book in your bedroom."

(ii)

The enemy staged an air-raid for Miss Morrison's first night at Merle Dower House. She was awoken out of deep slumbers by a bang which caused her bedroom windows to vibrate. Overhead an aeroplane was droning on a deep periodic note. The bang was followed by a succession of cracking noises suggestive of a Guy Fawkes party of some pretensions. Mary, who had been shown the Shelter erected by the Dowager's orders for the use of her staff, turned over onto her other side, and said to herself, "Thank heaven there's no question of having to go on duty. I'll get up if I hear anything more."

The next thing she heard was a breakfast-in-bed tray being bestowed by a maid on the table by her side. She said, rubbing her eyes, "They did come again last night, didn't they?"

The maid replied, "Yes, miss, but nothing like as close as Tuesday, and no lives lost, the milkman says. Her ladyship has told us that they'll come, no doubt, every night at present. On the first night her ladyship dressed, and came down to the dug-out to set us the example. But her ladyship has now told Macnaughton not to wake her. 'I'm eighty-seven and stone deaf in one ear,' says her ladyship. 'If this house gets a direct hit, the end will probably be painless.' Will you be wearing the green silk, miss? It's very warm out, this morning."

The green silk which Mary donned an hour later was the same which she had worn at the Went Park sherry party and at Gold Cup Day, in 1939, Rosemary Wright, in South Africa, or rather Rosemary Wright's husband, was proving a serious drain on Mary's finances. As she looked at herself m the full-length mirror, Mary heard the sound of a car being brought round to the front door. Lady Merle had offered her guest the loan of the twelve horse-power saloon for the day, and said, as they parted last night, that they would meet again for dinner at eight p.m.

"Just ourselves to-night?" Mary had asked, foreseeing the possibility of being detained at Crossgrove.

"As far as one can ever tell, in these strange days," had been the Dowager's Delphic reply.

The morning was, as the housemaid had promised, very warm. Mary was conscious of a sense of complete unreality as she drew slowly towards a scene which she had last beheld in the grip of the glazed frost. On Westbury Hill she met little Dr. Greatbatch, who came striding towards her, and after shaking her hand enthusiastically, said in his fiercest manner, "Well,

I daresay you'll think not much has happened to us since you went away."

"On the contrary," said Mary. "I feel like Rip van Winkle. Last night, when I drove the Taylors home, I was stopped in Dead Woman's Lane by a party of highwaymen headed by Major Mimms, who demanded to see my Identity Card and Driving Licence. Lady Merle, whom I have never seen before with a knitting needle in her fingers, has completed eleven of the very thickest grey fisherman's jerseys you can imagine. Tell me about Florrie Squirl and her baby. No news yet of Ted, I suppose?"

"No," said Dr. Greatbatch, looking solemn. "However, perhaps he'll fetch up yet. Mrs. Harker came in to see me last week, to tell me that all the other boys from the village, in Dick's regiment, were back, and she'd lain awake three nights. When I called at her cottage a couple of days later, to tell her the not very encouraging result of my enquiries from the officer in command at the barracks in Went, I found Master Dick hanging out his mother's washing. He'd returned with the rest, and the populace had pressed hot drinks and fruit and sandwiches and cigarettes upon him, at port and railway station, and he'd written a letter to his mother to tell her he was alive. But as he had no English money and no stamps, he'd kept the letter in his pocket for three days."

"How like a Harker!" exclaimed Mary. "But Ted wouldn't do a thing like that."

"No," agreed Dr. Greatbatch. "However, his wife has got the baby now. That was a very foolish affair! I mean her 'keeping the baby dark,' as Mrs. Potts expresses it. As Florrie was in a bad way when I got to her cottage, I sent for her mother. It turned out that Mrs. Potts had never known that a baby was expected. Odd thing, considering they live only five miles apart. It only proves what I've always known. Folk about here can keep a secret when they want. Florrie had been very close. It seems that she and her mother had had words about Ted throwing up his job and going off to fight for his country. Florrie had backed Ted up, and she and Mrs. Potts had not met or spoken since. Florrie told me that she had intended that the first Mrs. Potts should hear of her being a grandmother was from the postman. She said The Potts have a morbid strain. But as I didn't know anything about all this foolishness, I just said to Mrs. Potts when she arrived, 'My good woman you ought to have been here long ago.' She didn't let me see that she had received a surprise. She just pursed up that mouth and said, 'So I see, sir, and they'll be all right now. I left them all three howling happily together—baby loudest, and the cottage enveloped in blue smoke. Florrie had put something in the oven overnight, and forgotten it when her pains came on. Luckily I smell very little these days.

"Oh! Dr. Greatbatch," said Mary sympathetically, "how sad never to smell a bunch of violets."

"But think how few bunches of violets I smell, how many cottages," chuckled Dr. Greatbatch, as he withdrew in nervous haste.

Mary's next halt was at the Westbury Hill Post, where she found Mrs. Bates and Amy Squirl on duty, Muriel Bidding and Mrs. Mimms also present. Violet Jackson's unbelievably plain and solid married daughter, who looked perfectly square in a khaki uniform, had called in to see if anybody here would volunteer to house two school-mistresses for the month of August, when her own spare-rooms required for her public-school nephews.

"Well, I think I could take 'em, so long as Johanna Pratt is not with me still then," decided Mrs. Bates, busily flicking a duster around her shelves.

Miry, who had not thought of Johanna for months, was so much interested that she interrupted without greeting, "How is Johanna Pratt?"

When greetings had subsided, Mrs. Bates reported, "Johanna went with an ambulance to Finland, and returned through Norway. She had the most amazing escapes, but the day after she got back, broke her leg in the Black Out outside an Underground station. She's been down with me for eleven weeks now. She's astonishingly cheerful, considering that she now knows that she's got a permanently shortened leg and a stiff knee for life. 'Come on in,' she shouts from the sofa, 'this is not an Illness. It's just an Accident.' She's paying for her own telephone calls, which are many, and I've taught her to sew. She's hoping to get an office job. She's not married yet. I must say I'm surprised, after Norah Hill finding a husband—quite a rising Glasgow specialist, I hear. I imagine you heard about the Heap children charging in here, and sticking Norah's dachshund in one of my clean beds, dressed out in my sterile dressings as an Air Raid Casualty?"

"I hadn't," said Mary, "but I must confess that a load was lifted from my soul when Norah wrote to say that she wanted poor Otto back, and Marcelle telegraphed that Dr. Heap was sending her children to Canada."

"I suppose," said Lady Muriel in the voice of a drill-sergeant, "that you all got cables from my mother? She told me in her last letter that she was simply handing her address-book to her secretary, and telling the woman to cable everyone with English addresses, saying, 'I will take your dear children for the duration.'"

"It was very kind-hearted, and just like her," said Mary, "though at my hospital the one addressed to me caused some surprise."

"That is what I came to see you about," said little Mrs. Mimms to Violet Jackson's daughter, in tremulous tones. "When your mother's cable arrived at our house, it was literally an answer to prayer. I'm accepting. I'm sending them at once. My husband wants me to go too, but I've decided against that, though I shall never know a happy moment while I am separated from my children. Mrs. Bates, I came in to say that now I shall be able to come and help you here. But don't ask me to do anything for several weeks."

Mrs. Mimms, a piteous little figure, left the hut, attended by firm, khaki-coloured Lady Muriel.

"Humph!" said Mrs. Bates to a bottle of Dettol. "Don't know that she'll be much good up here." Mary followed Amy Squirl into the Quartermaster's store, and said to her, "Amy, I'm so sorry to hear that you've no news of Ted yet. I shall be passing through London again, on my way back to hospital next Monday. Would you like me to make any enquiries up there for you? There's a department opened now, I know, for—for tracing people."

"Something's happened to our Ted, of that I'm sure, miss," said Amy Squirl heavily. "Our Ted wouldn't let five weeks pass without slipping a letter into the box, if 'e was able, not even if 'e'd got no stamp. 'E'd know 'is dear ones was listening for the postman's knock. Would you like to see Ted's last letter to me, miss?" asked Amy, feeling in the pocket beneath her apron. "I was the last to get a line from 'im. I'd sent 'im a wrist watch for 'is birthday."

Mary took over to the light of the window the letter written in pencil on cheap, blue-lined block paper, much folded and creased. She had to stand at the window for a long moment after she had read the letter. The view was not particularly interesting, as it was principally composed of sheds, but Westbury church spire was just visible between two walls, on which some self-seeded snapdragons were flourishing. Mary had never known before that lads like Ted Squirl—twenty-five and married—still ended their letters to their only sisters with a row of hearty kisses.

"Well, I must be getting on to Willows. I've not been there yet," she explained to Sally Bates a few seconds later.

"The painted chairs look very nice in your parlour," nodded Mrs. Bates. "Wasn't it thoughtful of Captain Hungerford to tell Wookey to remove them from Woodside before the military took it over? I saw him when he came down to say good-bye to Corisande, Lady Merle, on his embarkation leave. So amusing, and so full of life. She must be terribly anxious."

"She is, I'm afraid," admitted Mary. "Until Pamela told me last night, I'd never even known that Kit had rejoined his old regiment, let alone gone abroad."

"You'll find that a lot of damage has been done in your pretty home," said Mrs. Bates ghoulishly.

"Never mind," said Mary, steeling her heart. "They're only worldly possessions, and the Battle of Britain is about to begin."

"When is your sister-in-law leaving for South Africa?" asked Mrs. Bates.

"As soon as she can get a passage," said Mary. "I only hope she may succeed."

"Rosemary is expecting her baby any day, I hear," said Mrs. Bates. "Is it true that the husband drinks?"

"Yes," said Mary helplessly to Mrs. Bates, who was always right.

(iii)

Noon—dinner-hour for most of those who dwelt on the Green—had sounded before Mary drove in between the scarred gate-posts of Willows. There was a brick-red canvas Sport Pool, half filled with water, lying in the sun exactly outside the dining-room. Under the shade of the big walnut, now loaded with fruit, a wooden plank attached to a ladder formed another noticeable new feature of the front garden. The little lawn displayed signs that the Heaps, who had been unable to remove these trophies of playtime to the New World, had enjoyed good bathing and many slides.

Mary studied the face of her house in detail. Brilliant sunshine lit it. Every window was open to the hay-scented air. Upon the whole, she could not say that Willows looked much the worse of her absence. The *clematis montana* around the parlour lattice bore a thousand pale pink stars. The wistaria had attained her bedroom sill, as she had planned. The veronica in the corner by the kitchen had failed to survive last winter. Its bare brown branches were a melancholy spectacle. It ought to have been dug up and thrown away long ago, but the ceanothus and honey-suckle over the porch had behaved just as she had intended.

She lingered for some time in the small front garden, pacing slowly from spot to spot with her hands sunk in her pockets. Nobody seemed to have heard her arrival, and a curious disinclination to enter her deserted home oppressed her. At length she laid a hand on the front door, which was standing ajar, and stepped into the house, quietly as a thief.

The parlour looked smaller than she had remembered, and the air within its pale green painted walls was heavy with flower scents. She perceived that Marcelle had arranged an effective group of cottage lilies, jasmine and moon daisies in a white alabaster urn of Italian origin. The urn had been mended with glue, and around its base, which occupied the top of Mary's walnut bureau, gleamed a swelling puddle of water. Automatically, Mary pulled open the drawer in which she kept a glass-cloth. The drawer now contained many scattered hairpins, an opened box of chocolates and several back numbers of women's magazines, with mutilated covers.

The glass of the needlework shepherdess picture had been broken, and in the corner of the room the grandfather clock stood mute. Mary had realized from the moment she entered the room that some familiar sound was lacking. The little ship, Kit's ship, no longer rocked its incessant passage across troubled waves. As her glance fell upon the painted chairs, the door from the dining-room opened and Marcelle entered, bearing in her hand a table-napkin and a telegram.

"Ah! there you are, Mary, at last!" exclaimed Marcelle, kissing her sister-in-law in a preoccupied way.

"I waited in all morning. As you said you couldn't lunch, I naturally supposed that you would be early. Did you know that that big vase is a perfect death trap? Whether I like it or not, I have to put it on the top of the desk now, because there's a large white patch on the polish. I've tried with every tool upon which I can lay hands, but I can't get your old clock to go. That queer little woman Higgs, in the village, told me that her son was a perfect wonder at mending clocks, so I telephoned to Crossgrove. It turned out that the young man had gone off to make munitions weeks ago. She might have had the sense to tell me and save me the telephone call, in these days. I've been longing to show you this horrible telegram. I don't know now whether to go or not. I suppose, in a way, it's more than ever my duty now."

The telegram which Marcelle handed to Mary was from Rosemary, and simply said that her husband had died suddenly yesterday.

"It's peculiar her not saying what he died of," fretted Marcelle. "In her last letter she said that the doctor had warned her that unless he pulled himself together, he would kill himself. I hope she didn't mean really kill himself. I suppose that since I heard this morning that I've got my passage, I may as well go. It's not very pleasant here now, with the Heaps gone and the guns banging every night."

While she discussed with her sister-in-law their arrangements for shutting up Willows, Mary's attention wandered. She heard herself agreeing that a "let" was very improbable at present, and heard herself saying the words, "If I ever return here."

"I wish I could persuade you to come out to Africa with me, Mary," said Marcelle, who had needed very little persuasion to adopt the role of the devoted parent hurrying to a widowed daughter's sick-bed. "I don't like the thought of leaving you here while I go off to perfect safety and security."

"I've had forty-three years of the best," said Mary, "and I'm beginning to be afraid that a great many of us here have come to think too much of those two words for some time past."

"Mary dear, I don't see how you can say that you've had the best, when you've never married," objected Marcelle, looking her most intense, and sitting down for a good chat on the edge of the sofa.

"I once received an offer of marriage," divulged Mary, "from the most fascinating young man in the world. At least I thought so. However, I was only sixteen and three-quarters at the time, so he had a lucky escape."

"Do you mean that you refused him?" asked Marcelle.

"I did," admitted Mary. "But I didn't mean to. However, he didn't linger. . . . That reminds me, while you finish your lunch, do you mind if I collect some papers from the desk which I locked up?"

She was able, in a moment, to lay her hand on the unfinished letter to Kit, written from her Scottish bedroom, and pushed, months since, into the pigeon-hole labelled "difficult." "Dear Kit," she read. "It seems incredible that this should ever reach you. . . ."

"That's right," she said aloud. Looking up, she saw that Marcelle had taken her advice and she was alone. Drawing up the painted armchair to her old desk, Mary began to pen a postscript. She was thus engaged when the door from the dining-room opened again, and Doris stood before her.

"If you please, miss," said Doris, "Mrs. Morrison forgot to give you this telephone message, which came from Merle Dower House over an hour ago."

"Thank you, Doris," said Mary. "How are you, Doris? You're looking well, I'm glad to see. You've grown, too."

"I'm very well, thank you, miss," smiled Doris. "If it was true that you was thinking of shutting up the house, Rose and me was wanting to go to the Went aeroplane works. My friend has been called up," she added explanatorily.

"Have you got a friend, Doris?" asked Mary, who well knew that in Westbury-on-the-Green this word always betokened a suitor.

Doris spoke the name of the small and grubby boy, who had, some years past, been engaged by Sheilah Hill to look after her kennels.

"Good gracious!" exclaimed Mary. "But he's only—"

"Harry's turned nineteen, miss," said Doris coldly. "He's taken me to supper with his mother. Mrs. Brink was inclined to be nasty, but Harry says that's natural and she'll get accustomed to me. Rose and me was sorry to hear that you was looking so tired, miss. Is it very hard work at the hospital?"

"Not at the hospital," answered Mary absently. Pulling herself together, she added, "All the patients are sailors, you know. They're wonderful, and do everything they can to help the nurses."

But when Doris had disappeared to fetch Rose, and she stood in front of her mute grandfather clock, trying vainly, with a single finger, to make her little ship move again, Mary did indeed feel languishing. She told herself that re-visiting familiar scenes is notoriously trying, that Sally Bates always got one down, and that Marcelle could be recommended to reduce the Laughing Cavalier to tears. "These are uphill days," she decided. "Funny to think that Shakespeare was in London when the Armada was expected. I wish I didn't feel so strongly this morning that if Kit's gone, as far as I'm concerned, there is nothing left remarkable beneath the visiting moon."

Rose's step sounded in the passage. Returning to her desk, Mary discovered that Doris had laid down upon it the telephone message from that undaunted warrior, Corisande, Lady Merle.

As the significance of its single sentence dawned upon her, plenty of colour returned to her face.

"Will Miss Morrison call at Went Junction on her road home from Crossgrove, to pick up Captain Hungerford, who will be coming down by the six-fifteen?"

THE END

FURROWED MIDDLEBROW

Milton Keynes UK
Ingram Content Group UK Ltd.
UKHW011516100424
440935UK00001B/10

9 781913 054175